MARVEL

AN ANTHOLOGY OF THE MARVEL UNIVERSE

THE SHIELD OF SAM WILSON

NOVELS OF THE MARVEL UNIVERSE BY TITAN BOOKS

Ant-Man: Natural Enemy by Jason Starr
Avengers: Everybody Wants to Rule the World by Dan Abnett
Avengers: Infinity by James A. Moore
Black Panther: Panther's Rage by Sheree Renée Thomas
Black Panther: Who is the Black Panther? by Jesse J. Holland
Black Panther: Tales of Wakanda by Jesse J. Holland
Captain America: Dark Design by Stefan Petrucha
Captain Marvel: Liberation Run by Tess Sharpe
Captain Marvel: Shadow Code by Gilly Segal
Civil War by Stuart Moore
Deadpool: Paws by Stefan Petrucha
Doctor Strange: Dimension War by James Lovegrove
Guardians of the Galaxy – Annihilation: Conquest by Brendan Deneen
Loki: Journey Into Mystery Prose Novel by Katherine Locke
Marvel's Midnight Suns: Infernal Rising by S.D. Perry
Marvel's Secret Invasion Prose Novel by Paul Cornell
Spider-Man: Forever Young by Stefan Petrucha
Spider-Man: Kraven's Last Hunt by Neil Kleid
Spider-Man: The Darkest Hours Omnibus by Jim Butcher,
Keith R.A. Decandido, and Christopher L. Bennett (forthcoming)
Spider-Man: The Venom Factor Omnibus by Diane Duane
Thanos: Death Sentence by Stuart Moore
Venom: Lethal Protector by James R. Tuck
X-Men: Days of Future Past by Alex Irvine
X-Men: The Dark Phoenix Saga by Stuart Moore
X-Men: The Mutant Empire Omnibus by Christopher Golden
X-Men & The Avengers: The Gamma Quest Omnibus by Greg Cox

ALSO FROM TITAN AND TITAN BOOKS

Marvel Contest of Champions: The Art of the Battlerealm by Paul Davies
Marvel's Spider-Man: The Art of the Game by Paul Davies
Obsessed with Marvel by Peter Sanderson and Marc Sumerak
Spider-Man: Hostile Takeover by David Liss
Spider-Man: Into the Spider-Verse – The Art of the Movie by Ramin Zahed
The Art of Iron Man (10th Anniversary Edition) by John Rhett Thomas
The Marvel Vault by Matthew K. Manning, Peter Sanderson, and Roy Thomas
Ant-Man and the Wasp: The Official Movie Special
Avengers: Endgame – The Official Movie Special
Avengers: Infinity War – The Official Movie Special
Black Panther: The Official Movie Companion
Black Panther: The Official Movie Special
Captain Marvel: The Official Movie Special
Marvel Studios: The First Ten Years
Spider-Man: Far From Home – The Official Movie Special
Spider-Man: Into the Spider-Verse – The Official Movie Special
Thor: Ragnarok – The Official Movie Special

AN ANTHOLOGY OF THE MARVEL UNIVERSE

Sam★Wilson Captain America

THE SHIELD OF SAM WILSON

Original short stories edited by

JESSE J. HOLLAND

TITAN BOOKS

MARVEL

CAPTAIN AMERICA: THE SHIELD OF SAM WILSON
Print edition ISBN: 9781803363875
E-book edition ISBN: 9781803367712

Published by Titan Books
A division of Titan Publishing Group Ltd
144 Southwark Street, London SE1 0UP
www.titanbooks.com

First hardback edition: January 2025
10 9 8 7 6 5 4 3 2 1

FOR MARVEL PUBLISHING
Jeff Youngquist, VP Production and Special Projects
Sarah Singer, Editor, Special Projects
Jeremy West, Manager, Licensed Publishing
Sven Larsen, VP, Licensed Publishing
David Gabriel, VP, Print & Digital Publishing
C.B. Cebulski, Editor in Chief

Sam Wilson created by Stan Lee & Gene Colan

Cover by R.B. Silva & Jesus Aburtov

A CIP catalogue record for this title is available from the British Library.

Printed and bound by CPI Group (UK) Ltd, Croydon CR0 4YY.

This book is lovingly dedicated to all of the individuals who protect and symbolize the United States of America, but especially to those Black men and women who have loved, fought, and died for this country both at home and abroad but whose contributions have never truly been acknowledged by their fellow citizens. Your sacrifices are appreciated.

TABLE OF CONTENTS

INTRODUCTION

JESSE J. HOLLAND

WHEN I first heard that Sam Wilson was going to be the next Captain America, I was furious.

I wasn't angry because Marvel Comics was sidelining a beloved character like Steve Rogers, the Star-Spangled Avenger, and giving his title to the African American man who was created to be his sidekick (though many other people were upset by this). I wasn't even upset because Marvel was retiring one of the first African American heroic identities in the comic-book industry and turning Sam Wilson into just another replacement for a World War II-era white super hero.

I was mad because I thought this would be an ignoble end to a great character like Sam Wilson.

You see, I'm a longtime comic-book fan. I started reading comic books as a child, and five decades or so later I still have a pull list—digital, not paper—and I'm a longtime devotee of Marvel Unlimited, the electronic catalog of Marvel Comics, so I read backward into the past as well as forward as I keep up with the most recent adventures of my favorite heroes and teams. And there's one thing I know for a fact, given all of my years of reading comic books:

The status quo always returns.

And that's where I thought they were going with Sam Wilson. He would be Captain America for a while, his falcon, Redwing, on his arm, but Steve Rogers was going to be back, and he was going to be Captain America. Which meant Sam was probably going to have to die, break his back, lose a leg, or go insane, and probably at the hands of Steve's greatest enemy, the Red Skull—all to inspire Steve Rogers to remember and prove to the world that he was the one and only Captain America.

And Sam Wilson deserved better.

I've always been a fan of Sam's. He and the Black Panther were the first characters of color I encountered in my early days of reading the Avengers, and unlike T'Challa—who was very proudly Wakandan and not American—the Falcon was the only Black American super hero that I knew of for a very long time. I would eventually discover Luke Cage and Monica Rambeau, but Sam for the longest time was the only super hero who looked like me and was from a real place that I recognized—Harlem—instead of a made-up country from a continent that I had never visited. That gave him a special place in my heart, and I always paid attention when he showed up.

Gene Colan, the artist on that issue and co-creator of the Falcon, described what was going through his and Stan's minds when they came up with the character in the introduction to *Marvel Masterworks: Captain America Volume 4* (2008):

"In the late 1960s, [when news of the] Vietnam War and civil rights protests were regular occurrences, and Stan, always wanting to be at the forefront of things, started bringing these headlines into the comics … one of the biggest steps we took in this direction came in Captain America. I enjoyed drawing people of every kind. I drew as many different types of people as I could into the scenes I illustrated, and I loved drawing

Black people. I always found their features interesting and so much of their strength, spirit and wisdom [was] written on their faces. I approached Stan, as I remember, with the idea of introducing an African American hero, and he took to it right away. … I looked at several African American magazines, and used them as the basis of inspiration for bringing The Falcon to life."

It was only when I was older that I discovered how special Sam Wilson actually was. Not only is he a cool super hero and an awesome character, but he also holds a special place in the pantheon of characters of color in the comic-book industry's history books.

Many comic-book and movie fans now know that the Black Panther, King T'Challa of Wakanda, was the first Black comic-book character in mainstream comic books, debuting in *Fantastic Four* #52 in July 1966. But T'Challa wasn't the first African American comic-book super hero… because he wasn't African American. That hero was Sam Wilson, the Falcon.

Sam Wilson was introduced by Stan Lee and Gene Colan in *Captain America* #117, which hit stands in September 1969. And from the beginning, Sam was a hero. He didn't have to lose his parents to murder (that came later in the rewrites). He didn't have to avenge the fridging of a girlfriend or wife. He didn't even start out fighting racism or running from corrupt cops or Klansmen in the United States.

Sam started out his career as a hero fighting for freedom for natives in a foreign land in the tropics, for no other reason than it was the right thing to do. Steve Rogers came along and gave him a costume and some training, but Sam was already a falcon-wielding hero when he met Captain America. Steve Rogers—and later the Black Panther—only gave him the training and, eventually, the mechanical wings and flight suit to make him a better-equipped hero, not a hero. Sam did that all by himself.

That, for a teenaged and young adult me, was very refreshing. Sam Wilson didn't need a tortured backstory of pain and sorrow to usher him into the world of heroics. He was a Black American who saw injustice and was fighting it not just for his own personal interest but for others, using whatever he had on hand. To quote him from his debut issue of *Captain America*, #117, "We'll make weapons! Out of sticks 'n stones if we have to! Anything's better than not fighting back!"

Here was a Black man who did good because he *was* good. That's Sam Wilson, especially when compared to the streetwise, down-with-it, ghetto-dwelling, Afro-wearing, blaxploitation superstar that was Luke Cage.

Cage, aka Power Man, holds his place in history as being the first African American to have his own self-titled superhero comic, *Luke Cage: Hero for Hire*, which debuted in June 1972. Luke was created to be a stereotypical man of his time, a jive-talking, disco-shirt-wearing, muscle-flexing convict who bemoaned the evils of the Man who set him up and kept him from being his true, authentic self. Luke didn't want to be a selfless hero working for the betterment of mankind and his neighborhood; Luke did good because it paid better. Oh, he wanted to do the right thing—and eventually would—but he would also let you know that the right thing came at a cost as he flexed his biceps and complained about how hard life was.

Sam, meanwhile, did good because good needed doing. He had a selfless job (he was a social worker in Harlem), palled around with Captain America for years, and even became a member the mighty Avengers, although Falcon became an Avenger solely because they needed a minority member to satisfy U.S. government regulations—not because they needed his skill or power but because they had a "Black" hero slot, and Black Panther didn't want to fill it. I was embarrassed to read that. The Avengers were reluctant to have Falcon forced on them, and indeed Sam Wilson had enough pride in himself to walk away from the Avengers a few issues later because of that situation.

But I digress. Since his inception, Sam has been beloved. Eventually, he became so recognizable that, while he didn't get his own comic book like Cage, he gained a co-credit in one of Marvel's most popular comic books, which was renamed *Captain America and the Falcon*, a title pairing that lasted so long that today people are just as likely to say "the Falcon" as they are to say "Bucky" or "the Avengers" if you ask them to complete the phrase "Captain America and..."

That's why I was mad when I found out that Marvel Comics were going to make Sam Wilson Captain America. I figured it would be yanked away from him through his death, his maiming, his insanity, or some other stupid thing that wouldn't honor all of the work done by his character and all of the writers who had crafted him into the righteous, courageous super hero that he was. I, in my position as a journalist back then, even put the question directly to Axel Alonso, then editor-in-chief at Marvel Comics.

Alonso, who was steering Marvel through a significant cultural shift, assured me that Sam Wilson's tenure as Captain America was not a mere placeholder until Steve Rogers' return. He emphasized Marvel's commitment to reflecting the evolving world and diversifying its roster of super heroes. But while his words provided some comfort, my skepticism remained.

However, as time went on, my perspective began to change. Sam Wilson's Captain America was not just a fleeting gimmick. The storylines explored the way he struggled with the mantle, not just due to his race but also through the weight of carrying such a significant legacy. It delved into what it meant for Sam, a Black man from Harlem, to wield the shield and represent American ideals that had often failed people like him.

One of the most poignant arcs appeared in *All-New Captain America*, where Sam faced enemies old and new, including a resurgent Hydra, while dealing with public perception, a key aspect being how different communities saw him. For some he was a symbol of progress while others viewed him as an impostor. This duality added depth to his character and the narrative.

Sam's interactions with Steve Rogers were also telling. Steve supported Sam, acknowledging that his time had passed and that it was Sam's turn to lead. This mentor–mentee relationship was heartening and demonstrated a passing of the torch that felt genuine and respectful.

In the broader Marvel Universe, Sam Wilson's Captain America became a symbol of modern heroism. He wasn't just fighting super villains; he was addressing social issues, standing up for the marginalized, and making Captain America relevant to a new generation. This was a departure from the traditional super-hero narrative and was something only Sam could bring to the iconic role.

Looking back, my initial anger was rooted in a deep respect for and protectiveness toward Sam Wilson as a character. I didn't want to see him used as a narrative tool only to be discarded. However, Marvel's treatment of Sam has, for the most part, been respectful and forward thinking. He wasn't just a replacement; he was a redefinition of what Captain America could be.

Sam Wilson's journey from the Falcon to Captain America represents a broader shift in the comic-book industry toward more inclusive and representative storytelling. It's a testament to the evolving nature of heroism and how legacy characters can be reimagined to reflect the times. Sam Wilson didn't just become

Captain America, he redefined him, and in doing so he earned a permanent place in the pantheon of Marvel's greatest heroes.

In the end, my fears proved unfounded. Sam Wilson has proven himself a worthy successor to Steve Rogers, not by mimicking Steve but by bringing his own unique strengths and perspectives to the role. He embodies the ideals of Captain America in a way that is relevant and inspiring for today's world, ensuring that the legacy of the Star-Spangled Avenger continues to evolve and inspire future generations.

Each author who contributed to this anthology has infused their narrative with personal insights and cultural nuances, offering a multifaceted portrayal of a hero who transcends traditional boundaries. The stories herein not only celebrate Sam Wilson's role as Captain America but also explore his origins, challenges, and triumphs. His ascension to the mantle of Captain America is more than a change of guard; it symbolizes the breaking of barriers and the broadening of what it means to be a hero. Through these narratives, the authors examine how Sam navigates the responsibilities of his new role while staying true to his roots and values. His journey is a reflection of the broader struggle for equality and recognition faced by many in the African American community.

At its heart, this anthology underscores the importance of legacy, exploring how, by taking on the role of Captain America, Sam Wilson not only honors Steve Rogers but also forges his own path. The stories reflect on the weight of this legacy and how Sam makes it his own, blending the old with the new. The authors explore how Sam's unique experiences and perspectives enrich the legacy of Captain America, making it more inclusive and reflective of today's world.

The diverse voices in this collection ensure that each story offers a fresh and compelling perspective on Sam Wilson's character. The authors, with their varied backgrounds and storytelling styles, bring a richness to the anthology that mirrors the diversity of the world we live in. Their contributions are a testament to the power of storytelling in shaping our understanding of heroism and representation.

I am proud to present a collection of stories that explore the diverse and powerful legacy of Sam Wilson's Captain America, written by some of the best up-and-coming African American authors, each bringing their unique perspectives and personal connections to Sam Wilson. These stories delve into different facets of Sam's character and the impact he has made as Captain America to create a rich tapestry of narratives that honor his legacy. This anthology is a testament to the enduring power of representation and the ever-evolving nature of heroism.

Jesse J. Holland, Editor

LOST CAUSE

KYOKO M.

SAMUEL THOMAS Wilson knew how to make an entrance.

It was a scorching-hot day in Colorado. It felt like the sun was trying to cook him sunny-side up as he rounded the last turn that put the Pueblo Memorial Airport firmly within his sights. He'd already been cleared to land by the faithful ground-control staff, spotting his final destination through the heads-up display in his goggles. When he reached the last leg of the flight, he let his body naturally straighten out for wind resistance and righted himself to land on his feet in front of the prison bus and the small throng of people waiting on his arrival.

The first man he spotted was one he knew all too well: a bald middle-aged Black man with perfectly straight posture, his leather duster flapping in the wind every so often, a black patch over one eye, the rest of his attire all black as well. He had a gun on his hip and a no-nonsense look on his face, though Sam knew S.H.I.E.L.D. agent Nick Fury had an actual sense of humor when he felt like it.

The second man was tall and lithe, wearing a white button-down shirt, jeans, and brown cowboy boots with a light blue sport coat over the ensemble. A shiny silver star winked out at Sam on the approach, proclaiming him to be a U.S. Marshal. He had brown hair and a goatee, his blue eyes sharp and observant as they watched Sam descend.

The last person on the tarmac was a Black woman with her hair in a bun, dressed in the uniform of the very institution he'd be supporting today—the USP Florence ADX, aka a federal supermax prison from which no convict had ever escaped.

Not yet, anyway.

Sam's boots touched down a few feet from his welcoming committee, a broad grin on his lips as he stepped forward and offered his hand to Nick Fury. "Morning, sir."

Fury offered a small but genuine smile as he shook it. "Morning, Cap. Nice flight in from the hotel, I see?"

"Except for this heat," Sam agreed. "I know Harlem gets hot in the summer, but *man*. This is something else. Not used to this Midwest heat."

"We'll make sure you don't melt," the marshal said with an easy smirk, offering his hand. "Marshal Franklin David Robertson, sir. Call me FDR. Good to meet you."

"Same to you."

"I'm Alcina Cirillo," the Black woman said, shaking Sam's hand as well. "I'm the ringleader for this veritable circus."

"Good to meet you, ma'am." Sam turned to the direction the group was facing to size things up. There was a small plane already on the tarmac with the inmates being transferred from the Raft to ADX for their permanent new digs. There had recently been a prison break perpetrated by the super villain Shocker, meaning that most of the Raft's security was now compromised, and it would be weeks or months before it could be restored.

"What's the final head count?" Sam asked.

"Six prisoners," Alcina said. "We tried to keep it small to lessen the work. And the hot tamale himself has a habit of converting people into his corner, so the fewer, the better."

Sam's brown eyes narrowed as he caught sight of said hot tamale exiting the airplane. He was a man of insurmountable stature, seeming to tower over everyone not just with his height, but with his presence. Naturally, he wore a burgundy prison jumpsuit, his arms chained to his waist, his legs shackled to one another. He had brown eyes and a bald head, with small beads of sweat falling forward onto his forehead. A shark's grin formed on his lips as the four guards walked the six criminals toward the bus.

"Well, if it ain't Discount Captain America," Brock Rumlow aka Crossbones said, his beady eyes beaming down unpleasantness. "How's it going, sucker?"

"Even my worst day is better than your best, smart-mouth," Sam replied with a cool, unbothered look.

"Don't worry," Fury said, tucking his hands in his pockets. "That smart mouth won't be so smart after he gets a load of his new digs."

Rumlow shrugged. "Iso ain't bad. I've had worse."

"That's what you think." Fury showed his teeth.

Rumlow gestured to Alcina. "Who's the babe?"

"Your new best friend," Alcina smiled, removing her night stick and pointing to the bus.

Rumlow licked his lips and winked. "I like the sound of that." He then turned and started to shuffle for the bus.

Sam shook his head. "Good to know he's still as charming as ever."

The small group chuckled. Alcina gestured to the four guards, all white men forty or older dressed in identical guard uniforms. The shortest stood at the end. He had blond curls and blue eyes, freckles dotting his nose. The one beside him was over six feet tall with his sandy-colored hair in a buzzcut, his eyes a rare shade of green. The third man was heavyset with brown hair and brown eyes. The last man was average height and weight, shaved bald, with dark blue eyes. "These are my men that will be backing you up."

She started from the left. "Robert Pettengill, Quentin Bell, Matthew Collins, and Justin Brandt."

Sam nodded to them respectfully and they nodded back. He gestured to Pettengill—who, like all the other guards, had a semiautomatic rifle strapped to his back. "I thought prison protocol was for non-lethal weapons?"

"We were given the go-ahead for a little more firepower considering the circumstances," he replied. "It's Rumlow."

"You're not wrong. Let's hope it doesn't get to that point. Thanks, fellas."

With that, they went back over to the bus to make sure the inmates filed in.

"What's the word on the distance we're covering?" Sam continued.

Fury pulled out a tablet and tapped a few things, showing him the highlighted route. "It should be a forty-five minute drive. The perimeter will be monitored by S.H.I.E.L.D. personnel using drones; they're small enough to avoid most detection by any party crashers and they'll ping you if there's incoming."

Sam turned to the marshal. "What kind of resources do we have if there's an attack?"

"We can call in a chopper for backup if things get hairy. There will be Fremont County SWAT officers on said chopper."

"Roger that. What's the last thing we heard from our intel?"

Fury sighed. "That's the trouble. We caught word of a jail break, but S.H.I.E.L.D. wasn't able to narrow down a source.

There are plenty of people who want Rumlow out, starting with the Red Skull and working through a lot of the criminal underbelly. The guy's a valuable mercenary and so having him loose benefits too many entities stateside for us to give you a dossier on who might be the culprit. We have to assume any hostile force that's used Rumlow before could be on their way."

Sam whistled. "That's an ugly thought. If I had to guess, though, I'd agree that Red Skull would want Rumlow bad enough to cross swords with us. Baron Zemo or Taskmaster might too. They've got the best toys, enough men to make it a successful jailbreak, and the motivation to git 'er done. I've crossed paths with them enough to know this is a golden opportunity they won't want to miss. I read the file on our perps, but there is one last thing I want to ask."

He turned to Alcina. "Our other five prisoners... I've read their rap sheets and psych profiles, but you've spent time among supermax convicts. I want your perspective on the other prisoners we're transporting."

Alcina blinked in surprise. "Hmm... well, ADX Florence is reserved for basically two kinds of criminals: the truly violent lost causes and the high-profile criminals that the authorities want to make absolutely sure never see the light of day again. It houses mostly terrorists and men too dangerous to be sent anywhere else, as well as those who sold U.S. secrets. Our other five prisoners consist of two bombing terrorists, an ex-C.I.A. officer, a serial killer, and a former Mexican cartel enforcer."

She peered at the bus, pausing in thought. "Their mentalities are certainly mixed. I would say of the five, the one most likely to gravitate toward Rumlow would be the serial killer, Wayne Clayton. Clayton has yet to make any escape attempts, but he hasn't displayed any psychological indications that he accepts his fate. I think he's biding his time, waiting for a chance to strike."

"Meaning we've got our work cut out for us," FDR said with a sigh. "We can expect non-compliance if someone does attack the bus."

"If given the opportunity, do you think all five would try to bail if someone hits the bus to get Rumlow out?" Fury asked.

Alcina nodded. "They may not think they'd get far, but I think all five would take the chance."

Fury regarded Sam seriously. "Then you make sure you watch your back, brotha."

Sam grinned. "Already got that covered."

He whistled again—but a short, loud blast this time. A moment later, a shadow cast itself over the group. They squinted into the blue sky as they spotted a falcon circling above, then descending like a torpedo. His wings opened at the last second and then he landed neatly on Sam's left shoulder, cocking his head as he observed the newcomers. "Redwing's ready to rock and roll."

FDR glanced at the others, mystified. "Uh, how's a falcon gonna help?"

Sam lightly petted the front of Redwing's feathers. "We have a special bond."

FDR grinned. "Oh my God—are you like Ant-Man, but for birds?"

Sam shrugged, slightly miffed at the comparison to the tiny hero. "More or less."

"I can't believe that rumor is true. This is amazing. Just wait 'til my kid hears."

"Text him. We've gotta get moving." Alcina shook Fury's hand and nodded to him, then raised her voice. "Let's get this show on the road, boys!"

The other guards filed into the bus, with Alcina and FDR bringing up the rear. Fury shook Sam's hand a last time. "Good luck."

"Thanks, Fury. We'll keep you apprised." Sam stepped back and nodded to Redwing, who took flight first, then he followed. The bus coughed itself to life on the tarmac and then began to follow the signs and directions from the flight crew to exit Pueblo Memorial Airport and enter the forty-five-minute route to ADX Florence.

o————o

FOR THE first fifteen minutes of the ride, everything was fine.

Sam had the video feed from Fury's drones cast into his goggles' heads-up display to keep an eye on the perimeter. Redwing had gone up to a higher altitude, letting Sam see through his eyes that it was all-clear for now. Sam had a comm-link to Alcina and FDR in the bus below and they'd told him everything looked normal from the ground level so far. They'd gone against the usual policy for a police escort in order to minimize how noticeable they'd be on the road.

Their surroundings, however, were the much larger problem. The route to ADX Florence wasn't completely clear, it would have them passing by several smaller cities in the area. It left plenty of opportunities for enemies to camp out and spring a trap. The bulk of the drive would be spent on U.S.-50: a six-lane highway with a divider that would account for about half an hour of drive time. They'd already gone past modest houses and a few businesses, passing some empty fields and a train track that ran parallel to the highway.

At the sixteen-minute mark into the drive, Sam's comm-link sparked to life. "Sam, it's FDR."

"Go ahead, marshal."

"It may not be anything, but check Camera Four in your feed. I'm seeing some interference that looks suspicious."

FDR and Alcina had live feeds to the drones as well,

accessible from a tablet; a precaution in case Sam had to engage the enemy and couldn't provide that information for them. He used the controls on the digital pad built into his right forearm to highlight Camera Four and bring the feed up.

The four drones formed a moving quadrant that followed the prison bus along, observing the general space along Highway U.S.-50, and Camera Four was south of them. When the feed filled the top corner of his vision, he could see why FDR flagged it as odd: the picture flickered every few seconds.

"What are the chances that's just a random technology glitch caused by being in the middle of nowhere?"

FDR snorted. "Slim to none, Cap."

"Yup, that's what I thought. I'm calling Redwing to take my spot; I'll go check it out."

"Roger that. Be careful."

Sam concentrated and reached out to Redwing via their telepathic link, and the falcon started to descend to Sam's current altitude. Once Redwing arrived, Sam turned around and flew for Camera Four's position bringing up the rear.

He slowed his flight to the same speed as the drone, then flipped upside down as he came within range. He let it fly above him and then checked the outside of the hull for anything suspicious.

And suspicious, he did find.

"There's some kind of object on the bottom of Camera Four," Sam told FDR and Alcina as he peered up at the bottom of the drone. "It's mechanical and about the size of a silver dollar. Has a black interface covered with glass. Don't see any numbers or identifying marks."

"Crap," Alcina hissed. "Someone's probably tampering with it. We have to assume it might be compromised. I recommend we decommission it for now."

"I can try removing it, but I don't know what it'll do. Might be worth the—" Sam fell silent as the previously blank face of the device acquired a red glow. Sam's instincts and experience told him that was a bad sign. He boosted his flight suit to fly faster, away from it.

His instincts were right.

Camera Four exploded not three seconds later.

"Whoa!" FDR exclaimed. "Was that what I think it was?"

"Yep, the cat's outta the bag," Sam said, watching tiny pieces rain down on the pavement below. "We're on, folks. Keep your eyes peeled. I'm gonna go check the other three cameras—"

Before he could finish the sentence, three explosions rocked the area simultaneously.

"All cameras down!" Sam shouted, twisting in the air to observe the gouts of smoke in the vicinity. "We're officially under attack, people. Sweeping the area now with Redwing to find the culprit."

Sam telepathically called to Redwing and the falcon joined him as they flew down to the top of the bus and then landed. Sam could overhear Alcina and FDR instructing the prisoners to keep their heads down and stay quiet as they tried to identify the threat.

Given that the tiny bomb had been attached to the bottom of the drone, Sam scanned the upcoming stretch of the highway. He had a hunch that someone had been carefully placed to wait for them to fly overhead and then shot the bombs onto the cameras, meaning multiple teams: one for when they'd already passed and another for trying to set up a blockade. They were now twenty minutes into the drive, the halfway point, and Redwing's sharp eyes spotted the first assailant.

There was a cell phone tower not far from the highway, and

perched at the top stood a Hydra agent with a jet pack. The prison bus veered to the furthest lane away from the tower, but it meant nothing as the Hydra agent blasted from his perch and landed on the rear of the bus, aiming a rifle at Sam when he landed.

"Morning," Sam said in a faux-friendly voice over the rush of wind around them. "I see you're someone who believes that imitation is the sincerest form of flattery."

"Only gonna tell you this once, Wilson," the Hydra agent sneered as he peered through his scope. "Tell them to stop the bus and let Rumlow off. If you don't, I'll kill you and everyone in this bus and on this highway."

"Charming ultimatum, but I think people might frown upon Captain America letting an international killer loose."

He wrapped his wings around his front as the Hydra agent opened fire, flying closer. Sam did a front-flip over the agent's head and landed behind him, kicking the back of his right knee. The agent stumbled and Sam grabbed the rifle, disarming him, and slammed his right wing into the man's temple. The Hydra agent tumbled off the side of the bus and fell into a nearby ditch, unconscious. Sam unloaded the ammo and then chucked the gun into a ditch further up.

"Made contact with a Hydra agent," Sam said into the link as he and Redwing continued scanning the route.

"Yeah, we heard the gunshots," FDR said in a snarky tone. "They're never alone, you know."

"Never," Sam agreed. "My best guess is that guy was the welcome wagon to see if we could be reasoned with. That means they're gonna send the big guns next."

"Or start trying to distract us with civilian casualties. I'm having the driver pull ahead. Think we need to scramble the SWAT chopper?"

"Send it ahead to shut down the highway. That'll keep any possible hostages out of their hands. Let's see if we can keep it contained. I don't want any cops or civilians taking a bullet."

The next stretch of the highway consisted mostly of desert on one side where a local ranch made its home and some scattered houses on the other. Sam's HUD lit up when it spotted an irregular heat signature up on top of a hill they were about to pass. "Redwing, move out."

The falcon took off from his perch on Sam's shoulder and launched into the air. Sam zoomed in until he could see more clearly, then cursed under his breath. He touched the link in his ear. "On my mark, tell the driver to take evasive action in three… two… one!"

Sam heard a sonic boom and the bus veered into the far right lane just in time. The missile missed, hitting the side of the road instead. Dirt and smoke kicked up into the air and the nearby cars all slammed on their brakes, swerving to avoid it.

"Alcina, FDR, I'm headed over to that hill. Get someone to watch the front and rear of the bus until I get back."

"Roger that," Alcina replied.

Sam took off just as a second missile hit the other side of the highway, and the bus switched to the center lane to stay out of its path. He smirked as he spotted Redwing go into a dive and hit the Hydra agent right in the face, clawing at his eyes with those sharp talons. It distracted him just long enough for Sam to get close enough to shoot a grappling hook at the missile launcher. He hauled on the other end of the line and snatched the weapon from the agent's grip, then flew straight and true and front-kicked him off the top of the hill. The man tumbled head over foot down the rest of the hill and then sagged at the bottom, out like a light.

Sam landed beside the agent and knelt, poking a finger into his ear. He ripped out the man's comm-link and put it in his left ear, listening in. He could hear someone speaking in Hungarian; they were asking for a status report of the bus's current position. Sam picked up the man's limp arm and checked the digital interface on it, seeing there were six other agents in the area, each in pairs. "From bad to worse. Hoo boy."

He held out his arm for Redwing as the falcon landed. "I'm gonna go take these jokers out; I need you to head back to the bus and keep an eye out for me, okay?"

Redwing took off. Sam, his shield firmly on his back, did as well, having memorized the Hydra agents' positions on the map he'd seen. The first pair were a half mile ahead of the bus, hiding behind an enormous shrub at the entrance to a nearby ranch. He heard them shouting over the comm-link on the approach and spun as they opened fire from behind the shrub. He flew straight for them and his wings took them both out before a single bullet could touch him. Sam paused long enough to unload their weapons, pocketing the ammo, and then flew for the next agents.

The highway had a small underpass where it formed a bridge. The agents were crouched underneath waiting for the bus to pass overhead, both equipped with grappling guns. They shot out cables that latched onto the roof of the bus and then rappelled upward.

Or, rather, they *tried.*

Redwing landed on the side of the bus where they were reeling themselves up and gripped the grappling hooks in his talons, snatching them free. The agents screamed as they fell from the top of the bus onto the burning, cracked pavement of the highway.

"Nice work, Redwing," Sam said as he flew past the injured and angry Hydra agents. The falcon let out a fierce call and resumed his watch of the bus.

"Wait, does he actually *talk* to the bird? Out loud?" Alcina asked.

"I did say they had an Ant-Man thing going on," FDR answered.

Sam grinned. "Hey, don't hate. The bird just saved your butts, you know."

"For which I am grateful," Alcina said dryly. "But it's still kinda weird that Captain America *talks to birds*."

"We live in a world where gods, aliens, and mutants are real," FDR reminded her.

"...Point taken."

The last pair of Hydra agents were a mile ahead behind a cluster of shrubs, about to toss down caltrops to blow the bus's tires. He knew he wouldn't get to them fast enough before they'd lay them out, so he hailed his associates again. "How good of a shot are you, FDR?"

"Depends. What's the target?"

"There are two agents behind a shrub coming up on your right. Any chance you can lay down some cover fire while I try to get to them?"

"Be happy to. Pettengill, can I borrow your rifle? Thanks, man." Sam could see the bus's double doors open and the barrel sticking out just as the Hydra men jumped out to toss down the caltrops. FDR opened fire, winging one of them in the right arm. They raced back to cover as he kept shooting, giving Sam just enough time to pull the Captain America shield from his back and fling it with the utmost precision. The shield bounced off one man's head. He collapsed in the dirt. The shield broke the other man's right collarbone before rebounding into the air. Sam caught it when it arced back toward him and then landed behind the solo injured man. The Hydra agent's right arm hung limp, but he still threw a sloppy haymaker at Sam.

Sam casually dodged it and just arched an eyebrow as the guy stumbled, struggling to stay upright from the pain.

"Really, dude? Hydra must pay extremely well."

"Fogd be a szád!" The man tried to hit him again, but Sam just rolled his eyes, ducked the punch, and then grabbed his arm as it breezed by. He slammed the guy into the dirt with a hip toss that knocked him out and then disarmed him before launching into the air again.

"That takes care of this batch of Hydra agents," Sam said as he started to close the distance between him and the bus. "All quiet on their comms, so I'm heading back to you. How are the inmates?"

"Chatty and twitchy, but fine for now," FDR said.

"And the guards?"

"All quiet on the western front," Alcina said. "Until the next batch of murderers comes along, at least."

"Good." Sam checked the route ahead. Just another ten minutes to the prison and they'd be home free.

And, of course, as soon as the thought flickered through his mind, Redwing told him about an approaching object.

The falcon had gone back up to a high altitude after Sam returned to stay with the bus. Redwing said he couldn't identify it yet, but it wasn't a jet or a drone.

Sam flipped on his back in the air and narrowed his field of vision at the sky, attempting to locate the anomaly where Redwing had approximated its approach. "Look alive. I think we have another party guest."

"Just one?" FDR asked, sounding flabbergasted.

"Looks like. I'm going to try and intercept—"

Sam quieted as he heard movement through the comm-link and then FDR cursed loudly. "Whoa, what's going on? Talk to me."

"Pettengill, what in God's name are you *doing?*" Alcina snarled.

"What does it look like I'm doing, Alcina?" Pettengill replied far-too-casually.

"Robert," FDR said through his teeth. "You need to *think this through.* If you don't put that rifle down, we're going to open fire. I know your colleagues don't want your blood on their hands and neither do I."

Pettengill let out a bitter laugh. "That's just the thing, marshal. I'm pretty sure none of these men give a crap if I live or die. Why do you think I took the deal they offered me in the first place? I'm overworked and underpaid. So what if Rumlow's loose? It ain't like he's gonna kill anyone who don't already deserve it."

"Hear, hear," Rumlow said smugly.

Sam didn't wait any longer; he flew down to the side of the bus, facing the doors, and rapped his knuckles on them. The bus driver, a portly white man in his fifties named Paul, hurriedly let him in and he closed his wings, stepping inside to see the current standoff.

Alcina had gone to the back of the bus to provide coverage of their rear. She stood with the rifle's muzzle just under her chin, Pettengill's arm around her neck to hold her in front of him. Most of the other prisoners had vacated the area since they knew he was in danger of being shot… except for Rumlow, who stood proudly beside them. FDR stood just inside of the gate that separated the riders from the driver, his service weapon pointed at Pettengill's head. The other three guards stood in the bus seats nearby, their guns also pointed at him, keeping the aisle clear in case someone had to bum rush them.

It was then that Sam figured out what was likely going on; the second cell tower they passed had been a landmark for the person dropping in from a nearby plane. They had probably instructed Pettengill to wait until they'd reached that section of road and then he'd confirmed their position to whomever was airborne so they could take over the bus.

The question remained, just who had organized the jailbreak?

They were about to find out.

"Alright, I need everyone to just *calm down*," Sam said firmly, holding his hands out in supplication. "This doesn't have to end in violence."

"Oh, but it's so much more fun if it does," Rumlow said, grinning.

"Well, no one's asking you," Sam snapped. "So keep your mouth shut or you'll be swallowing teeth when I'm done with you."

Rumlow sneered at him. "You're pretty high and mighty for someone who had to get saved by a *girl* last time we fought."

Sam stared at him blankly. "I *dare* you to call Misty Knight a girl to her face. I double-dare you, Rumlow."

The mercenary swallowed hard. Sam could tell even he knew it had been a weak insult. Misty Knight was one of the two Daughters of the Dragon and was not to be fooled with by anyone with a brain.

Sam turned his eyes on Pettengill. "Come on, man. You're smarter than this. I get it—this is a crap job and it's hard and you don't get the pay or the recognition you want."

He took a step closer, his voice iron. "But this is not the way to get what you want. Even if your employer promised you money and an escape route, this is a federal crime. Not only will the feds be after you, but S.H.I.E.L.D. will hunt you down like a dog. Don't do this."

"You're wasting your breath," Alcina hissed. "Shoot him. I don't care if you hit me. We can't let Rumlow out. You know what he'll do."

Rumlow stroked the side of her cheek. She jerked her head away, glaring. "Aww, that hurts, gorgeous. I was just starting to like you."

He then tapped Pettengill. "Handcuff key."

"Right pocket." Rumlow dug the key ring out and unlocked all his cuffs, tossing the chains aside.

"So you gonna gimme a gun or what, moptop?"

"There's a backup on my ankle."

Rumlow crouched and plucked a .22 snub-nosed revolver free, checking that it was loaded before snapping it closed with a flourish. "Aight, here's how this is gonna go. My ride's on the way. You stay right there and don't move and we'll let everyone get to ADX Florence in one piece."

Rumlow's expression darkened. "If you try anything, Pretty Girl goes first, then I start poppin' my fellow inmates. There is a lot of blood that I can shed today, Cap. Don't try me."

Rumlow raised his voice. "That goes for you too, bus driver. I can hit you from here. Just keep driving unless you want to breathe through the hole I blow out of your throat."

"Franklin," Alcina said, seething. "Shoot. Him. *Now.*"

FDR gritted his teeth, stepping closer to Sam and keeping his voice low. "Your call, Cap."

"We've got to get them away from the hostages," he said quietly. "The helicopter is still on traffic duty, so that's one asset out of play. I hate to say it, but I think letting our mystery guest collect Rumlow is our best bet. It's still a long way to freedom from here."

FDR nodded towards the inmates. "What about them?"

"That's what I'm worried about," Sam murmured. "These men are in prison for life. They don't care if they make it to ADX Florence or not, so if anyone gets the idea to be a hero or just get revenge, we're in trouble."

"If you're done chit-chatting, I want you to toss me your weapons," Pettengill ordered, jabbing the muzzle of the rifle harder into Alcina's jaw. "Starting with you, marshal."

FDR growled. "Don't suppose you have any bright ideas, Cap?"

"Not any good ones."

FDR sent him a cross look. "If he kills me, I'm coming back to haunt the crap out of you."

"Noted, my man."

FDR sighed and popped the clip out of his Glock 17. He snapped the one in the chamber out and then tossed the empty weapon at Pettengill's feet. "There. Choke on it, Judas."

"No hard feelings, I see," Pettengill said with the utmost sarcasm. He motioned to the other three guards. "You lot next."

In the midst of muttered curses, the men unloaded their ammo and tossed the empty guns at his feet as well.

Pettengill continued. "Wilson, drop the shield and kick it over."

"Yeah, yeah, keep your shirt on." Sam unhooked the shield from his back.

Rumlow shifted his weight, looking uncomfortable. "That might not be a good idea—"

Sam flung the shield at Rumlow.

His aim was perfect. The shield bashed into Rumlow's hand and knocked the gun loose, the subsequent gunshot punching a hole in a nearby window. The shield then bounced off the side of Pettengill's head, allowing Alcina to rip herself free. She scooped up one of the fallen empty guns and slammed it into Rumlow's face when he tried to grab for her. Blood spurted out of his nose as he fell back with a groan of pain. The guards all tried to rush forward to reach their weapons or the .22 Rumlow dropped, but Rumlow kicked the pile of guns under the seats. Sam and FDR hopped over the top of the seats to get at their adversaries; FDR pouncing on Pettengill while Sam went after Rumlow.

"Just don't know when to quit, do you?" Rumlow hissed as Sam slammed his head back into the leather seat. Rumlow hit him hard in the ribs twice, then Sam twisted so the next punch missed and drove Rumlow's head into the side of the window, cracking it. Rumlow elbowed Sam in the temple to drive him back, then front-kicked him into the seat across from them. Rumlow pounced on him and wrapped his hands around his throat, using his weight to hold him down while he tried to strangle him.

"This is just what I wanted," Rumlow murmured, leaning in close to make it as personal as possible as Sam struggled to breathe. "Another shot at being the man who killed Captain America. Maybe I'll keep the shield as a trophy once you're finished."

"You want that shield?" Sam said roughly. "Then pry it from my cold, dead hands, Rumlow."

He kicked at Rumlow's left knee which made him buckle, loosening his grip just enough for Sam to get a gulp of air. He then slammed the top of his head into Rumlow's already busted nose and the big man recoiled in pain. Sam rolled onto the floor and grabbed the shield, bringing it up just in time to block another vicious punch from the mercenary. He rammed it into Rumlow's already injured knee and then shoved himself to his feet. Rumlow came for him with quick, brutal blows that reverberated off the shield.

"Is that all you got, Captain America? Huh? Come out from under that thing and fight like a man!"

Sam dodged another punch and then kicked Rumlow in the lower belly, making him wheeze and double over in pain. "What was that, Brock? Speak up, can't hear ya."

Rumlow roared and tackled him, slamming him into the nearest window. Sam saw stars for a second before Rumlow went in on him, punching the side of his head until he felt his brow split, blood running down into his right eye. Rumlow caught him once in the nose, making their faces match, but unlike Rumlow, Sam could think on his feet. He spat a mouthful of blood right into the mercenary's eyes and Rumlow jerked away, rubbing at them. Sam then kicked him into the aisle between the seats and raised the shield above his head, straddling Rumlow. "Stand down or you're done, Brock."

"You ain't got the nerve to kill me—"

WHAM!

Sam brought the end of the shield down a mere inch from the top of Rumlow's head. It left an enormous dent in the floor of the bus. "I've had a bad day. Try me, punk."

Rumlow grimaced, but didn't move, giving Sam a split second to check on the rest of the chaos erupting around him. Pettengill and FDR were in the middle of a wrestling match on the floor of the bus, with FDR crouched over the latter having gotten him into a half-nelson. Alcina and the other guards were now tussling with the inmates, who had tried to grab for the guns. The only people not in a fight were the bus driver… and the serial killer, who sat up front, staring out of the windshield as if he were on an enjoyable and leisurely Sunday drive. Sam felt something cold and slimy go down his back and couldn't have explained why.

But everything around him came to an immediate stop when everyone heard a loud thud on top of the bus. The mystery guest had arrived.

All eyes landed on the bus driver and the double doors. A moment later, a gloved fist reached down from the roof and knocked hard on the doors twice. The bus driver swallowed hard and called back, "Uh, guys?"

"It's alright, Paul," Alcina said. "Let them in. We don't have much choice."

"Aye, aye." He turned the crank to open the doors.

And the Taskmaster stepped onto the bus.

Tony Masters was a tall man in a mask that looked like an eerie grinning skull, wearing armor from head to toe, his sword in a scabbard on his hip and a bow and arrows strapped to his back. He wore a jet pack, but one that was more sophisticated than the one Sam had seen on the first Hydra agent.

Taskmaster pulled the gate open and stepped inside, surveying the damage. "Well, well. Looks like I crashed the party a little late."

"Every party needs a pooper, that's why we invited you, party pooper," Sam deadpanned, narrowing his brown eyes at the villain. "You know I can't let you take Rumlow."

"I do know that," Taskmaster replied. "But it's not as if I'm asking, Wilson. I'll make this simple: you give me Rumlow and my associate Pettengill and we walk out of here. Everyone lives, no further injuries, no loss of life."

"And if I don't?"

Taskmaster cracked his neck. "I kill everyone on this bus and take my men with me anyway."

Sam glanced around. "No offense, but you're a little outnumbered, you know."

"I know. It just doesn't matter. Decide, hero."

Sam worked his jaw, running the scenarios through his head one by one and determining the most likely outcome of each. He knew he could surrender them and try chasing after them once there were no potential hostages, but he also knew Taskmaster. Redwing confirmed he'd planted an explosive charge on the roof of the bus, intending to kill them after he retrieved his men. They were between a rock and a hard place.

That is, until Redwing reached out to him with a *different* sighting.

Sam started to smile, unable to help himself. Taskmaster tilted his head. "What's that look for, Wilson?"

"How about my counteroffer? You and me, *mano y mano*. Winner take all. If you win, we stand down and let you take Rumlow and Pettengill. If I win, you pack up and head home empty-handed."

Taskmaster continued to scrutinize him. "I'm supposed to believe you'd keep your word?"

Sam shrugged. "Of the two of us, who's more honorable?"

"Point taken. Do you expect me to keep my word?"

"Not really, but I'll humor you anyway to avoid more bloodshed."

Sam got the impression Taskmaster was grinning beneath his mask. "Alright, Wilson, you're on."

Sam stood up and secured the shield to his back again. Rumlow dragged himself into a nearby seat, glaring daggers as he went, but not putting up another fight. The two factions split apart to opposite sides of the bus to watch the confrontation. The tension in the air was palpable as Sam settled into a judo defensive stance. Naturally, Taskmaster mirrored him, as that was his infamous unnatural ability. For a moment, there was nothing but the clank of the bus's engine and the rumble of the road beneath it.

Then Taskmaster struck.

He lashed out at Sam with lightning-fast kicks aimed at his solar plexus. Sam parried the blows and took a step back so the next roundhouse kick missed his head. Taskmaster tripped him, so Sam let it carry him into a backroll and came up on one knee, punching Taskmaster's right shin. As he staggered, Sam landed an uppercut right on the chin, driving him back several steps.

Taskmaster shook his head, then snorted, seeming impressed. "Not bad, Wilson."

He rushed Sam, landing two vicious hits to his ribs that made him grunt in pain. Sam clasped his hands and brought them both down across the side of Taskmaster's head. Taskmaster shook it off and rammed his palm into Sam's injured nose. Sam reeled, his eyes watering, grabbing the top of a nearby seat to stay upright. He managed to block the next kick, but his blurry vision made him miss the incoming flurry of jabs. His ribs screamed in protest beneath the suit, so he brought his forearms up like a boxer, forcing Taskmaster to back up so his fists wouldn't fly past him. Sam adjusted his stance and ducked the next punch, then wrapped his arm around Taskmaster's throat when he had an opening and threw him to the floor of the bus using a *koshi guruma* throw.

Taskmaster blocked Sam's boot when it came down, aimed at his throat. He twisted his legs up around Sam's lower body and then dragged him to the floor beside him, leaping atop him and shoving his forearm into his throat to choke him.

"A valiant effort, but you have to know you're outmatched, Wilson," Taskmaster gloated as he pressed down even harder. "You can't win."

"Not trying to win," Sam rasped, smirking. "Just trying to stall."

Taskmaster hesitated. "Stall for what?"

As if on cue, the sound of the SWAT helicopter finally reached his ears.

Taskmaster turned his head to see the helicopter as it drifted into view of the bus windows. There was an officer with a high-powered, armor-piercing rifle pointed right at him. The officer gave a sarcastic wave that made Taskmaster growl. The SWAT officer beside the rifleman whipped out a loud hailer and addressed them. "This is Fremont County police. You are under arrest. The bus is going to pull over and we are going to extract you from it. If you do not surrender, we will use deadly force."

Rumlow spat on the floor in disgust. "Ain't no party like a pig party, is there?"

Taskmaster's shoulders dropped as he let out a weary sigh. "You're more trouble than you're worth, Rumlow. Someday, you'll realize that."

The villain pushed to his feet and straightened his armor. He then offered a hand to Sam. "Well played, Captain America. Well played."

Sam took his hand and let Taskmaster pull him to his feet, clearing his sore throat. "Can't take all the credit. Gotta thank FDR and his fast phone fingers."

FDR waved cheerily. "You're welcome!"

Taskmaster sent Sam a gimlet stare. "Our score is not settled, but it will be at another time."

Sam bared his teeth in a grin. "Looking forward to it."

"Hey, hey!" Pettengill cried. "You can't just leave us here! We had a deal."

Taskmaster spared him an annoyed look. "Had you done your part correctly, the deal would still be in play, but you didn't, so I am not obligated to hold up my end of the bargain. Find your own way out of this mess."

He stalked for the gate… but stopped when he noticed the serial killer was now blocking his path.

Wayne Clayton was a tall, gangly man shaved bald with sleeve tattoos running down his arms. He still wore the same serene expression as before and spoke with an uncharacteristically soft voice as he addressed Taskmaster. "Might I make a request?"

Taskmaster couldn't help but sound bewildered. "And that would be?"

Clayton smiled. "Might I have a souvenir? I have never met a super villain before."

Taskmaster turned toward Sam, who just shrugged. "I mean, the prison's gonna confiscate it as soon as he gets there anyway."

Taskmaster reached into his quiver and offered the man an arrow. "Will this suffice?"

Clayton's smile widened. "It will indeed. Thank you, sir." He sat.

"You're welcome." Taskmaster shoved the gate open and Paul obligingly opened the bus doors for him. With a blast of his jet pack, he vanished into the burning hot Colorado sun.

The SWAT officer with the loud hailer gave a start. "Cap, are we pursuing him?"

Sam waved his hands and shouted back, "Stand down! Let him go."

"Roger that. We're coming in for pickup."

The bus then eased onto the shoulder, slowed, and came to a stop.

Just as Alcina, FDR, and the guards were marching him down the aisle to the outside, Pettengill grabbed the prison guard Justin and ripped the gun from his hand, jamming the muzzle against his temple. "Nobody move!"

They all froze. Pettengill squinted at the chopper that had landed in front of the bus. "Tell them to stand down."

"Robert," Alcina said in a measured voice, her gun unwavering as it pointed at him. "Listen to me. There is no way out. You have to accept what you've done and live with the consequences. If you don't put that gun down, one of us will blow you away. And I don't want you to be surprised or assume that we're bluffing. We *will* kill you. Take the easier path."

"If you don't want Brandt dead, then you'll make sure that

doesn't happen," Pettengill said as he slowly backed up toward the gate. "I'm walking out of here."

"Listen to her, man," Sam urged. "This is your last chance. If you walk out that door, they're gonna just shoot you both and you know it."

Pettengill swallowed hard. "No," he said as he kept inching for the gate. "I'm not going to the slam. I've seen what it's like. Better off dying on my feet than living on my knees."

"As you wish," Wayne Clayton said quietly, having surreptitiously appeared behind Pettengill. Before anyone could move a muscle, he stabbed him in the side of the throat with the arrow.

Justin jerked himself loose and whirled around to see Pettengill hit the floor, blood pouring from the wound. "Oh God, someone get the First Aid kit! Call an ambulance, now!"

Clayton returned to his seat, humming an upbeat tune as the rest of them went into action to try to save his victim. The other inmates watched on wordlessly, any semblance of a fight no longer present after seeing the bloodshed up close and personal.

o————o

"I'M SORRY," Sam said quietly.

Alcina watched as the paramedics pulled the body bag closed and prepared to load Pettengill's corpse into the ambulance. "Why? It wasn't your fault he was a turncoat."

"More like a lost cause," FDR said gravely, shaking his head. "What the hell was he thinking?"

Sam petted the front of Redwing's feathers. "What all men think when they're desperate: that they can get something for nothing."

He turned to look back at the bus. "But it could've gone a lot worse, if you can believe it."

"I can and I do." Alcina offered her hand. "Thank you, Sam. We couldn't have survived if you hadn't been here."

"You underestimate yourself," Sam said as he shook it, then FDR's hand next. "You both handled this debacle like champs."

FDR elbowed him. "Does that mean we get to become Avengers?"

Sam laughed. "I'll ask, but no promises."

Alcina checked the map on her tablet. "Just a mile to go before we're there. God, I hope it's smooth sailing."

Sam patted her shoulder as the three of them walked back to board the bus that would bring Rumlow and the rest to their new home. "It ought to be. After all, the storm's gotta pass sometime."

"Amen, Cap. Amen."

EVERYONE'S HERO

MAURICE BROADDUS

"WELL, IF *it isn't Mr. Chickens Coming Home to Roost," S.H.I.E.L.D. Director Maria Hill said, sitting at the center of the room as if on a throne of intel. Sitrep and telemetry reports streamed all around her like tickers on CNN. Agents scurried about with important faces and determined strides, on their way to conduct official business. The S.H.I.E.L.D. helicarrier was built like a flying detention center, able to withstand an attack from just about anything short of a nuclear weapon. S.H.I.E.L.D.'s logo branded every wall, as if once they turned a corner its agents might forget who they worked for. Who owned them.*

They didn't own me.

"Clever, Director Hill." My shield nestled comfortably into place across my back. "See? How hard was that to respect someone's name and title? Especially when you were the one who asked me here."

"Sorry to upset your delicate sensibilities, Falcon—I mean, Captain America. It still takes some getting used to." Maria got this tone when she was about to serve someone up. The woman was a superspy; lied for a living. Probably as a hobby, too, just to stay in

practice. So if she revealed a tell, it was because she wanted you to know. "But allow me a gentle correction. You weren't asked, you were summoned."

"I'm a free agent now. Got better things to do than run S.H.I.E.L.D. errands."

"True, you no longer have to cooperate with S.H.I.E.L.D. or the U.S. government. You fight for the everyman now. You have the revoked security clearance to show for it."

I folded my arms across my chest. Redwing settled onto my shoulder. "So why have I been called to the principal's office?"

"This is General McAllister Groves."

Ramrod straight, his hands clasped behind his back, the general still cut an impressive silhouette in his uniform. Barrel-chested, hair a little grayer about the temples, he stepped closer but didn't extend a hand. 'Nam. Desert Storm. C.O. of the Joint Chiefs. One of the most accomplished military men, Black or otherwise, ever produced by this country. "Hello… Captain. Long time."

"Hello, General." I turned back to Maria. "Once you've been strapped to missiles with a payload of anthrax with someone, it creates a bit of a bond."

A terrorist calling himself Hate-Monger had captured General Groves and used his access to a Stark–Fujikawa cleanup op in Russia to acquire anthrax.

"Good times. I don't miss them at all."

"So why have you called the band back together?" I asked.

The general strode around, gesturing at screens. Images of farmland, militia movements, and an array of faces rotated through them. "We've been looking to be more proactive in stemming the tide of extremism."

"Okay…"

"We're taking the fight directly back to 'Hate-Monger' and folks like him rather than wait for them to set up a base of operations.

We have infiltrated several organizations and networks, stepping up operations on various fronts."

"This sounds… problematic," I said.

"Why? These are the exact sort of folks we thought the 'new' Captain America would love to go after," Maria said as she climbed down from her throne, all but saying the word "Black."

"I'm uneasy because it almost looks like you all are searching for fresh methods for your counterterrorism operation."

"Literally our mandate," she said.

"In my experience, whenever this level of resources, intelligence, and mandate are brought to bear, it creates a massive dragnet, trampling ordinary citizens, usually the Black and Brown ones. COINTELPRO dressed up for more acceptable targets."

"Hmph." The general snorted with derision at the accusation. "Yes, we just have to use the tools correctly."

"What have you done?" My tone was a mix of exhaustion and exasperation since I'd seen this dance before. Getting in front of being caught with their hands in the cookie jar.

"What makes you think—" Maria asked.

"It's me. What have you done?"

"We have a situation brewing in Woodsberg." At the general's direction, the cameras panned the scenic streets of AverageSmallTownVille. "We have a missing asset on the ground."

"This seems… beneath my paygrade. I'm usually brought in for more 'punch the super-powered villain' scenarios. It's not like I can go undercover there."

"We're counting on that. We are talking about…"

…Woodsberg, Indiana. No one could point it out on a map, not even if the map was of Woodsberg. The city was laid out under the name of Bear Creek in 1853 (switching to its current name in 1869). This being America, the story took the usual turn in the

1880s, when Woodsberg fully embraced being a sundown town. Black folks couldn't reside within the town and any who worked within its borders were told they had to be out by the time the sun's last rays of the day hit their backsides. It was a KKK headquarters not too long ago. Up until recently they still had a sign that read "…don't let the sun set on you in Woodsberg" …with a hard 'R'. They may no longer be a sundown town, but beneath the surface they were still sundown in spirit.

"Are you lost?" A woman whose blonde hair needed touching up at the roots tugged her baseball cap lower onto her head. It read "Join the Front." She walked up to me like she had been deputized to conduct a stop and frisk.

"This has got to be one of the most hospitable and concerned towns I've ever been in." It didn't matter that I was wearing my civvies, albeit with the shield on my back: my presence was conspicuous to the point of discomfort for them. To wear the uniform, to be a symbol, automatically invited hate. That was the way it was whenever anyone stood for something, operated on principles. But there was an extra irrational energy and dimension to the criticism of *me* in the uniform. "You know you're the fifth person who's stopped to make sure I knew where I was going?"

"You're a lippy one. Wait, you look familiar," she squinted her eyes, searching her memories, then clocking the shield.

I braced. This point in the interaction only went one of two ways, and from the way her mouth soured, she would not be thanking me for my service.

"Now, before you call me racist…"

"Ma'am, I hadn't called you anything yet."

"I'm just saying that you should know that I don't see color. You're just not *my* Captain America. Don't get me wrong, you were fine an' all for being the Falcon. But moving up the ranks to Captain America, that's Affirmative Action heroing. You should stick to being your own people's hero."

"Remember my place."

"Exac—that's not what I meant." Ambling off in a huff, she wasn't halfway down the block before she pressed her cell phone to her ear. The general was right. My presence alone kicked over rocks. I only had to wait to see what crawled out from under them.

Ostensibly, "the asset" was supposed to make an appearance at the same spot U.S. Republican presidential candidate, Thomas George Finkmeister III, did in 1940 when he made a ten-hour speech about the political missteps committed by President Franklin D. Roosevelt. The moment was meant to leverage the symbolism: to illustrate how much had changed and demonstrate how much hadn't. This was where the trail ran cold. I held up the dossier in vain hope, but apparently my target also didn't sport any of S.H.I.E.L.D.'s fancy tracking tech.

Redwing circled overhead. Through our special connection, he alerted me to the approaching truck. A red Ford which had seen its share of rough, off-road adventures. Two flags waved from its bed: an American flag and a blue and black one that read "Join the Front." The truck circled once and sped off.

God, family, country. That was how I was taught to live my life. My father drilled into me the tenets and values of faith. My mother drilled into me the responsibility of serving others. My time as partner to the first Captain America, Steve Rogers, drilled into me the duty to defend the ideal of what the U.S. stood for.

I often found myself in the parts of the country that failed to live up to that ideal.

The truck returned. It screeched to a halt and a welcoming committee of "Good Guys with Guns" hopped out.

"You're trespassing." Despite the fatigues, their leader stepped toward me with the cocksure bravado of someone who knew military folks but hadn't served a day in his life. He thumped a metal bat into his hand.

"I'm on a public sidewalk." I carefully tucked my scanner into my jacket. "Though I'd always wondered if I might meet my end by PWB."

"PWB?" Fatigues Guy asked.

"Pokémon-ing while Black."

"Look here, Sambo..." His friend was a squat figure with a bulbous face and blotchy complexion. His breath was rank with recently imbibed courage.

"Cute. Unoriginal and typical, but probably the best you got."

"Wait, he looks familiar," Squat Guy said as Fatigues Guy spread out, trying to circle me. A poor attempt to distract me from the others dismounting from the truck.

"I'm pretty sure we all look alike to you." I held my arms out, not quite tamping the air. "Fellas, allow me to assure you that you don't want to do this..."

Fatigues Guy tapped his bat against the ground. Satisfied with the delicate metal clink it made, he charged, swinging in an upward arc. Even as I pivoted, I was aware of his buddies swarming me from behind. Grabbing Fatigue Guy's batting arm at the wrist, I squeezed the nerve there, sending a convulsion of pain through him. I launched him into his buddies. Bounding onto the largest one, I slammed his head into the sidewalk before he could recover. Redwing swooped down, tearing at the face of Squat Guy.

Redwing cried out, veering upward as a figure marched up the block. It barreled towards us like a freight train. People barely had enough time to clear the sidewalk. Its face only a crude approximation of a human, the robot wore a blue uniform over its metallic chassis.

"I am the Zone Enforcement Response Option. Cease all illegal activities."

I'd read about this "Officer Z.E.R.O." in the Avengers files. Basically a one-man assault unit. Enhanced strength and reflexes, virtually indestructible. Constructed to handle hazardous police duty. Its rollout was halted due to design flaws—namely that its cerebral inputs were based on someone with a resentment for police. Its hands whirred to become a launcher with a series of canisters around it. "You all must disperse immediately."

Without waiting for compliance, Officer Z.E.R.O. launched several canisters. Upon landing, they exploded and released plumes of tear gas. The locals scattered. "We are committed to non-violent dispersal of protestors," it said.

Its hand mount rotated, and it began to fire sponge bullets that exploded around me. The impact alone might have put me down. Each shell released foam containment, followed by balls spewing CS gas. A foam discharge locked up my left arm.

"You need to take it down a notch. Innocent civilians are going to get hurt." No matter the situation, there were innocents. I couldn't just paint everyone in Woodsberg with the same brush. That was easy. Compassion was the true, hard work.

Officer Z.E.R.O. locked in on me as its sole target. Its shoulder mount targeted me. "You have caused me to fear for my life. Initiating self-defense protocols."

I managed to raise my shield up as its emitters glowed and the world exploded. Pain burst through me like a tidal wave. Every nerve receptor lit on fire. The latest in police crowd control measures: an invisible beam of short-wavelength microwaves. They only heated the outer surface, penetrating skin just deep enough to affect pain receptors, making me feel as if I'd been dangled into open flames. I dropped to my knees. The officer sprang on me. Used its baton to choke me.

"You are under arrest." As it reduced my world to complete blackness, it said, "You are now a prisoner of..."

"...the operation?" I asked.

"Codename: Xeon." General Groves tossed me a dossier. The device looked like a scanner the size of a cell phone.

"Xeon?" Turnabout was fair play as the name slapped me with the weight of my own past failures. The dossier emitted a holographic image of the man I once knew. Xeon was the leader of Legion, a gang that ran the streets of Harlem back in the day. I had been working with them, as Sam Wilson and as the Falcon. They were on the verge of turning the corner when the police confronted them. In the altercation, an officer shot and killed one of the Legion members. Xeon always blamed me. I always blamed me. "Wait, how is he your asset?"

"You mean because your old friend was involved in a conspiracy to kidnap the president?" Maria couldn't hide the snide sneer in her voice.

"No one was harmed. It even initiated a fruitful dialogue in the community," I said.

"You're thinking like a social worker. Try thinking like a trained government agent. The full weight and resources of the U.S. government landed on his head..."

"He would have been buried under the jail." My voice was reduced to a resigned whisper.

"And then the jail's existence denied." The general transferred the dossier to the nearest screen. Xeon's image leered over me.

I chided myself. Not once since that incident had I even bothered to check up on him. There was always something—the next mission, the next bad guy, the next world-ending threat—to keep me busy. "You turn him?"

"We provided an opportunity." General Groves scrolled through Xeon's file, a series of images documenting his evaluation. "He was enrolled in a special program, becoming a Presidential Management Fellow at U.S. government agencies. On the ground, he works as a well-placed community organizer. In our rooms, he reports to the State Department."

"He's a snitch." I sucked my teeth, not sure who I was more disgusted with. "At least that's how his old friends in Legion might see it."

"He's our asset."

"By any other name." I remained skeptical, waiting for the other boot to fall, probably aimed at my behind. None of this added up. Maria Hill, Director of S.H.I.E.L.D. General Groves, of the Joint Chiefs. Two heavy hitters brought in for what amounted to a search and extract. "So, what did he stumble into?"

"It began with a DM." Maria blew up a message, its metadata scraped down to the nanobyte.

"When will we learn that Chirp is the devil?" I asked.

"An anonymous user sent a message implying they had sway with a State Department official. The UNSUB claimed full access to classified information and computer systems. To prove he had access to intelligence outside his purview, the unknown user sent some preliminary intel on the National Front."

"Did it check out?"

"That's what Xeon was investigating for us," General Groves said.

"In short, you need me to reconnect with my old friend. I just hope that the..."

"...spirit that I have seen. May be the devil..." I read out.

My head lolled forward, hanging heavy against my chest, as I stirred from unconsciousness.

"... and the devil hath power." A man lounged in a corner, not bothering to look my way. Xeon. His posture that of a person completely unbothered by his circumstances. Turning to me—calm and confident—his thick, muscular build still displayed traces of his days running the streets with Legion. His face—framed by his strong jawline and weathered eyes, steely and determined—sported a beard unkempt by days without access to a razor. Scars marred his arms. His former cornrows were long shorn off, leaving his hair trimmed low and respectable.

"You never struck me as a *Hamlet* fan," I said.

"What can I say? I defy people's expectations of me. Any particular reason you reciting it?" Xeon's voice thickened with a mixture of gravitas, weariness, and wisdom.

"Trick of mine. If I get knocked out, it's my way of knowing everything's still in place."

"This part of your rescue plan?" Xeon gestured to my chains.

"I don't know what you're complaining about. My brilliant detective skills led me right to you. Now we just have to get out of here." I closed my eyes. I sensed Redwing nearby through our special connection. He was fine and would be my true north, guiding me out once I escaped these chains. I tested the restraints. They were securely fastened to the wall, but situations like this were just about finding the weak link. "You've come a long way, working for General Groves now."

"I hear the judgment in your tone. I'll tell you like I told him: he don't own me. Despite what any of them think. He ain't got as much juice as he thinks, neither. Like I don't know if they put a Brown person in charge, there must be nothing left to lose. When people are absolutely desperate, that's the only time they bet on people like us."

"I wasn't judging you. I was… sorry." Our captors had taken my shield: they thought me disarmed. Common mistake. Removing the lockpick from my belt buckle, I went to work. "Since we got time to kill, I was curious about how you fell in with the general."

"You won't get it any more than my so-called masters do," Xeon said.

"Try me."

"When you left, I was done. I fell out with Legion. I understood that I couldn't keep living life like I was. Problem was, I couldn't figure out how to do right by the community. Man, I was just out there floundering. Then another one of you neighborhood do-gooders, Kamal Rakim, got with me. He managed to get me to see what being in a community, what serving our community, actually looked like.

"Made me understand that even if we had a seat at the table, that table was literally built to profit off our suffering. That's the world we're living in. He showed me how to do the real work of changing lives. Not just slapping Band-Aids on gunshot wounds thinking they made a difference in someone's life."

Xeon wielded his words like a dagger aimed at my heart. Refusing to give him the satisfaction of even a grimace, I nodded and he continued. "So, when the general approached me, Rakim reminded me that I was going to fail. That there was no way I couldn't. Not as a cog propping up their machine. My only choice was to figure out how to be truly me, make the role my own. So, yeah, I'm in their fancy program and all, but it's to leverage all of those excessive government resources and intel for my community."

"You're trying to do the role you've been tapped to do, but on your own terms. I get that better than you think."

"Don't try to 'bond' with me like we in some sort of similar situation. You fight for *them*." Xeon turned his back to me, returning to his thoughts.

"I fight for everyone."

"I'll give you that Sam Wilson fought for us. But as Falcon, as Captain America, you're with them. You're *their* hero. Tell yourself what you need to."

"Here's what I tell myself: I had to let go of my anger. Yeah, I used to be like you back when we met. Mad. After centuries of wrongs without reparations, I've lived in—worked in—the trauma. But I realized that I couldn't work from that place. Hostility polarizes rather than unifies. There was no healing in lashing out. It was no better than living with no hope, slowly poisoning my soul. My faith."

The lock clicked.

"Whatever. In the end, you solve *their* problems," Xeon said.

"Saving the world is in everyone's best interest."

"After that, how do you make *our* world better?"

"That's not fair."

"It never is. Now get me out of here. Before..."

"...this mission sounds like a mess you made," I said. "One you expect me to clean up."

"Is that so bad?" General Groves glared at me. "Hate-Monger is out there."

"Is that so bad? You sent Xeon on some rogue op to ferret out the National Front without giving him sufficient backup," I said. "You made it personal."

"It's personal in spades. Did you forget? He had us stretched out and chained. Left us completely powerless to remind us of our place. He was going to kill and destroy, and have the world blame us for it. Us and our people. He humiliated me. Us."

"I get it. Don't think I don't. But..."

There were still times when I wondered, What would Steve do? *I couldn't help myself. For years I worked alongside him, trained alongside him. He was a mentor and partner and friend I admired, even looked up to. He'd probably have given some rousing speech about how we had to rise above and be better, or else we'd be no different than the people we fought against. And he'd be right, of course. Yet I couldn't just spout words in a poor impersonation of him or else I'd always feel like I never measured up—like I was an imposter. I had to find my own voice and my own way. Instead, I remembered my father's lessons on becoming a living sermon, a faith lived out well. To protect "the least of these." That was the dream fulfilled.*

"I'm going after Hate-Monger because it's the right thing to do. He has someone who was once my friend, a man I owe a debt to. Lives are in danger, ones I've sworn to protect. What you've done, how you've done it, is on you. So I guess that leaves us..."

...skulking through halls. The labyrinthine corridors didn't surprise me. These types always had huge financial backing to build their death traps and secret lairs. It was almost as if money wasn't the point for them. Redwing circled high above, anxious and impatient. It'd only be a matter of time before he tired of waiting and met me halfway. He was a dependable partner. I wished I could swap him for my current company.

"We're too often defined by our trauma rather than our aspirations. Oppression is not a prep school," Xeon whispered.

"Look, ghetto Yoda, I don't need the running commentary. I need to focus on getting us out of here."

"I'm your conscience. You know, in case you forgot where you came from."

"You think I see myself as a Black super hero? Man, I'm a super hero, period."

"That's how they get you: try to get you to forget who and

what you are. Compartmentalize your two identities… it don't work. You have to own who you are."

"Tell me, can I punch you in the face and it not be a political statement?"

"No. Violence to defend the ends of the status quo is a political statement. Your problem is that you're still a 'save-the-world' type. You run the Man's errands, save a life here and there, and pat yourself on the back. Never seeing the big picture. Only now you have wings."

"And a shield." I held up my balled hand when we neared a junction. "If you want me to stop saving the occasional life, starting now, just let me know. Otherwise, let me do my thing."

I wasn't a true believer, not like Steve was. Take away his shield, the uniform, he was still Captain America through and through. He was what the country thought it was. I was its reality. But I still believed in the dream of America. I wasn't loyal to a flag, but an idea. An ideal. The dream was old. Unfulfilled.

Inching my head around the corner, the hall opened into a massive ballroom, one large enough for a town meeting. A man stood on the dais, my shield resting at its center like a trophy. Officer Z.E.R.O. stood sentry, unmoving as if powered down, protecting a felon I'd recognize anywhere.

Josh Glenn. Hate-Monger. He's not the only Hate-Monger, nor the first, and certainly not the most original—that's probably the Hitler clone. Glenn is just the sad reboot that no one asked for. A fanboy of the original, living out his wretched, pathetic dreams.

Prowling about under the crowd's adulation, his every step filled with a sense of entitlement. The strut of a man who owned the world, whose authority was inevitable… His tailor-made suit cost more than I made in a couple months (the super hero 'biz' is more like an unpaid internship, ain't no hero whose last name isn't Stark swimming in cash. Especially now I'm off S.H.I.E.L.D.'s payroll). Every iota of Hate-Monger displayed the arrogance of the so-called "superior" race he believed he belonged to, wrapped up with the disdain belonging to the most virulent member of the Klan.

What made it worse: he looked so… respectable.

"You can come on out of the shadows, Captain Quota Hire," Hate-Monger announced. All eyes turned to me.

I strode toward him. His audience parted for me. Xeon trailed, ready for action to jump off. "You've lost your hood."

"I don't have to wear a hood. Not these days. The country has finally embraced what I've always been about."

"Divisiveness?"

"That's you, not me. I'm an Americanist; a Western chauvinist, if you will. Look around you. I'm not gearing up for war. I'm gearing up for messaging. I have a whole marketing department and social media farm developing and pushing out those brands. It's about crafting social narratives. And there's nothing illegal about that."

This wasn't the first, or the fifteenth, time I'd heard versions of that speech from people like him. Like a nest of snakes: as soon as you'd chop down one viper, another one would stick his head up. But fools like Hate-Monger would always have lackeys to sacrifice for them, to take the fall for them, which made him even more dangerous. I never worried about being punched or shot by Hate-Monger.

His words, the ones that made the lost and misunderstood adopt his particular brand of hatred and violence, made him dangerous.

A wall of TV panels had been set up in the front of the room. Data streamed all around him. Crop yield projections. Real-time security footage from nuclear reactors. Fatigues Guy and Squat Guy glanced over at us, smirked, and returned to hastily put-together workstations in the ballroom's rear, under the baseball cap lady's supervision. Social media apps filled their displays alongside a list of talking points.

"I see you're up to your same tricks," I said.

"Not at all. You misunderstand—I want what is best for the country. I don't believe in violence as a means to any social ends. We have nothing to hide here. We're operating completely out in the open. Like all true patriots who want to see this country survive and thrive, the National Front is worst-case-scenario planning.

"We're specially funded to examine public policy. We're like a thinktank of ordinary citizens, the ones politicians too often ignore."

"Terrorists?" Xeon asked.

Hate-Monger ignored him and continued his tirade. "My people, the ones you claim you're also sworn to protect, are scared. They see rioting but watch the media call it rebellion. Or a reckoning. We oppose these movements designed to chip away at law and order and the security of our nation. It's un-American. We propose... different solutions."

"Genocide?" Xeon inquired sarcastically.

Hate-Monger continued, ever louder. "For example, should the National Front discover a plot to poison America's breadbasket, fomenting civil unrest by attacking energy facilities or a move to damage our national economy to stoke divisions, it will be met by our cadre of Officer Z.E.R.O.s."

I glanced over at it. The robot continued to stare out impassively. "But there are laws against assault, kidnapping, and detainment."

"We'll see what a court has to say, if it gets to that. Your friend was an accidental, though appreciated, test scenario. We hadn't realized our activities might also flush out so-called civil rights activists. We now know our enemy's face. Luckily, we had to 'stand our ground'; we 'feared for our lives' and all that. We had to hold you for our own safety, until we could verify who you were and determine who the appropriate authorities were to call."

I wasn't a lawyer, but at the moment, Hate-Monger was beyond any punchable offenses, except on general principle.

"You believe his bull?" Xeon asked.

"He is a familiar non-solution. We may not have a choice. I can play Whac-A-Mole with villains and it won't change a thing. My mission was to find you. As far as the law is concerned, the rest of this is probably complicated," I said.

"America used to be simple," Hate-Monger said.

"No, it had the illusion of simplicity. That worked for some."

"He's whiter than his privilege." Xeon seethed next to me.

What Hate-Monger refused to accept was that we shared the same story. Born from the grim parts of history, I too grew up in an America built on settler colonialism, racial slavery, and the repercussions of historical trauma. I lost both parents at a young age. My father, Paul, was a minister of uncompromised faith who dreamt of a better tomorrow. He was gunned down while stopping a fight. A mugger shot my mother, Darlene, a year later. I knew the anger. It was my constant shadow. But I also had role models who surrounded me, grounded me in the idea of resistance and what it truly meant to be free.

"There was a time when someone like him used a Cosmic Cube in an attempt to rewrite my memories. Created a persona called Snap Wilson. Gang member and drug dealer, the product of limited imagination. People were so ready to believe it because they expected it. That story fit into their narrow narrative of who we were. A nation that turned to fake news and misinformation because the truth was too hard. But that's their problem. We're leaving." I stormed up to the dais and reached for the shield. "I'll just be taking this."

"Theft in progress." Officer Z.E.R.O. flared to life. "Subject attempting to flee incarceration."

Officer Z.E.R.O. dashed toward me, firing bean bag rounds that exploded in a flurry of metal pellets all around me. I flung my shield at its face, but the robot batted it away. Xeon scrambled toward my shield. Turning toward him, Officer Z.E.R.O. swung its metal fists. Xeon slid under the blows and scooped up my shield. The robot pummeled away at my unbreakable shield as I ran toward them. When I collided with Officer Z.E.R.O., it was like wrestling a tank. It elbowed my stomach. Tumbling away, I recovered to my feet.

"Catch!" Xeon threw my shield toward me. Not a great toss, but I could work with it.

With me staying out of range of its microwave weapon, the battlebot switched weapons, launching flashbang grenades.

Removing his jacket and tossing it to the ground, Xeon grabbed keyboards from nearby workstations and threw them at the robot. Officer Z.E.R.O. turned to him. Despite its size, its speed was phenomenal. The robot maneuvered behind Xeon and slammed him to the ground in a chokehold. It drove a metallic knee into my friend's back and then threw him away like a ragdoll. While it was distracted brutalizing Xeon, I slammed my shield into Officer Z.E.R.O.'s back. My momentum drove the shield through much of its body. Officer Z.E.R.O. froze as if calculating the extent of its damage before it keeled over.

"No!" Hate-Monger screamed.

I helped Xeon to his feet. When he locked eyes with Hate-Monger, Xeon lunged at the dais and drew back his fist to punch

Hate-Monger. With a high screech, Redwing reared up, clawing at Hate-Monger's face until he toppled from the dais.

"You hitting him was what he wanted. Enough to get you arrested."

"Ain't no rule against me punching a Nazi," Xeon said.

"Well, there shouldn't be. But meanwhile, let him press charges against a bird and see how far he gets. Let's go. I have to decide if I want to..."

"...accept the mission?" General Groves asked.

I took the dossier scanner. "Life, liberty, and the pursuit of happiness. Liberty. The dream of being truly free. That's what I fight for. A friend of mine once told me that to be a hero you have to make sacrifices for something greater. To me, to disgrace the shield is to disgrace the dream. But most importantly, to be a Captain America for the people, I have to be responsible to those not in the room. The forgotten."

Without so much as a backward glance, I headed out.

"Sam." Director Maria Hill snagged my arm, stopping me as I passed her. "The shield looks good on you."

EXCLUSIVE CONTENT

SHEREE RENÉE THOMAS

"HOW DID dinner and a show become a cross-country road trip?" Sam asked.

Laden with two red suitcases and a leather satchel large enough to carry his shield, he followed Misty into the boutique hotel suite, relieved this debit card had gone through.

I gotta keep up with my account balance, he thought with a defeated sigh as they walked past vintage vinyl, music memorabilia, and antique jukeboxes. Life was decidedly different without S.H.I.E.L.D. and their financial backing.

"I never said where," Misty answered, directing Sam to set her luggage by the window.

He nodded as he opened the curtains, staring out at the Nashville skyline. The afternoon sun warmed his face and flooded the room with golden shafts illuminating the tiny dust motes in the air.

"Come on, Sam," Misty said, excitement in her voice. "Let's go. We're gonna miss the meet-and-greet." She stood behind Sam and hugged his neck, planting her full lips against his cheek. "I want all the merch," she said. "Some vinyl for my turntable, a T-shirt, and Xclusiv DYG's autograph. I know you can make that last one happen!"

For three months Misty had talked about catching one of these shows somewhere in the country. Xclusiv DYG was her favorite rapper. His music put Sam in the mind of a hip-hop, country-and-western punk fusion. Misty called it "Country Punk Trap Music."

Like his music, Xclusiv defied all categories, comfortably morphing sounds and looks as he pleased. Xclusiv's debut album, *Straight Out the Woodshed*, had debuted at number one on the pop music charts a year ago and was still holding on to top ten status.

Misty played Xclusiv's album so much, Sam had memorized every word of every song. He was an old-school hip-hop and classic jazz fiend, but Misty wasn't the only person jamming that hit record. Everywhere Sam went, he heard Xclusiv DYG, rapping, singing, humming and moaning, strumming his guitar, left-handed like Jimi Hendrix, picking it expertly like an old-school bluesman.

"Whatever you want, Misty." Sam smiled.

OUTSIDE THE hotel, afternoon sunlight filled Sam with newfound vigor. Cars scuttled through the Nashville streets. Pedestrians populated the sidewalk, walking to and fro, some in cowboy hats and boots, others rocking various kinds of swag from other eras. Their numbers didn't quite compare to what he was used to seeing back in Harlem, but the character and eclectic energy of the crowds was just as thrilling. It was a people-watcher's heaven.

Sam stared at the sky and imagined himself soaring over Nashville, the wind in his face, his best friend Redwing by his side.

"There's our Uber." Misty pointed at a silver Toyota Highlander pulling into the hotel parking lot. The pair slid onto the back seat, Misty greeting their driver while Sam shut the door.

"You're here to pick up Mercedes Knight?" she asked.

The driver looked at the glowing GPS system displayed on the dashboard. Then he eyed Misty through the rearview mirror.

"Yes," he said, his dark eyes baggy, and bloodshot. He looked like someone who hadn't rested for days, whether riding customers around, partying all night, or both. A weary smile spread across his unshaven face. "If only I had a *Mercedes* to scoop you up."

Misty shook her head and stared out the window. Sam understood the irritation he saw in her eyes. People were always making lame jokes with her name. She pulled a pamphlet from the breast pocket on her jacket, unfolding the glossy brochure across her lap.

"This concert is going to be amazing," she said, pointing at the smiling faces and musical instruments spread in front of her. Xclusiv was a musical polyglot, expert in the guitar, piano, and kalimba, among others. "Our VIP tickets guarantee us front-row seats for all Xclusiv DYG goodness. Thank you very much. Of course, we'll start with the before-the-show shindig. That's when I'm getting my album and my T-shirt autographed. Yes!"

She poked Sam playfully in his side. "After that, we've got two hours to kill before the concert. We can grab something to eat, maybe some of their famous hot chicken, and have a few drinky-drinks and see the city up close. You up for a rodeo ride?" She winked.

Sam glanced at Misty and raised an eyebrow.

"How are you going to come to Nashville and not try your chances on a mechanical bull?" she asked. "They have all kinds of pubs and cool bars. We can have a drink or two before the show," Misty said, patting Sam's knee. "We're vacationing, remember?"

"You two going to the Xclusiv DYG concert?" the driver asked with sudden excitement.

"Yeah, are you?"

"I wish, but the bills keep calling." The driver cut the radio on, rocking in his seat as the music blared throughout the SUV's cabin. "*When it's late at night and the spirits rise up to walk*," he sang along with the stereo.

"*Just listen to the shadows and you'll hear those sweet memories, walkin' and talkin'.*" Misty joined the driver's song, snapping her fingers, grooving in her seat.

Sam wanted to jump out of the car. It wasn't the ear-worm music or even Misty and the driver's dissonance. An intangible feeling knotted Sam's stomach. He found himself gripping the armrest as some of his earliest memories stirred in his mind: riding to Charleston to visit his grandparents, playing in the fire hydrant in front of his stoop, warm oatmeal and Saturday-morning cartoons. Good memories, the kind that made your soul strong, right alongside the kind that made his heart ache.

Sam was surprised at the flood of memories that hit him now he was actually paying attention to the words and rhythm. The images felt so real, he couldn't help wondering if the music affected Misty. Every time she listened to Xclusiv DYG, she got a nostalgic look on her face and scratched her prosthetic arm. A wistful gesture she didn't seem to notice herself. Sam wondered whether she might be reliving some past experience that occurred before the bombing that took her arm, her career in law enforcement, and nearly her life.

When the SUV pulled up in front of the venue, Sam jumped out first, eager to escape the memories. A moment later, Misty hopped out, and the pair stared at a red-brick building that loomed before them, glittering in the approaching twilight.

"Southern Rock Music Hall," Misty said. "Do you know what it means for an artist like Xclusiv DYG to perform here? It's more than progress. This is history in the making, Sam, and we get to participate."

"Making history is wearing me thin." Sam scratched the back of his head.

Southern Rock Music Hall reminded Sam of his family's old church back in Harlem with its arched windows, red bricks trimmed in alabaster, and spired roof. His mind cast him back to that last Sunday afternoon with his dad. How they had laughed and talked with friends and family until the sun had set lazily behind the church roof. The next evening masked assailants would gun down Sam's father while the pair were walking home.

A group of eager fans gathered in front of the concert hall. Xclusiv DYG T-shirts, fitted caps, and airbrushed backpacks bounced around the auditorium's facade. The crowd spilled over a set of stone steps down to the sidewalk.

Sam imagined the next few hours wasting away in country-trap purgatory. "By the time we get inside, the show's gonna be over," Sam complained.

"They're not letting anyone in yet. That's why the crowd's so big," Misty replied, coolly. "Besides, we got VIP passes." She flashed the tickets and raised her eyebrows.

Sam followed Misty up the stone steps to an ornamented set of white double doors where four bouncers dressed in black suits and sunglasses grimaced at the swelling crowd. Misty offered one of the bouncers a wide grin as she presented the tickets.

"Welcome to the Xclusiv DYG experience," the staff member said with a proud smile. He opened both white doors and gestured for Sam and Misty to step inside the venue.

"How much money do you plan on spending?" Sam asked.

"You're not paying for anything, so don't worry," Misty said.

"Look at that line. Instead of standing back there, you get to walk straight in with no hassle. Thank me later." She turned her back to Sam and disappeared inside the concert hall.

"Wait a minute?" a man dressed in a black suit asked, lowering his shades to the tip of his nose. He wore a fresh crew halfmoon Ceasar faded to perfection. A latticework of tattoos stretched from his button-down collar to the meat under his chin. "You're Captain America."

Sam smiled and nodded. No suit, no shield, it didn't matter. Captain America was larger than life, inescapable, even at a country-trap concert.

"Take it to the hotline," the staff member shouted, pointing a finger covered with more tattoos.

Why did I make that video?! Sam laughed and shook his head. Standing up for his beliefs, going viral at the same time, had changed his entire life—including his career and his friendship with the original Captain America, Steve Rogers. Even his perception of himself was different. He'd spent months weighing the decision, but in the end he chose to take a stand. If he was going to represent America, it had to be all of its people or none, and the country needed to know that.

"Come with me. I'm taking both of you back myself." The man with tattoos peeking from his black collar and sleeves shook Sam's hand. "X is gonna flip. We got Captain America in the building."

"And who are you?" Sam asked.

"Head of security, call me Hammer," he said, shaking Sam's hand. Then he cupped his hand around his mouth and whispered, "X said you would come. Some of the others doubted, but not me, not for a second."

HAMMER LED Sam and Misty through the crowded hall filled with dim lights, walls of smiling faces, glasses shining like starlight. Around the auditorium, arched windows lined the walls, rows of seats—filled with patient onlookers—rose from the floor.

Everyone's attention was focused on the stage where Xclusiv DYG sat in a green armchair. He wore a black and red body suit made of polished chainmail that glittered under the stage lights. His hair, a shocked flourish of black and red streaks, sprung from his head and fell around his shoulders. Platform boots covered in red and black gems adorned his feet.

In the armchair across from Xclusiv, a woman wearing a white skirt suit with purple and blonde hair nodded attentively. For some reason Sam found himself drawn to this woman. She was stunning. High cheekbones, full lips, striking eyes, she looked like a supermodel. It wasn't just her beauty, though.

Unbidden, Sam thought of his parents again. Their deaths, the pain, his grief. Rubbing his eye, he had to focus to bring himself back to reality. Offering Misty an uneasy smile, he hoped she had missed the sudden change in his demeanor. Misty wasn't psychic, but she had that woman's intuition. Coupled with a career in law enforcement, her powers of perception proved just as formidable as Professor X's.

Considering his partner's uncanny sense of perception returned Sam to reality just as quickly as the vision on stage had sent him spiraling.

"I recognize that woman. I can't quite place that face, but I know it for sure." Staring at the stage, Misty bit her bottom lip.

Sam turned to his partner. He didn't like the sound in Misty's voice. If she did know the woman on stage, the acquaintance wasn't a friendly one—not at all.

"I've dreamed of playing on this stage since I was a child," Xclusiv said in a hazy voice, staring at the crowd like he was daydreaming. "So many greats have performed here. So much music history happened right here in this auditorium, and tonight we're going to make history again."

The crowd cheered as Misty squeezed Sam's arm and whispered, "Told ya." The foreboding that had just filled her voice had vanished.

"This building is filled with a rich history that stretches back over a century," the blonde interviewer said. "So many great talents who've impacted Southern Rock Hall with their music. What makes Xclusiv DYG different?"

"Just look at me." Xclusiv DYG spread his arms while the crowd cheered. "Seriously, though, tonight's concert will be like nothing any of you have experienced anywhere in the world. All of you will remember this night for the rest of your lives."

Xclusiv stood and moved to the edge of the stage, sitting with his legs dangling over the side and chatting with onlookers.

"Impressive, huh?" Hammer asked, squeezing Sam's shoulder. "Y'all ready to meet Xclusiv DYG?"

Sam and Misty followed Hammer down to the stage where Xclusiv sat, signing autographs and conversing with a circle of adoring fans. After autographing a backpack painted with his own smiling image, Xclusiv DYG noticed Hammer leading Sam and Misty through the crowd. The country-trap rapper greeted the trio with a warm smile, shiny eyes, and outstretched arms.

"Finally!" Xclusiv wagged. "I was wondering when you'd get here."

Sam and Misty turned to each other, confusion filling the space between them.

"Yes, we've been expecting you, Sam Wilson and Mercedes Knight," Xclusiv DYG continued. "The ancestors are good all the time!"

"You can call me Misty." She spoke slowly, her voice hesitant and cautious. "How did you know we were coming? I mean, you could have pulled my name when I bought the tickets, but how did you know about Sam?"

"No need for alarm, diva. I saw it in a song I wrote on my kalimba. I saw you standing here, just like you're doing now." Xclusiv wrapped his hands around Misty's before turning to Sam.

"And you, Mr. Wilson. Thank you for being *our* Captain America. I can only imagine the responsibility that comes with your job and that fancy shield."

Sam sighed. He always carried the shield's weight, sometimes on his arm, sometimes in his heart.

Misty rubbed Sam's back. "He's been through so much, but he keeps pushing. The world couldn't ask for a better Captain America."

"I've been following your career since that first video." Xclusiv extended brown spindly, jeweled fingers for Sam to shake. "You took a stand for all the people, even the ones living in the margins like me."

"You're a hero in your own right," Sam chuckled. "Trust me. You got way more fans than I do."

"I don't know about that," Xclusiv replied. "But I must admit, I do get it in."

"Well, I've been a fan since your underground days, when you were releasing music on social media," Misty said. "You've come a long way."

"I appreciate the love, Ms. Knight." Xclusiv leaned toward Misty, examining the earrings she wore carved into the shape of bullets. "Girl, you are killing them *dead* with this ensemble."

"That's you, with this red and black," Misty replied, gesturing to the singer's outfit. "It's like you're laidback but still fly. I can't wait to see what you wear on stage tonight."

"Diva, lemme show you." Xclusiv took both of Misty's hands in his own. "Hammer's going to take you to my dressing room, hook you up with food and drinks. After I finish meeting and greeting, I will join you."

Misty turned to Sam, joy shining in her eyes. "I knew this was gonna be a special night."

OVER TWO hours had passed before Xclusiv DYG burst into the dressing room. He accepted a fluted glass from Hammer, even as the red liquid bubbled over the rim and ran down the country-trap rapper's hand.

The dressing room reminded Sam of his first studio apartment but much, much nicer. The side of the room where he sat with Misty on a green sofa served as a reception area. Beside the couch there was a matching armchair. Both pieces of furniture faced a coffee table and a walk-in closet.

Xclusiv DYG plopped into the armchair and kicked his feet until both shoes fell to the floor.

He took several gulps of his bubbling drink. "This whole year has been one big mess. If you only knew what I have to deal with on a daily basis."

"Care to share?" Misty sipped her own drink.

"Hammer, can you give us a few?" Xclusiv DYG spoke to his assistant but smiled at Misty. "Make sure no one disturbs us."

"No problem, X." After nodding at Sam and Misty, Hammer closed the door behind him.

Setting his own drink on the table, Xclusiv leaned forward.

"First, I wanna share some things I didn't before." He pulled his feet up into his chair, crossing his ankles.

Sam raised his eyebrows when Xclusiv began to hum. The sound was deep and guttural, much more spiritual than Sam would have anticipated. When a keyboard leaning against the wall played its own ghostly tune by itself, Misty's hand went toward her jacket's breast pocket, but Sam caught her wrist. They both watched as Xclusiv rose from his seat, floating over the armchair. Electric blue light surged from his eye sockets and spread over his body.

"Is this part of the VIP package?" Sam asked, eyes wide with disbelief.

"I don't think so." Misty shook her head.

"This is the all-access pass." Xclusiv pointed his open palms at Sam and Misty.

Before either Sam or Misty had time to react, Xclusiv's electric blue aura flooded the entire room. When the light cleared, the pair found themselves in a garage someone had converted into an improvisational music studio. They stared at the drum set that blocked the garage door and the keyboard and guitars that took up the middle of the space.

"You asked if I wanted to share, diva." Xclusiv's disembodied voice spoke through everything in the room, the walls, the garage door, the scattered array of musical instruments. "Funny thing is, sharing and collecting stories is my job."

"Who are you, really?" Sam asked the disembodied voice. *Did he put something in my drink?* "Whatever you turned on, you need to turn off right now. No one's been harmed. We can still go back and enjoy your concert, no harm no foul."

"I bought tickets to watch you perform." Strolling past the drum set, Misty thumped a cymbal, releasing a metallic hiss that echoed through the converted garage. "I've shown you nothing but respect and love, and you were just setting us up?"

"It's not like that at all." Xclusiv DYG materialized right before Sam and Misty. The country-trap rapper morphed from a glimmer to a spectral outline whitewashed in lucid pastels to detailed flesh and red spandex. His eyes, bright with sudden fear, followed Misty around the room. "It wasn't safe to talk out there."

Misty frowned. "Okay, this is the part when you tell us what's going on, no riddles, no puzzles. We want the straight up-and-down version."

"When we met, you said you were expecting us," Sam said.

"I did. I'm glad you're here. Thank the ancestors." Xclusiv took a deep breath in through his nose, out through his mouth. "I'm on the run, sort of. The forces chasing me come with the job, but lately things have gotten way out of hand."

"Still too vague," Sam said.

"I'm sorry. It's just... I'm scared, you know?" Fear shone in Xclusiv's eyes and shook his voice. "Truth is, I am Jali Iggawen. Our order is ancient, and we are known by many names. I bet you two are familiar with the term 'griot'."

"West African poets, singers, storytellers," Misty responded. "The discipline originated around the thirteenth century, I think."

"The griot's job was to preserve their nation's history and culture, and ultimately its people. They served as counselors, healers, even leaders themselves in some cases," Sam added.

"Okay, you two," Xclusiv laughed. "Somebody made good use of their time working with King T'Challa."

"You still haven't told us where you've taken us," Misty said coolly.

"Don't worry. We're all safe here," Xclusiv said. "I'm sorry, but I'm still new to all this. In college I studied ancient African music. One of my professors invited me on a trip to Mali. After we got there, she explained that she was really searching for an artifact called Seita's kalimba. I had read stories about the griots of old unleashing the ancient instrument's power, but I thought those were myths, you know.

"I wish I would have known." Xclusiv stared at the kalimba, inconspicuously arrayed with the other instruments. "I would have never followed my professor into that temple, but she was so excited. We spent days searching the catacombs under one of the oldest temples in Mali. We actually found the instrument. Somehow, I knew how to work the instrument. That's why she invited me. I remember striking those keys thinking it was the greatest moment of my life.

"That's when I met The Ancestors for the first time. Come to find out they'd been watching me since I was a kid. Training me the whole time without my knowledge. My professor was actually a priestess. I had been chosen the entire time, since my birth, maybe even before. I accepted a lifelong mission to gather, protect, and share the stories we tell, the histories we live, and the collective memories we all share.

"I also inherited a few enemies in the process. A few weeks ago, The Ancestors came to me in a song. They specifically said the two of you would come and assist me and add your own stories to my collection. Only problem is, the threat that we must face together is definitely my toughest so far."

"And that would be?" Sam asked.

"It's an ancient threat with a new face," Xclusiv said. "I did an internet search, and found her and her sister pretty easily. They aren't hiding these days."

"I knew I recognized the woman who was interviewing you." Misty snapped her fingers.

"Oh no." Sam covered his face with his hands. "This can't be good."

"That was Regan Wyngarde, the Lady Mastermind," she said.

"The mutant illusionist?" Sam asked.

"I didn't recognize her because this isn't her normal type of gig. She's normally harassing the X-Men or running some kind of scam to raise money to harass the X-Men. She's bold to be showing her face like this, but with her powers, it's not much of a risk."

"Why would a sometime mutant terrorist and scammer be interested in collecting stories?" Sam asked, turning to Xclusiv DYG. "And who are these Ancestors you keep talking about?"

"What better way to control the world than to control the world's narrative?" Xclusiv answered. "And The Ancestors, those are the spirits of our people. Collective spirits that stretch back to the very beginnings of this world."

"Oh well, that explains everything," Sam said.

"Either way, we've got your back," Misty said.

"So you're going to help me for real?" Xclusiv DYG clasped his hands like a beggar.

"That is what we do," Sam said slowly.

"Yes! That means it's time to leave my safe space," Xclusiv said, pumping his fist before turning to Misty. "Are you ready to see my outfit, diva?"

Another flash of electric-blue light returned the trio to Xclusiv's dressing room. He opened the walk-in closet, revealing a lifelike mannequin rendered in his image. It wore a white bodysuit covered with white jewels. Gleaming bracelets and rings adorned the mannequin's wrists and fingers.

The bodysuit shone like a ghost, bright and translucent. Sam imagined Xclusiv on stage, emerging from a trapdoor, singing to a crowd of screaming fans.

Misty stepped forward, her face and voice filled with white light. "You are going to slay in this."

Sam imagined Xclusiv blinding someone with the light beaming from the suit. Those features could help the country-trap rapper defend himself, but Sam had seen extraordinary feats of creativity when it came time to hurt others.

"What does DYG stand for?" Sam didn't know exactly why this question had come to mind. Maybe there was something in Xclusiv's name that would provide some greater insight on how to assist the situation.

"Da young griot," Xclusiv said with a wide grin.

"Duh?" Misty said, pulling the rubber back on her slingshot. "Enough talking, we got work to do."

o———o

HAMMER HAD driven Cap and Misty back to the hotel in one of Xclusiv's armored SUVs to get their armor and weapons. As Sam donned his uniform, he noticed Misty pull out a slingshot from her suitcase.

"What are you gonna do with that?" Sam asked.

"A sling and leadshot packs just as much power as .45 caliber." Misty offered a mischievous grin. "I got a bag of lead ball bearings and a bag of marbles, just in case. Either will do."

Now Captain America, not Sam Wilson, stood offstage beside Misty Knight, scanning the crowd ready for any sign of trouble. If Sam could have had his way, they would have canceled the show altogether, but Xclusiv had refused. The country-trap rapper had a job to do. But Cap felt like they were using Xclusiv DYG as bait.

"Knight, you good?" Cap asked, turning to his partner. Even with the chaos of stage personnel running around backstage, and one of the world's most powerful telepaths lurking somewhere nearby, his eyes were still glued to Misty Knight.

"Still trying to wrap my head around everything." Misty spoke softly, rolling a lead ball bearing between her thumb and forefinger. "I just found out that my favorite singer's a griot sorcerer protecting the power of collective history. I mean, how do you protect stories?"

Sam thought about the memories that rose in his head every time he heard Xclusiv's music. "Case like this, we need Blade and Brother Voodoo," he said as the lights in the auditorium went black.

Screams and shouting, whistling rang through the dark as colorful smoke spread, and the neon lights flashed across the stage. Sam tensed up for a moment but relaxed when he heard the screeching organs and shock waves of 808 bass ripple through the auditorium as the crowd cheered. Underneath the haze and glitter, the crowd fell silent… until Xclusiv DYG appeared on the stage, amidst a sea of renewed applause, screaming, and faces drenched with tears.

Dressed in a black shroud, hood pulled over his head, Xclusiv Da Young Griot sauntered from the dark to the stage's forefront, where a single spotlight cascaded over the country-trap rapper. Spreading his arms, Xclusiv basked in the crowd's adoration. The scene reminded Cap of the chiaroscuro paintings he had learned about in college: Xclusiv DYG, Southern Rock Hall, consumed in ecstasy.

Wheels churned in Cap's head as he watched the scene unfold. *How did I get drawn into this mess?* Then he thought about the hotline and the island where he met Steve Rogers. He had been helping people his entire life. That's all he knew, and this moment was no different.

Leaning forward, face obscured by shadows, Xclusiv grabbed the microphone with both hands. The stage lights flared, revealing a full band dressed in their own black robes. More cheers rose from the dark, swirling mass.

"Cashville, Tennessee, are you ready to make history?" Xclusiv stretched his hand toward the screaming crowd. "We have to be careful, though. Some wanna stop our movement, but they're gonna learn tonight. We can't be stopped."

Xclusiv nodded at the raving faces, as the band dove into a driving groove that threatened to rip the auditorium apart.

"This is a rock concert on steroids," Cap said, craning his neck for a better look at the raving audience.

"Even I wasn't ready for all this," Misty admitted.

All at once, silence filled the auditorium. Everything froze in place, ecstatic faces, knees and elbows bent in thousands of dance poses. On stage, Xclusiv DYG posed with the microphone raised to his mouth and one hand reaching above his head.

Cap and Misty Knight, however, were surrounded by a gleaming dome. Knight's arm and the dome shared the same yellow light as she projected a powerful forcefield from her bionic arm.

This lady never runs out of tricks, Cap thought.

Misty Knight stared into the audience, jaw clenched, seething with rage. Cap followed her line of vision to the rafters half-circling the stage and the arena floor, where he spotted two figures standing on the balcony.

The first, a tall, slender woman dressed in glittering yellow, stood with her feet spread apart and balled fists set against her hips. Her hair, a wellspring of blonde curls, fell around her shoulders. Lady Mastermind's outfit reminded Cap of the costume Xclusiv had shown off earlier in his dressing room.

Behind her, one of the biggest men Cap had ever seen stood with his arms folded across his chest. His hair was blonde and curly, cropped close around his ears, save for a pair of bushy sideburns. Staring down at Cap and Misty Knight, the man offered a malicious grin. He reminded Cap of a middle school bully.

"There she is," Misty growled under her breath. She slipped a ball bearing into the rubber cup on her slingshot.

Sam stared at the woman on the balcony. Mastermind was one of the world's most dangerous mutants, with illusion-casting and psychic abilities that rivaled those of her terrorist father, who was strong enough to gain the respect of Magneto, one of the world's most powerful beings. Her S.H.I.E.L.D. file read like a full-length novel.

"Who's the other one?" Cap asked, tilting his head.

"Falcon," Lady Mastermind called from the balcony, her refined accent caressing each word. "It's really you. I was so excited when I saw you earlier. I was dropping by to do some homework, and I'm glad I did. I could hardly believe it, city slicker like yourself traveling hundreds of miles for a country-trap show. I would've pegged you for an East Coast 90s fan."

"Good music is good music, and I go by Captain America now," Cap answered, his fists balled at his sides, defiance rising in his voice.

Misty raised her steel hand and gestured. Neon light surged as she sent a piece of the forcefield surrounding herself toward the stage, and watched as it enveloped Xclusiv in an orb of glowing yellow light.

"Well, *Captain America*, I hate to interrupt the festivities, but we have a job to do. Returning empty handed is not an option." Lady Mastermind leapt from the balcony and landed in the middle of the frozen crowd. "Forgive my manners. Have either of you met my friend, Sabretooth?"

While Lady Mastermind sauntered through the frozen crowd, Sabretooth leapt from the balcony and landed behind her. He had a strong jaw shaped like a wooden box, and a hooked nose. Even his eyebrows were curly blond. He wasn't wearing his normal fur-lined costume, but his black turtleneck and blue jeans combined with his razor-sharp fangs and vicious-looking claws somehow made him look even more deadly than normal.

"I hate to say it, Sam, but this is about to get ugly real soon." Misty raised her slingshot.

"You're probably wondering why we're here. Let's just say our investors are interested in spinning their own narratives. Like that old saying goes: 'History is written by the victors.'" Lady Mastermind smiled, twisting a blonde lock around her finger.

The light around Misty Knight's arm surged, and the bubble encasing them broke into two domes, one surrounding Knight, the other Cap.

"This will protect us from her illusions. Whether it can stand against Sabretooth's pounding is another story."

"It'll have to," Cap said, hoping it wouldn't be too restricting. He would need as much maneuverability as possible to beat Sabretooth. "Who are these investors you keep talking about?" Cap pointed at Lady Mastermind.

"None of your business, hero," Lady Mastermind answered. She smiled as white light filled her eyes, and her voice filled the auditorium like she was speaking through her own microphone. The frozen audience started moving again. Now their cries were filled with terror instead of ecstasy as she filled their minds with illusions of horror, each one seeing their worst fear. The mob rushed forward, attacking Cap and Misty Knight.

A series of flashing orbs burst from Misty Knight's palm, blinding the crowd. They ducked for a few seconds, shielding their faces, before they groped their way toward the stage. Cap waited as the bubble around him dissolved. Once free, he spread his wings in a quick flurry and flew to the heights of the rafters. From there he flung his shield at Lady Mastermind. Just before the shield struck her chest, Sabretooth pushed her out of the way. The shield bounced off the wall, and back to Cap's waiting hand.

But as Lady Mastermind got up, slightly worse for wear, the psychic hold she had over the audience waned. Ceasing their attack, the crowd, confused and horrified, stood around staring at each other.

"You see what I see?" Misty Knight's voice buzzed in Cap's ear.

"I do," he answered. "Maybe that's the out we need to get this situation under control."

"Maybe," Misty said. The dome of light shrunk to fit her form. It still covered most of her body like an armored suit, but her hands and her slingshot were left exposed. She hopped onto the stage, shielding Xclusiv DYG with her own body, and firing several lead shots into Sabretooth's chest, reloading her slingshot with uncanny speed. Point blank range, the lead balls struck the snarling strongman and sent him falling to the floor

"That won't stop him permanently," Misty yelled. "Let's neutralize Mastermind first. Then we can handle Sabretooth together."

"What do you have in mind?" Cap asked.

"Keep her distracted long enough for me to get Xclusiv off the stage. After that, I'll handle the rest."

Alright, Cap sighed, as he flew toward Lady Mastermind, catching her off-guard and slamming her into a row of empty seats.

Without Lady Mastermind's illusions, hysteria swept through the crowd. By the time Cap got a clear view of the stage, the entire space was empty. The instruments were still there, but Xclusiv, the band, and Misty Knight were gone.

"He won't be able to hide for long," Lady Mastermind yelled as she swung at Cap's head, missing by less than an inch. She winced as she punched an empty seat. "My big, strong man will find him. After that, Xclusiv DYG will become official music history himself."

Cap dodged Lady Mastermind's next punch, smacking her in the back with his shield. The blow sent her stumbling until she tripped over a young man wearing an Xclusiv DYG T-shirt, scurrying for his life.

Cap smiled until he saw Sabretooth pulling himself to his feet. Lady Mastermind crossed her arms and chuckled. Sabretooth joined his comrade laughing, until he coughed up a glob of blood at Cap's feet.

"Do not worry, my dear Captain," Wyngarde said, amused. "Xclusiv DYG will not die in vain. The stories that he collects will be used to write a new narrative, an epic tale that will recreate the world anew."

Cap heard a zipping sound as something flew past his ear. Wyngarde's eyes went wide and fearful. She fell backward, convulsing and staring at the ceiling, bewilderment and terror twisting her face.

Sam heard the growling just in time to raise his shield and block the massive hand and claws swinging toward him. He blocked Sabretooth's first blow, but the second sent Cap flying over several rows of auditorium seating.

Before he had time to move, Sabretooth pounced toward him again. This time Cap managed to duck the punch and connect a right cross of his own with Sabretooth's jaw.

He heard the sound again, lead shot zipping through the air. Twice this time. *Thewp! Thwp!* Sabretooth roared and grabbed his face. Puzzled for a moment, Cap thought the strongman was trying to claw his own eyes out. Blood ran through Sabretooth's fingers and down his cheeks. Looking to the spot where he had first spied Lady Mastermind, Cap found Misty Knight standing on the balcony railing. Posing with one eye shut, she held her slingshot in one hand and pulled the rubber back with the other.

"Like I said, the power of a desert eagle," Misty called out, as Sabretooth pulled himself across the floor.

The strongman leapt to his feet, blood running down his face and neck, matting his blonde curls against his forehead and neck.

"I don't need eyes to see," he said as he lunged toward Captain America.

Sidestepping the clumsy attack, Cap smacked Sabretooth with his shield. Misty Knight released the slingshot's rubber cup, hurling another metal ball that lodged itself between Sabretooth's shoulder blades. Sabretooth stood up straight with the sound of metal puncturing the flesh below the nape of his neck. He fell to his knees, shook his head, and smiled. Cap raised his fist and his shield, ready for another attack. Misty loaded another lead ball into her slingshot. He started to fling his shield, but found it more entertaining to watch Misty fire another lead shot into Sabretooth's rear end.

Instead of attacking Cap or Knight, Sabretooth grabbed Lady Mastermind's unconscious body and leapt into the air, disappearing over the same balcony where the villains had first appeared.

"Should we go after them?" Knight asked. "We could detain them and call in some S.H.I.E.L.D. agents to wrap all this up."

"Call them, but first we need to check on Xclusiv. Where'd you stash him anyway?" Cap asked.

Misty Knight led Captain America back to Xclusiv's dressing room.

"Open up," she said as she rapped on the dressing room door. "It's Misty Knight and Captain America. You're safe now. We've taken care of everything."

After a few seconds of worrisome silence Cap thought about breaking down the door, but stopped when the locks clicked.

The doorknob twisted, a small crack appeared, then Hammer's fearful eyes peeked through. When he saw his saviors, he opened the door and stood to the side, watching the triumphant duo saunter into the dressing room.

Xclusiv DYG sat on the same couch, huddled together with his bandmates. They were still dressed in the black robes they'd worn on stage.

"Did you get my diamond back?" Xclusiv said, jumping up from the couch, bright eyed and hopeful.

"What do you value more, your jewelry or your life?" Misty Knight retorted.

"It's not like that, diva," Xclusiv said. Voice deflated, he raised his hands in acquiescence. "I'm just saying. That was a four-hundred-thousand-dollar diamond."

"Four-hundred-thousand-dollar diamond?" Cap asked, a puzzled frown twisting his face.

"How else was I supposed to take out Lady Mastermind?" Misty Knight asked. "I'd used up all of my ammo and needed something to help save you from seeing your defeat."

"Why didn't you tell me what you were planning?" Cap asked.

"No time," Misty Knight said.

Xclusiv stood up and looked at his bandmates. "Alright, let's get this show on the road."

The band members rose from the couch and walked out of the dressing room.

"You're still going to perform, after everything that just happened?" Cap asked.

"I have to," Xclusiv said. "I accepted this responsibility, and I'm going to see it to completion."

Back in the auditorium, the crowd was patiently waiting. Cap was still dressed in his uniform, which felt really weird, but the people around him were all cheering, patting him on the back, snapping his picture. For a moment, Cap felt like he was the celebrity, like the people there had come to see him.

When Xclusiv DYG returned to the stage, the crowd cheered so loud and for so long, Cap thought his eardrums would burst. The country-trap rapper grabbed the microphone resting in front of him and addressed the crowd.

"They tried stealing our history tonight. They would have killed me and my band and some of you in the process, but they did not realize The Ancestors had already sent not one but two guardian angels to protect us. Y'all show some love for my new friends Misty Knight and Captain America. Misty, Cap, come on up here and let the people thank you properly."

Misty leapt onto the stage and hugged Xclusiv, rocking the country-trap rapper from side to side. Cap followed his comrade and stood next to Xclusiv. He spread his wings full-length and hovered above the stage while the audience cheered.

Dad, I wish you could see me now, he thought.

As soon as Sam landed, the band resumed the music that had been cut off earlier in the night. Xclusiv disrobed, revealing his all-white catsuit. He flung the black garment into the crowd and poured his heart into the music. Misty sang the words to every song, and before long even Captain America joined in, off-key but word-perfect. In his mind, he saw his dad and his mom. Cap let the memories take him gladly. His parents were with The Ancestors now, and wherever they were, they were doing just fine. This time when the tears came, he did not try to stop them. Instead, he grabbed Misty Knight's hand and danced until The Ancestors themselves took the stage, showering themselves in a wealth of music and collective memory.

BY ANY MEANS UNNECESSARY

GAR ANTHONY HAYWOOD

SAM HADN'T seen Carmen Hall in a long time. Before he was Captain America; before he was the Falcon; before he was the Sam Wilson he was today. They'd been a thing in high school, two kids fighting to keep their heads above water in the murky, turbulent seas of Harlem, New York. They both wanted out but only Sam made it.

Carmen put down roots she couldn't tear loose and Harlem was where she'd remained. They lost track of each other, the way old friends do. Sam heard Carmen had gotten married some years back and had a son. That was all he knew.

When she wrote to him via Avengers headquarters two weeks ago, not knowing how else to contact him, he didn't waste any time answering back. Her letter said she was in trouble and needed his help, and Carmen Hall wasn't the kind of lady to ask for a hand if she wasn't actually desperate for one.

Now she was living in a one-bedroom apartment on 139th Street in Central Harlem. Sam found her cooking something on the stove when he arrived at the agreed-upon time, twelve noon on a Tuesday in May. The years hadn't been cruel to her, but they'd left their mark; Sam could see the charismatic Black pixie he used to love behind the tired eyes and weary demeanor of this full-figured mother and matriarch, but he had to look hard.

"I thought you'd be in uniform," she said, smiling sheepishly. "I was kind of hoping to see you in all that red, white, and blue."

"And the shield?"

She laughed. "Yeah. And the shield. It ain't every day Captain America comes by the crib to see a girl."

"Is it that bad, Carm? You need Captain America's help and not Sam Wilson's?"

"Both." The smile vanished from her face. "I need you both."

They sat in the living room while she explained. Whatever she was cooking simmered on a low flame, smelling like the best part of Sam's past in this place he'd wanted so desperately to escape forever.

Her son Leon was dead. Just nineteen years old. His body had been found in the early morning hours one month ago in Jackie Robinson Park. It was the way Carmen had for years been afraid he would wind up; he'd been a thief and a drug abuser since his early teens and the crimes he'd been willing to commit to satisfy his demons were only getting worse. But he hadn't simply lost his life to another thug or a cop, with a knife blade embedded in his chest or a bullet in the head. He'd been torn apart. Arms and legs ripped from his torso like he were a giant doll, left on the park's dewy grass in bloody, shredded segments.

"Wait," Sam said, beginning to understand. "I've heard about this. There's some crazy vigilante up here doing this to people. He calls himself Mission—"

"Critical," Carmen said, nodding. "The police say Leon was his fourth victim."

It wasn't the kind of news that could escape an Avenger or anyone associated with S.H.I.E.L.D. The accounts of the four killings Sam had come across hinted at a mass murderer with superhuman powers. NYPD was downplaying the possibility, suggesting the mutilations were merely the work of multiple killers, rather than just one with the strength of five, but Sam's instincts told him this was wishful thinking.

Still, there'd been no official call to investigate. Sam was here on his own, for reasons that were strictly personal. Were he to ask Steve Rogers, the former Captain America would be right there at his side but this wasn't the kind of mission a man from the 1940s would be particularly useful for. Rogers was on an undercover mission with a covert Avengers undercover squad.

People never expected anyone who was an Avenger to care about anything that was a street-level threat—only tackling marauding super villain teams and invading aliens, Sam thought. His government contacts would probably advise him to hold off on getting involved until more intelligence could be gathered. They'd warn him that Captain America couldn't be going after every homicidal maniac roaming the streets of New York, like Daredevil or Spider-Man seemed to do. But, Sam knew there was nowhere else he should be and nothing that would be more important.

This was Carmen asking, and this was Harlem being preyed upon. Sam could not deny either one.

Neither could Captain America.

SAM SPENT the next three nights on watch. He'd made a map of Mission Critical's crime scenes and was sticking to those areas. Flying from one perch above the city of his birth to another, watching. On the streets below, Harlem writhed and howled, lights of every color flickering to the drumbeat of music and sirens, laughter and outrage. It was both beautiful and sorrowful.

People scraping by to build a life, some struggling to rise above it all, others going under willingly, making victims of whomever was handy just to feel a dollar richer today than they had the day before.

Sam watched and waited, reminded yet again why he'd chosen the career path he had, why he'd first donned the Falcon's uniform and now that of Captain America. Somebody had to stop the madness that had taken both his parents. Enter the fray to save the innocent from the predators in their midst, rather than turn and look away. You could be a hero just for trying, but if you could try armed with powers and weapons beyond those of average men, you could make a difference. One victim at a time, or by the thousands. Sam had been blessed with such powers and weapons and he wasn't going to squander them.

Somewhere down there, a monster was lurking, thinking of Harlem as his own private hunting ground, and Sam Wilson was going to find him.

ON THAT third night, Sam did almost call Steve Rogers for help. Theirs was a symbiotic relationship, after all. The man with the wings and shield, bolstered by the voice of wisdom in his ear, originating from the control-room to end all control-rooms, where information of every kind could be drawn at a moment's notice. Steve would have been happy to assist, if only after he'd delivered a brief scolding for not having been consulted earlier about Sam's mission, but Sam had become eager to rely on Steve only when circumstances demanded it. A Captain America who could never get things done on his own was a Captain America in name only.

So tonight he held off, standing on rooftops and crouched on hi-rise window ledges, surveilling Harlem alone. And eventually, as the clock was approaching 3 a.m., his patience was rewarded. A dark, lithe figure slipped in and out of shadow along a half-mile stretch of Frederick Douglass Blvd, moving like no average person could move. Clothed all in black, two jagged white stripes running shoulder to inner-thigh, it propelled itself in leaps and bounds, low to the ground and fast. To Sam's mind, it was like a miniaturized version of the Hulk's favored form of forward momentum, only more graceful and less powerful.

Sam swooped down to get a closer look, taking care not to be detected. As he suspected, his target was on the scent of his next victim. Sam watched the dark figure turn into an alley off 147th and stop near the entrance, yards from where two people were engaged in combat, too intent on killing each other to notice another presence. Hovering above in silence, like a kite riding the air currents of night, Sam recognized the nature of the pair's altercation immediately, having seen this ballet too many times in the past to mistake it for anything else. Fights over money—especially drug money—had a look and sound all their own.

Clearly, Mission Critical recognized it too. Sam saw his body tense and then spring into action, bounding in a single leap to pounce upon the more aggressive of the two Black men in the alley, the big one swinging a knife with bad intent. Sam dove down to intervene as the other man fell back against the alley wall, eyes agape, and then scrambled off and away, certain he would be next on the costumed man's menu if he stuck around to watch.

The man with the knife was screaming, Mission Critical holding his throat in a right-handed vise, when the shield of Captain America shot into view. It slammed off the would-be killer's ribcage, separating him from his victim, and then returned to Sam's grasp in a series of ricochets just as he touched down. Sam closed in quickly on the man in black, expecting little resistance from someone who'd just taken a blow from a near-indestructible shield, and nearly paid for his overconfidence dearly.

Mission Critical was up and on top of Captain America in the blink of an eye. Sam was on his back, fighting to keep the costumed assassin from tearing his head from his shoulders. This villain had strength equal to Sam's, and along the outside edges of both gloved hands, blades sharp enough to cut Sam to ribbons.

"Well, now," Mission Critical said gleefully, behind a full-face mask that hid a grin Sam could feel if not see. "Captain America. Version three-point-oh. What an honor!"

He tried to pierce Sam's costume with a combination of quick slashes aimed at the hero's torso, but Sam avoided the attack, managing to take flight at the perfect instant and land a knee to his opponent's chin. The attack stunned the other man, who fell to the floor like a bag of bones, then immediately rose as if he'd landed on springs. Sam had seen all he needed to see. Mission Critical was not one to be taken lightly. He needed to finish this fast.

But a swift defeat was not in Mission Critical's plans. He gave Sam everything he could handle, the killer's razored hands and Captain America's shield leaving mark after mark on the other man. The man with the knife, like his friend before him, was long gone, Sam barely noticed.

"Who the hell are you?" Sam demanded, astonished.

"I'm the answer to our people's problems you only pretend to be," Mission Critical said. "I am the solution! I am the cure! I am the warning that evil will be met with even greater evil until this city is made safe again. Washed clean again."

Sam leaped into the air again, hoping his aerial abilities would give him an advantage. His wings propelled him directly at his foe with a burst of speed. But Mission Critical anticipated the move, raising his armored arms to block the incoming attack. Sam's shield met the exoskeleton with a resounding clang, the force of the impact sending shockwaves through both combatants. The difference was, Sam was expecting it. Mission Critical slid back slightly but maintained his footing, his eyes narrowing in focus in time to see Sam lunging forward again. Mission Critical blocked, wildly and instinctively. With the brunt of the impact on his arms, he was again knocked back.

Tired of playing defense, the villain lunged forward, the blades on his gloves slashing through the air with deadly precision. Sam dodged to the side, his wings folding close to his body as he maneuvered around the attack. He swung his shield in a wide arc, aiming for Mission Critical's exposed side. The villain twisted his body, the exoskeleton whirring as it adjusted to avoid the blow. The shield grazed his armor, leaving a shallow scratch.

Until finally, inevitably, the realization seemed to dawn on Sam's combatant that he could not win. Sam had called a pair of red-tailed hawks down upon his head and their attack proved to be all the pain and humiliation Mission Critical could endure. He was up against a greater, more determined force and so was doomed to lose. Finding one last reservoir of strength, he struck Captain America with a body blow that, like the impact of a charging rhino, could not be easily shaken off. Sam went down in a heap and did not get up, conscious but dazed.

Had approaching police sirens not chosen this moment to assert themselves, Mission Critical might have tried moving in for one last chance at a kill, but he chose to flee instead. Sam gathered himself just in time to toss a small object at the retreating man's back, a silver disk the size of a coin that, only on close inspection, could be recognized as a miniature version of Captain America's shield. It was a new toy from Nick Fury's skunkworks, a tracking device that bonded to any surface and could be used to pinpoint its location within a three-foot radius.

Mission Critical limped off into the night, his bounding gait slowed by pain and injury, unaware that Captain America would be able to follow him wherever he chose to hide.

THE VILLAIN'S trail led to a crumbling red tenement on 105th Street, as dark and silent as the post-wrecking ball demise it was clearly awaiting.

Sam, panting hard and ignoring the cuts and bruises from the fight, had to circle above the structure like a vulture on the scent for several minutes before he was convinced the tracking device he was following wasn't lying to him. On the ground, the homing signal led him directly to a basement apartment at the end of a short flight of stairs off the sidewalk.

There were no signs or sounds of life beyond the door and single window, but there were traces of blood at the foot of the entrance. Sam didn't bother knocking. He used his shield to pry the brittle door open, snapping locks and the doorframe like twigs in the process.

The apartment was pitch black and thick with the stench of abandonment; no one but the rats that scurried hither and yon had lived here for a very long time. Sam stepped through the place, room to room, with the care of a bomb squad tech defusing a live explosive. The tiny shield attached to Mission Critical's back finally called Captain America to the kitchen, a skeleton stripped bare of all fixtures and appliances.

Sam followed the tracking signal to a full-height cabinet in one corner and opened the door; the cupboard was bare, of course, but Sam wasn't fooled. He felt around inside until his fingers tripped the hidden release, stepped back and watched the cabinet's false interior slide away to reveal a narrow set of steps leading down, all the way down into the building's very bowels.

To his surprise, it was light and not greater darkness that welcomed his approach. This wasn't a basement but a cavern, a high-tech laboratory equipped like something out of a Hydra fantasy. Sam descended just far enough to take it all in without risking exposure.

Giant machines and computer workstations, towering columns of steel and power lines, dials and monitors glowing yellow and blue in the muted wash of overhead lights turned down low... And the unmistakable silhouettes of three people, two men and a woman, all Black, encased in glass cocoons, either dead or buried deep in an unnatural sleep.

At the center of this space, Mission Critical lay on a table under a bright light, enduring the examination of an older Black man in a white lab coat, whose frizzled Afro dotted his head like patches of dry sagebrush. Sam knew him. Not every subject of a S.H.I.E.L.D. Red Dossier was memorable, but this one was.

"Time to call Steve," Sam told himself wisely.

"DR. WILTON Lancaster," the familiar voice said in Sam's ear. "A borderline genius in the field of biotechnology who used to be one of ours until we cut all ties with him seven years ago."

Sam was sending Steve Rogers live video from the underground facility in Harlem and Steve had identified the man in the lab coat within minutes.

"Cut ties?" Sam asked. He was still perched high atop the staircase leading down from the tenement kitchen, in shadow, where he could observe without being observed.

"We basically shut down the program he was running and

gave him his release, with the usual admonitions about what could happen to him should he defy the terms of our NDA. Clearly, our warnings should have been more forceful."

"Why did S.H.I.E.L.D. cut him loose?"

"He was showing signs of becoming unstable. We liked his work but he was taking his project in directions it was never intended to go."

"Let me guess: His project had something to do with making superhumans out of the ordinary. People with powers not unlike Captain America's. Or the Hulk's. Or—"

"Yes," Steve said, cutting Sam off. "He wasn't close to creating anything like the Super-Soldier Serum, but he was getting there. Had he not lost focus on the prize, he may have become an invaluable asset to us."

"And how exactly did he lose focus?"

"He became obsessed with the idea of making the eradication of urban crime the sole point of his work. He began to sound more and more like someone committed to achieving that goal by any means necessary. Or *un*necessary."

"Okay. I think I've heard enough," Sam said.

"Hold on. You're going to need backup," Steve said. "I'm sending in a team to assist."

"That won't be necessary. I can handle Lancaster and his boy MC all by myself. But thanks for the intel, old man."

"Listen to me, Sam. We thought Lancaster would be rendered harmless once we pulled his funding, but obviously he's found another benefactor with deep pockets and motives as questionable as his own. Until we know who that benefactor is—"

"I've got to go," Sam said, pulling himself to his feet. "But thanks again."

He ended the comms connection with Steve Rogers in mid-sentence. The last word Sam heard him say clearly was "rogue."

Maybe this was a mistake, going solo on a mission that seemed to call out for a squad. But this Captain America had to cut the apron strings of his predecessor's support sometime, and there was no time like the present to try. If anybody knew how to go it alone in Harlem, it was Sam Wilson.

"IT'S OVER, Dr. Lancaster."

The man in the white lab coat spun around as if on a swivel. His patient was only barely conscious so he understood immediately that he and the Black Avenger were essentially alone. He had just discovered the silver homing device clinging to Mission Critical's back and he gestured with the tiny disk now, finding his composure.

"So you're the one who did this," he said.

Sam nodded. "He was about to claim another victim for you. His last."

"His last?" Lancaster smiled. "Oh, no. We are just getting started."

"Who's we? Who is paying for all this, Doctor?"

"Someone who understands the why of it. The fundamental idea that no nation can ever be secure while the poor are allowed to eat themselves, no matter who or what form of government is at the helm. An underclass plagued by crime will always rise up against those who wield power."

Sam paused to read between the lines of what Lancaster was selling. *No matter who or what form of government is in control…*

"You're being used, Doctor," Sam said. "Whoever's given you the resources to continue this work you started for S.H.I.E.L.D., they aren't interested in what happens to poor people. *Black* poor people, especially. Despots depend upon the subjugation of the poor, not their freedom from hardship."

"Brilliantly put," a disembodied voice agreed, echoing throughout the chamber.

Sam and Lancaster turned together as a giant monitor above their heads flickered to life and a face all-too familiar to Captain America filled the screen. Or, rather, the lack of a face, hidden behind a curtain of purple cloth.

"Zemo!"

Sam had no right to be surprised. He and Helmut Zemo had crossed paths several times before and the member of Hydra's high command had all the power and mad ambition necessary to bankroll Lancaster's work, and more.

"It seems you and I have destinies that will forever be intertwined, Captain," Zemo said. "No matter what path my plans take, there you are to complicate them."

Sam turned to Lancaster. "Do you know who this man is? *What* he is?"

"What I am is weary of your constant interference," Zemo said. "You and the old man who came before you. Doctor Lancaster's work for me should be of no concern to you or Steve Rogers. The vermin he has Mission Critical exterminating are unworthy of your desire to save them."

"Zemo is insane," Sam said to Lancaster. "We are *all* vermin to him. He'll take your research and use it to create an army of Mission Criticals, and their victims won't be limited to mere criminals and predators in urban neighborhoods."

"I don't believe you," Lancaster said.

Behind him, the body on the table began to stir. Mission Critical was fully conscious now, regaining his strength faster than Sam had thought possible.

"You look surprised, Captain," Zemo said. "He appeared so close to death only moments ago. Well, all the credit goes to the good doctor. His advancements in cell regeneration have exceeded even my expectations of late. Recovery time from even the gravest of injuries can be measured in minutes now."

Mission Critical got to his feet, wobbly but determined, and squared off with Sam directly. "Round two," he said.

Sam tried to dissuade him, but the man in black was on him instantly. Lancaster retreated to give them room and the battle between the pair was on again, this one more brutal and desperate than the last.

Sam could feel his focus tighten, slowing down their movements even as he knew their struggle was intensifying. He was focused, every muscle in his body tuned to the rhythm of the fight. However, he could feel the same focus from Misson Critical, keeping them on equal footing.

He launched into a series of quick, agile strikes, his shield a blur of motion. Mission Critical countered with equal ferocity, his blades clashing against the shield in a shower of sparks. The room echoed with the sounds of their battle, the metallic clangs and grunts of exertion filling the empty space.

Mission Critical activated a powerful thrust from his suit and pushed Sam back, creating a momentary distance between them. He activated a hidden mechanism in his suit, and the blades on his gloves began to vibrate at high frequency, humming with an ominous energy. He charged at Sam, the enhanced blades cutting through the air with terrifying speed.

Sam raised his shield just in time to block the first strike, but the force behind it was immense. The vibrating blades sent a shockwave through the shield, numbing Sam's arm. He gritted his teeth, using his wings to propel himself backward and gain some distance. Mission Critical was relentless, following up with a barrage of rapid slashes and thrusts.

Sam's agility was his greatest asset. He twisted and turned, using his wings to change direction mid-air, evading most of Mission Critical's attacks. But the villain was fast, and his exoskeleton granted him enhanced strength and speed. A glancing blow caught Sam's shoulder, the vibrating blade cutting through his suit and drawing blood. He hissed in pain as he felt the slippery substance drip down his arm but didn't falter.

As Mission Critical tried again and again to take Sam apart, limb from limb, as he had his other victims, Sam's emotions began to get to him, knowing all of this was simply a show strictly for Zemo's entertainment. The thought enraged him.

"Call him off, Lancaster! Now!"

But Lancaster was unmoved and Mission Critical was beyond being controlled. The killer kept coming, raining blow upon blow on Captain America while absorbing all the punishment Sam and his shield could inflict. Lancaster's lab was being dismantled beneath the crush of their engagement, clouds of glass and metal spraying in all directions around them. The mad scientist didn't care, he just wanted to see Captain America destroyed.

Finally, Sam had had enough. Mission Critical had become more vicious as the fight continued, with the villain's blades slashing through the air, aiming for Sam's throat. Sam barely raised his shield in time, but the vibrating blades struck with such a force it sent painful tremors through his already injured arm. Sparks flew as Sam was pushed back, gritting his teeth against the shock.

Mission Critical wouldn't falter or let up. For every strike Sam threw, the villain threw two, every slash intended to kill. One blade found its mark, slicing through Sam's suit again, deep into his side this time. Blood flowed freely, staining the ground. Sam staggered, pain searing through his body, but he refused to fall. He retaliated with a desperate swing of his shield, catching Mission Critical in the ribs and sending him stumbling.

Sam, aching and weary, knew he had to end this madness *now.* Whispering a quick silent prayer for forgiveness, he threw his adversary across the lab to put some distance between them, then flung his red-white-and-blue shield toward the gigantic monitor overhead. In a perfect arc, the shield sliced through the supports mounting the screen to the ceiling and down the monitor plunged, landing with a thundering crash upon the supine man beneath it.

Mission Critical did not move again.

Sam took a deep but ragged breath, his body warring between his desires to collapse and his instinct to rush and make sure that his enemy would survive. At heart, his social worker background pushed him to help, not hurt. But his experience as Captain America told him to stay alert and keep a wary eye on the true adversary, who had been watching the fight from safety with a keen eye.

In the shimmering shards of the massive monitor's display screen, the refracted image of Helmut Zemo flickered undaunted. "How disappointing, Doctor," the man of Hydra said ruefully. "You'd come so far. And yet, it appears, not quite far enough."

Sam understood his meaning immediately, but Lancaster only stood there, stunned and oblivious. The doctor had just been handed his walking papers, and Zemo was not the kind of employer who trusted Non-Disclosure Agreements to ensure the silence of people who had failed him.

Sam grabbed the older man by the waist and flew to the top of the staircase he'd used to enter the lab, pushing his wings to the limits of what they could do at speed. Tears fogged up his visor as he navigated through the halls and corridors carrying the only person he could rescue. This was a hard learned lesson from his social worker and super hero days: sometimes, you just couldn't save everyone.

The old man was the closest, and if he had tried to save anyone else, they would have all died together. His instincts, honed by years of work on the street and in the sky, told him there was no time to save anyone else; neither Mission Critical, nor any of Lancaster's other three experimental subjects.

He doubted any of them would have saved him, had the shoe been on the other foot. Indeed, Mission Critical had been trying to kill him, before Sam had taken him out. Sam would mourn them just the same, or at least the people they could have become, and their faces would be imprinted in his mind forever to be seen again in his nightmares as he questioned whether there was something else he should have done. But, Sam knew in his heart that he had no other options, as injured and tired as he was. That knowledge didn't always help. He blinked a tear from his eye as he twisted around a corner. A wry grin came over his face. At this moment, he wasn't sure that he had saved himself yet.

The instant Captain America and Lancaster reached the tenement's kitchen, the first explosion went off, reducing the cavern below to a roiling cloud of fire and smoke. With his ears ringing and Wilton Lancaster still in tow, Sam shouldered through one of the tenement's boarded-up windows and climbed skyward, outracing the two ensuing explosions that completed the destruction of the building's lower floors by mere seconds.

A swarm of unmarked, black SUVs that were the calling card of S.H.I.E.L.D. was pulling up in front of the burning building when Sam and Lancaster came back down to earth. Steve Rogers had ways of finding people who didn't want to be found, and helping them whether they wanted his help or not. He was bullheaded like that. His cavalry call had come too late in this case, but Sam couldn't help but feel grateful for the gesture, all the same.

o———o

STEVE AND Nick Fury grilled Wilton Lancaster for hours in a small, deliberately claustrophobic room at a local S.H.I.E.L.D. field office. Sam listened in to the tail end of his interrogation, after he'd paid Carmen Hall a visit to tell her Leon's killer had been found. She thanked Sam and asked him to stay a while, but, he refused her invitation. He knew from personal experience that a man could get stuck in Harlem for good if he hung around too long.

As for Lancaster, he proved to be an uncooperative witness. He'd made a deal with the devil to see his life's work come to fruition and Captain America and S.H.I.E.L.D. had seen fit to destroy it. He'd bought into Zemo's lies, and nobody was going to convince him he'd been a fool to do so.

In the end, when all of Steve Rogers' and Fury's questions had been asked and disregarded, Lancaster looked at Sam forlornly. "You have no idea, the opportunity you've thrown away. The good we could have done together, with the powers I could have given you."

And then it was Sam's turn to look upon Lancaster as if he were a child of no discernment.

"I have all the powers I will ever need," Captain America said.

THE WAY HOME

NICOLE GIVENS KURTZ

THE STARS and Stripes fluttered in the wind as Sam Wilson stood atop the S.H.I.E.L.D. Helicarrier, gazing out at the city below. The distance between the earth and the clouds wasn't lost on him. His growth from his roots in Harlem to symbolizing America as Captain America mimicked the chasm between the ground and the heavens, he thought. His stomach knotted into a ball as he thought about himself, an African American man, lifting Captain America's shield, a symbol of hope and justice for all Americans.

No, the irony wasn't lost on him at all.

As he donned his red, white, and blue costume, a surge of energy flowed through him. Any new journey meant closing a door on an old one. He'd always be Falcon, and Harlem would always be home. A quick flash of his parents flickered across his mind, and a twinge twisted in his chest, but he blew it out.

"You okay?" Steve Rogers stood beside him on the Helicarrier deck as it descended. He looked so ordinary in his cream sweater and jeans. "The shield can be heavy, but you're strong."

Sam inclined his head and uncrossed his arms. "That shield isn't just heavy, it's complicated."

He didn't need to go into detail. Steve had a long history fighting fascists.

And a long memory.

"It is." Steve said. "People are complicated, but the mission is simple—stand up for what's right and just, no matter the cost. Keep doing what you're doing."

A lump formed in Sam's throat. "Yeah."

With a final nod, Steve turned and walked away, leaving Sam alone on the deck. Sam took a deep breath. He didn't doubt his skills or abilities. Ahead lay many challenges. The landscape Steve encountered, even after his suspended animation, had changed. Mass shootings, fascism spread over social media, and other geopolitical crises, all combined with intergalactic threats and superhuman villains, kept his agenda full.

As Sam boarded one of S.H.I.E.L.D.'s small flying shuttles to go down to New York City, a sense of excitement and trepidation spread through him. He didn't need to prove his capabilities to the naysayers, but his success would shut a few mouths. Steve was right, being Captain America was a continuation of what he'd always done—stand up for justice and equality for all Americans.

The shuttle touched down on the landing pad to a roar of voices and an ocean of reporters. Scores of camera flashes lit up the late afternoon. Sam glanced back at the S.H.I.E.L.D. agents.

"What's this?" Sam gestured to the crowd.

"Someone must've leaked your arrival time," the agent said, frowning at the view. "Delphine, get me the AD."

Sam turned back to the crowd. NYPD police officers tried to keep distance between the landing hub and the reporters, demonstrators, and distractors. He took a deep breath and stepped out onto the deck. The shield had weight, but the legacy made it heavier. The crowd below erupted into cheers as they caught sight of Captain America, some for their first time.

Sam raised the shield. His agenda would commence tomorrow, during his first meeting with the mayor.

Flashes from cameras and cheers rent the air. He didn't bother speaking. No one could hear him without a microphone. The din drowned out his cellphone. The notification buzzed through to his watch. He glanced down, while continuing to smile and nod. He spied the identified number.

Jamal?

He hadn't heard from Jamal Quinn in nearly a decade. They'd been close once, back in the day, breakdancing and going to parties where the DJ spun magic and rap music, possessing everyone to dance. Those had been good times. Memories of block parties, bodegas, fountain drinks, and fried fish sandwiches came flooding back.

"Hey, Captain America!" someone shouted above the din, snaring Sam's attention.

He glanced up from his watch.

"You suck!" the heckler finished, before being drowned out by those agreeing and those who didn't.

Sam's smile froze on his face. He walked to his destination, past media microphones and cell phones being shoved in his face, into his person, along with shouted questions.

"Are you afraid to be Captain America?"

"What makes you qualified to be Captain America?"

"Do you support voting rights legislation?"

A S.H.I.E.L.D. communications representative swatted several of the vultures back and nodded a greeting at Sam.

"Sorry. You landed earlier than expected. Delphine Andrews."

She wore her braids tied up high in a bun, delicate makeup, and diamond earrings, with a typical black S.H.I.E.L.D. pantsuit and heeled black boots. She turned her attention to the reporters flocking around him.

"Captain America will not answer questions today. This is not an official press conference." Delphine stopped walking, drawing their attention to her, allowing Sam to escape into a waiting car. He climbed in the back, and another S.H.I.E.L.D. agent slammed the car door closed, slicing off the noise.

In the hushed quiet, the driver asked without turning around, "Where to, Captain?"

"The hotel."

"Yes, sir."

With a sigh, Sam took out his phone and listened to Jamal's voicemail message. Funny, his friend hadn't texted him, but left him a good old-fashioned audio.

> *Sam, I know it's been a minute, but I need you. These cops aren't doing anything, and I know you're Captain America now and probably busy. I don't know who else to ask... call me.*

The dread and desperation in Jamal's words pierced Sam's heart. He hadn't heard his friend sound so despondent in a long time, not since that horrific night.

Sam threw his head back against the seat and shut his eyes against the wailing sirens erupting in his memory. The warning urgency of the ambulance and its paramedics who arrived too late, much too late to save his parents, his way of life, or his childhood. On that night, with his world dissolving into a river of tears and agony, Jamal clasped him on the shoulder and offered his hand.

Jamal and his mom supported him in ways he could never repay.

But he'd try.

LATER, SAM Wilson flew over the rooftops of Harlem, his eyes scanning the streets below. The sky clear, blue and crisp in early fall. It felt like years since he visited his hometown, and he felt a mix of nostalgia and apprehension as he soared.

What did Jamal want? Why couldn't he tell me over the phone?

He landed on the roof of an apartment building and made his way down the stairs to the street level. As he walked through the crowded streets, a sense of familiarity and belonging enveloped him. Here was home. Several people passed by, and spoke with head nods and "What's up?" No one mobbed him.

"Welcome back, Falcon!" a young man shouted. Sam waved. His new moniker as Captain America would take time, but to some, he would always be Falcon.

He arrived at the address Jamal had given him, a small community center in the heart of Harlem. Jamal worked as a community organizer and loved it. The sound of children laughing and playing greeted Sam when he pushed open the door. Signs labeled "Office" pointed the way to Jamal. Music filtered from one of the back playrooms. Laughter erupted, and then shouts and decries of foul drowned it out. The place smelled of old sweat, sugar, and soda, like a mix of a gym and teenage hormones.

It brought back memories.

Sam rounded the corner, a smile flitting on his lips, when he nearly collided with someone.

"Sam!" Jamal exclaimed as he saw his old friend. He hugged him and stepped back, taking him in. "You came!"

"You know I was coming," Sam said. "You said you needed me."

His smile disappeared, and he nodded. "Come in here."

His eyes shining with unshed tears, he led Sam into his office, a closet-sized box with a barred window. Jamal walked around his desk and eased into his chair. For such a strong, tall man, he moved as if he was ready to shatter.

Jamal rubbed his face. "Thank you, man. I don't know what to do. My son is missing, and the police aren't doing anything to find him."

"I'll do everything I can to help." Sam sat down in the single folding chair in front of Jamal's desk.

Jamal sighed and sagged in his seat. "I'm glad someone gives a damn about Henry. Police don't seem to care, you'll find him before they even start looking."

"I know it's difficult, but I want to hear what happened from you, from the source." Sometimes people remembered more in the second telling than in the frantic first interview where emotions blunt a person's recall abilities.

"We're wasting time," Jamal said. His strained tone ached with rage and helplessness.

"The sooner you tell me, the sooner I can get started." Sam knew the frustrating hurt zipping through Jamal. He'd been there too. It wasn't his favorite destination.

"When did you see him last?" Sam tried again. He took out his phone and stylus ready to write down what Jamal told him.

"Three days ago. He had a date and left the house around, I dunno, eight. His curfew's midnight. He's 17, you know, so I..." Jamal pounded his fist on his desk. Watery eyes met Sam's gaze before turning to the barred window. "When he didn't come home, I knew. I could *feel* it. Something was wrong."

"He never missed curfew before?" Sam asked.

"No."

"He's 17. Wow."

Jamal smiled. "It's been a minute, Sam, since you saw him."

"Yeah, he was like, what six or seven?"

"Somethin' like that."

Guilt hit Sam like a brick. How did ten years go by just like that? Now he sat in Jamal's tight office and remembered that Captain America meant helping people, not only battling aliens and super villains. New Yorkers, and Harlemites in particular, took care of each other.

He'd find Henry.

"What about Tanika?"

Jamal coughed. He rubbed his hands on his pants. "His mom and I are divorced. Have been for about five years. Worst time to split up for Henry, but he sees her whenever he can."

"Does she know he's missing?" Sam figured Jamal checked with his ex-wife first, but he had to ask. He didn't want to assume too much.

Jamal nodded. "Oh, yeah. Believe me. She knows."

"When was the last time she saw him?"

Jamal looked out the window. "His birthday weekend, about a month ago. She's been traveling for a book tour, so she hasn't been home."

"Does he have places he hangs out all the time? Friends? Partners?" Sam needed somewhere to start. New York City, with her five boroughs, contained millions of people. Henry had become a proverbial needle in a haystack.

Jamal crossed his arms. "I searched those places, called the hospitals, the jails, 'cause you know…"

"Yeah, I know. What's Henry's girlfriend's name?"

Jamal looked Sam in the eyes. "Boyfriend. Kwame Ofori. Henry's bisexual. His word, not mine."

Sam shook his head. "Why ain't that your word? That's how Henry chooses to identify himself. Right?"

"Not you too," Jamal said.

Sam let the comments go, since Jamal was emotional and

stressed. "Was he having a hard time in school? Online?" Sam's mind was already working through possible scenarios.

"Teenager stuff. The ex-girlfriend made some posts about him breaking up with her for Kwame. Lots of teenage drama." Jamal shrugged. "Typical you know, he said, she said, rumors..."

"What kind of rumors?"

"I dunno. Here's his social media things." Jamal handed Sam a business card. "He started his own little business. He liked drawing for folks, so he took commissions."

"Thanks." Sam took the card, on which all of Henry's social media handles were listed.

"Here." Jamal handed Sam a "MISSING" flyer of Henry. "My most recent picture of him."

Henry looked like a teenage Jamal, same flat, wide nose, and thin lips. Same thick eyebrows and mischievous eyes. He wore a short fade haircut and diamond earrings, one in each ear.

"Look, I love him. Please bring home."

"I will," Sam said. The unspoken request, to bring Henry home *alive*, took too much to vocalize, too much strength, too much hope, Sam understood the assignment. Too many young Black people came home in body bags or not at all.

Both men stood up. Jamal released a deep sigh. His shoulders rose as if someone had blown air into him, puffing him up. Now with the stress lifted, or rather shared, his friend smiled, and the creases of worry in his forehead lessened.

"Thanks." Jamal presented his fist.

Sam bumped it with his own. "I got you."

SAM EXITED the recreation center. He scanned people's faces as he walked through the crowd. Maybe he'd spot Henry on his way to see his dad. He took out the flyer and asked people hanging out in front of stores. They knew Henry, from the neighborhood, but no one had seen him. A dog barked in the distance. Horns blared. The song of the city played on.

A group of young men huddled at the corner of an intersection. He approached them, with the flyer in his hand, trying not to startle them. They stopped talking when he reached them and eyed him warily. Sam understood the constant flight or fight mindset they maintained just to survive. Their hesitation at his approach didn't bother him.

"Excuse me," Sam said. He held up the flyer. "I'm looking for a young man who went missing a few days ago. His name is Henry Quinn. Have you seen him?"

The young men looked at Henry's picture, then shook their heads.

"I ain't seen him," one of them said. He was older than the others, rough, tall, and unshaven. "You should talk to Kwame. He know everything goes on around here."

"You know where I can find Kwame?" Sam folded the flyer and put it back in his pocket.

"Kwame? Works at The Buzz Barbershop," the young man said. "Used to be part of the game, but now he trying to help people get out of it. He got locs on one side of his head."

It sounded like Kwame was a lot older than Henry. It wouldn't be the first time a mentor took advantage of an innocent and impressionable mind. Sam pushed down the hot flash of anger. Jamal wouldn't let his son actively date a grown man.

"The Buzz," Sam repeated. "Thanks."

"No problem, bro. Anything for Captain America."

The men burst into laughter.

Sam stiffened. *What's so funny?*

The internal question must've appeared on his face, because the one who gave him Kwame's information stopped.

"Aye, sorry man, but yo, why you ain't Falcon no more?"

Sam paused. All eyes were on him, waiting. Whatever answer he gave would worm its way across social media, but more importantly into their minds. He'd been their hero and now, as Captain America, he'd become *everyone's* hero. Something else African Americans had that'd been taken by the majority.

"Listen, I'm always Falcon." Sam met the men's blank faces. "Being Captain America doesn't change that. Harlem is home. I'm still her guardian, her defender, and I'm here for you. That's why I'm looking for Henry."

"Yeah. We'll see," the leader of the group said with a shrug.

"Thanks for your help," Sam started down the sidewalk, his mind racing with possibilities. Kwame could be the key to finding Henry.

He leapt up into the air, his wings taking him higher than the congested streets and clogged sidewalks. *Redwing. Locate The Buzz Barbershop.* Sam sent the message telepathically to his winged companion. Redwing would lead him to the location. The scarlet bird swooped ahead, leading the way.

THE BUZZ Barbershop sat sandwiched between a hair salon and a beauty supply store. Sam landed on the sidewalk in front of the strip mall. Here, the crowds were thinned out and the pace slower. The barbershop's hand-painted sign peeled, and the shop's operations hours were faded by time and sunlight. Sam grinned. Here was where real community change happened. Barbershops, beauty salons, and churches had long been the hub of Black neighborhoods. The Civil Rights movement found its footing in places like this. It wouldn't surprise him if this was one such place. Somehow the strip mall avoided the creeping gentrification of Harlem's history and culture.

He folded his wings and walked in.

The overhead doorbell announced him.

"Come on in. Be right with you." An older Black man with a graying afro and round, black glasses was cutting a customer's hair. He kept his eyes on his work, not looking up to even see who the visitor was.

Sam looked around at those waiting. He nodded in silent greeting. Sports played on a mounted flat screen. Fake plants added greenery, but overall, the place resembled every barbershop he'd ever been in.

"Good day. I'm looking for Kwame Ofori," Sam said.

"What do you want with him?" a middle-aged man asked. He had long, shoulder-length dreadlocks with half of his head shaved along the right side. The tips of his locks were dyed blonde. He sat in the chair in front of a barber station, dressed in a black T-shirt and jeans.

Sam took out the flyer. "I'm looking for Henry Quinn. He's been missing for a few days now, and his family's worried. I was told to talk to Kwame."

"You look familiar." The man leaned back in his chair, studying Sam's face. His eyes were like coals.

Sam hesitated, not sure if the man was Kwame or not. "I'm a friend of the family."

One of the women, seated with a toddler and waiting for their turn, said, "Y'all stupid. That's Falcon! Y'all act like a man wearing wings and a damn flag come in here every day."

"Captain America," the older barber corrected her without looking up from the nape of his customer's neck. "Kwame?" the barber nudged his colleague's shoulder.

Kwame bolted upright. He got out of the chair and said to Sam, "Follow me."

Sam followed Kwame through an opening with door beads.

It revealed a makeshift breakroom with an old microwave, folding table, and a few chairs. Kwame turned to him.

"There are some powerful people involved." Kwame took a swig from a canteen, and grimaced. "Henry and my son, KJ, might be caught up in this."

"Your son?" Sam frowned.

"Yeah, Kwame Junior. We call him KJ."

"Ah." It clicked for Sam. Henry and Kwame *Junior* were friends.

Kwame quirked an eyebrow. "You got a problem with gay folks?"

"Not at all. I just want to find Henry."

Kwame nodded. "KJ came home, like I told Jamal. He said he got stood up."

"Did he text or call KJ?"

"Nah, but you know there's been missing girls in the past few weeks. These human trafficking rings take boys, too. Harlem could be looking at something like the Grim Sleeper."

"Urban legend," Sam said, to test Kwame's conviction. He knew without a doubt human trafficking happened, but he wanted to make sure Kwame had real information.

Kwame took another swig and swished the liquid around his mouth. "That's what they want you to believe."

Sam tried a different tactic. "How come you know so much about it?"

Kwame smirked. "You think 'cause I ain't Captain America I don't know anything?" His voice hardened and he walked away from Sam. "You so damn smart, you figure it out."

"Hold up." Sam reached out to him. "Can I talk to KJ? He might be able to give more insights, since he and Henry were friends."

Kwame paused and turned back to Sam. "Friends? KJ's gay as the rainbow, Mr. Captain Freaking America. You can say it."

"Just because your son is gay doesn't mean he and Henry were a couple," Sam said, his voice tight with rising anger. "Jamal made it sound as if their relationship was a recent thing. Young people today don't like labels, so I didn't push a label onto them. Friend is generic."

Kwame stroked his chin. "Yeah, okay. You can talk to 'em. Let me text 'em."

"Thanks." Sam blew out a sigh. Kwame's sensitivity to his son's sexual orientation had everything to do with a society that kept pushing the buttons of shame and guilt. He understood the man's trigger temper on the subject. It didn't mean Sam liked it being directed at him.

Kwame parted the door beads and headed back into the main section of the barbershop. He went to his station and picked up his phone. He punched the tiny keyboard as if he worked on an old school typewriter.

As Sam chuckled to himself, his own device lit up. The S.H.I.E.L.D. emblem appeared. *Not now.* "Kwame, uh, I have to run. Can I meet KJ here, a bit later? Here's my number."

Kwame took the card with Sam's phone number. "Depends on what he got going on. I know he's upset about Henry, so yeah."

"Thank you." Sam hurried out the door.

A black SUV with tinted windows came to a screeching halt about ten feet ahead of him. Horns blared in annoyance around it. The rear window rolled down.

Who the hell is this? Sam readied his wings for battle. The S.H.I.E.L.D. call could've been a warning.

"Get in the car, Sam!" The beautiful and very irritated voice of Delphine Andrews came seconds before her face appeared.

Sam dropped his defensive stance. *What now?* "I'm in the middle of something..."

"Now!"

It wasn't negotiable. Sam walked over and climbed into the back seat. Delphine scooted over to allow him room. As soon as he shut the door, the vehicle took off.

"Okay, so what's the 911?" Sam asked.

Delphine had two phones, one in each manicured hand. She glared at him.

"You're due to have dinner with the mayor, the police commissioner, and other city council members in an hour." She shook both phones. "And you smell like de la Harlem and sweat. You're still in the damn costume!"

"Hold up!" Sam interjected. "I'm meeting the mayor tomorrow at ten. Why are you giving me grief?"

Delphine took a deep breath and audibly released it. When she spoke, her voice had a scary calm.

I've clearly missed something.

"I have left several dozen messages as early as five hours ago to confirm the itinerary. I texted you—a lot. I came by your hotel room to tell you in person. If you would've answered *one* of those, you'd know!"

"Look, I have something I'm taking care of," Sam said. "I've been occupied. Sorry about that." *Scouring the city takes time.*

Delphine's eyes had no empathy. Only full-on annoyance. She was all business. "What the hell, Sam? You can't just fly all over the city."

"Why not?" Sam didn't like her tone and he *really* didn't like the assertion she had him on a leash.

"If you aren't paying for a product, you're the product," she said. "Who do you think funds S.H.I.E.L.D.?"

"I'm a man, not a product."

"You're not Falcon, a neighborhood hero and two-bit ensemble player anymore. You're *the* Captain America. You don't get to disappear into your little excursions without authorization. If you blink, burp, or breathe wrong, it'll trend all over the world." Delphine clicked her tongue. "Got it?"

"You're saying S.H.I.E.L.D. owns me now?" Sam turned to look out the window, at the sky, where he once could fly free and unencumbered.

Delphine softened. "No, I'm not saying that…"

"It sounded like that's exactly what you said. A product."

Sam thought back to his people, how for much of America's history Black people had been considered less than human: products and animals. Now, he bore the Captain America name and costume—an America that still considers Black folks products, consumables.

"I misspoke. You're an icon, a symbol, a beacon of justice," Delphine said, slumping back into the seat. "It's different from being Falcon. It's like moving up from the backup quarterback to the starter. All eyes are on you. We can't afford any missteps or slipups. Our detractors are waiting for that."

A notification lit up Sam's watch. Kwame. KJ was on his way to the barbershop in a half hour.

Sam smiled.

Delphine asked, "You got it?"

"I get it," Sam said.

The car came to a stop at an intersection. Sam got out of the vehicle and launched into the sky. Delphine scrabbled out of the car, after him. "Sam! Get back here!"

He'd remain untethered, even if he had to fight for it. Henry Quinn had been missing for three days.

Three days too long.

KJ SAT at the end table beyond the barbershop's door beads, dressed in loose jeans, white sneakers, and an oversized T-shirt with block letters. Tattoos snaked around his right forearm. Gold necklaces hung low around his neck. Kwame stood by the rear exit.

"Son, this is Captain America, Sam Wilson. He's trying to find Henry," Kwame explained. He gave his son a wan smile. "You want something to drink?"

"Yeah." KJ smiled, flashing a pair of dimples that gave him a brief look of childhood.

He had a swagger of youth and careless bliss of ignorance. His rigid stance spoke to his discomfort, despite his tough-looking exterior. He avoided eye contact with Sam.

"Yeah what?" Kwame paused, his hand on the doorknob.

"Yes, sir." KJ's smile disappeared.

"You?" Kwame directed his question at Sam.

"No, thank you. I'm good." Sam waved.

Kwame grunted as he left. Sam turned his attention back to the younger Kwame.

"KJ. Can you tell me about Henry?" Sam sat down at the table, across from the teen. He didn't want to antagonize him, but he had to get answers.

"What do you wanna know?" KJ took out his phone and began scrolling. "You look smaller in person."

"What about the last time you saw him? When was that?" Sam let the attempt to bait him slide by. He'd been a teenager once.

KJ shrugged as he put his phone away. "Like I told Dad, Mr. Quinn, and the cops, the last time I saw Henry was in school, Friday. We went to the café, and he asked if I wanted to go see a movie that night. I said yeah. At seven, I'm at the movie theater. I texted him. I called. You know?" KJ's voice cracked. The hard persona he projected faltered. He pushed himself to sit up from slouching.

"Hey. It's alright. We'll find him," Sam said. "Could he have run away?"

KJ shook his head. "No. He loved his momma too much to do that to her. He wouldn't leave her with…" KJ shifted in his seat and rubbed his chin. He pushed his hands into his jean pockets.

"With who?"

KJ shrugged. "Never mind."

Sam made a mental note to circle back to the topic, but at the risk of KJ shutting down, he moved on. "Do you know anyone who'd want to hurt him?"

"You for real? That suit got you messed up? We Black, queer, and male. Peeps be coming for us 24/7. Be for real."

"Anyone in particular? Give me a name," Sam said, letting KJ's personal attack slide. Like his father, the teenager was hyperaware of the dangers living in America posed. The same America whose stars and stripes blazed across his chest. He understood KJ's short and angry answers. But he was wasting time.

KJ wiggled. "Leona been giving him drama at school. Spreading bull about him, about us."

"Leona's the ex-girlfriend?"

"Yeah."

"What types of stuff?"

KJ cleared his throat. "Uh, you know, like I said, spreading lies. Okay, like on Friday, after school, Henry and I were outside Bruno's. Leona and her little friends came over and started harassing him. She was frantic, screaming at Henry and threatening to hit him. I told Henry I'm out and left. Ain't nobody got time for that."

Sam didn't like the sound of that. Love triangles bubbled with passion and anger. "You left him?"

"Yeah." KJ answered, his voice quiet.

"You don't know what they argued about?"

"Me, I guess. She didn't like getting dumped." KJ slouched down as if trying to slip under the table.

"For you?"

"Man, for *anybody.* Leona comes with bling and bougieness. The fact Henry even got the chance to date her was a scandal. And when he came out as bi? Boom!" KJ took his hands out of his pockets to demonstrate an explosion cloud.

Sam nodded. "Could she have done something to him or had something done to hurt him?"

"She smacked him."

"What did Henry do?" Sam didn't like the escalation of events. Leona could've had a relative harm him on her behalf.

"He called her some special names and stormed off."

"How do you know about this? Didn't you desert him?" Sam said, hoping to rattle KJ enough to get him talking.

KJ stiffened and pressed his lips together. He stared at the table for several seconds before looking up at Sam. "I walked away and when I got to the corner, I looked back to see if he'd left. I saw them all around him, pointing fingers and screaming at him. I started back, but… he'd gone already. Leona and her crew had started to walk to Bruno's."

"Earlier, you said Henry loved his momma," Sam changed the subject. "How was it between him and his dad?"

KJ blew out a "woah."

Sam waited and kept his face neutral.

"I'm not dumb. I know you and Mr. Quinn are friends," KJ said.

"Yeah, but I need to know everything. Sometimes what people say and do in the days and months before they go missing are clues to how to find them."

"All I'm gonna say is Henry hated living with that man. They argued all the time, you know what I mean? He'd been begging to move in with his mom." KJ stretched into a fake yawn. "Where's Dad? I got homework to do."

Before KJ could say more, the rear door opened. Kwame came in with a cloud of smoke and grease. He put two stained brown bags on the table.

"Aye, sorry about that. Bruno's was packed. I figured you ain't eat." Two pops were in a cardboard drink carrier. He took out two wax paper sandwiches from the bag.

Bruno's Burgers. It'd been almost a decade since Sam and Jamal went there. That brought back memories.

Once the food had been distributed, Kwame looked at KJ. "How's it going?"

KJ unwrapped his burger. "Fine."

Sam stood up. "I'm going to leave you to it."

He wouldn't get more out of KJ with his dad hanging around. Plus, the food reminded him that he hadn't eaten.

"Thank you."

KJ stumbled out of his chair. "You'll find him. Yeah?"

Fear glittered in the teenager's eyes, his body tight with concern. Either KJ cared about Henry, or he knew more than he said. Kwame placed a reassuring hand on KJ's shoulder.

"I'm going to do all I can. If you think of anything, please tell the police or your father."

"Yeah," KJ said, easing back into the folding chair. "Like they care."

"YOU WANT fries with that?" the server asked with all the interest of someone watching paint dry.

"No, a salad, please," Sam said. He ignored his cell phone's buzzing. Delphine's insistence would have to be dealt with, but not right away. *Right now—food!*

He sat in the rear booth at Bruno's, a local restaurant renowned for their thick burgers and fried fish sandwiches. Henry's assault by Leona happened outside this location and Sam half wondered if the teenager would show up here.

People came in with the bluster and noise of youth. Sam smiled as he thought back to the days when he and Jamal piled in here after school. They would scrape together their allowances and the change from the candy they sold at school to buy food here. Warmth flowed through him.

"Here you go, Falcon," the server said with a wink.

Sam said, "Thanks!"

The server placed the salad in front of him. "Burger be out in a bit."

"I appreciate it."

She left.

Alone, he had a chance to think. How much of what KJ provided was true?

Redwing. Any signs of Henry?

Sam closed his eyes. His telepathic link with Redwing revealed KJ approaching a brownstone's flat steps. The door was ajar, and behind it stood Tanika, Henry's mom. A shadow moved behind her, but Redwing's point of view didn't show the person.

Why would KJ be going to Tanika's?

Redwing's position across from the ebony-painted door and porch gave Sam a better view. KJ went up to the door and slowly pushed the door open. He now wore a hoodie with its hood up. The teenager glanced around and bounced on one foot to another in impatience.

A Black male, in jeans, a button-down shirt and socked feet let KJ in and hurried to shut it.

Sam inhaled. What were they hiding? Who was the man?

KJ had given him the impression he was headed home for the evening. Despite their solid conversation, Sam felt the teen knew more than he said.

Time to do some old-school surveillance.

"Alright, Falcon, here's the big Bruno," the server said.

"Great. Can I get it to go?" Sam said.

This fresh lead stirred the need to act. The cool evening sky embraced him. When he flew, he was free from the weight of the things holding him down—the racism, the violence, the heartache. Harlem unfolded below, her glittering lights and live music reached his ears. The brownstone was only a few blocks from the barbershop. Far enough away from the older neighborhoods. Redwing remained on the lookout.

No one had left or arrived.

Sam landed on the sidewalk. The tree-lined street stretched on in both directions, postcard perfect.

These aren't cheap.

Sam stood underneath the tree opposite the porch. He needed better cover. Pedestrians walked by, absorbed in their devices or in their conversations. No one appeared to take notice of him—a man with wings and wearing a red, white, and blue costume.

Just another day in Harlem.

Redwing called out in warning. Sam looked right, in the direction and his stomach fell. Jamal came marching down the sidewalk, heading directly toward him.

"What are you doing here?" Sam met Jamal before he reached the porch.

"My child is out here, Sam. I gotta find my baby. You didn't expect me to sit around and wait," Jamal said.

"Were you following me?" Sam couldn't believe it. *How did he get here? Coincidence?*

"For a super hero, you don't pay a lick of attention if I'm able to follow you." Jamal laughed. "No, man, I followed KJ. Call it dad's intuition, but I didn't think he'd been straight with me."

"You've been here before, right?" Sam nodded at the black-painted door.

"Yeah, it's Tanika's place. Well, hers and Jeffery's, her new man."

Sam glared at Jamal. "Why didn't you tell me about him?"

Jamal shrugged. "Look man. I'm only concerned about Henry."

The ebony door creaked open, interrupting them.

"If you're going to argue outside my home, you might as well do it inside," a woman said, her oval face somber. She wore a flowing green dress and flip flops.

"Tanika, I..." Jamal started, but she cut him off.

"Inside. Please." Taneka cut her eyes over to Sam. "You too, Captain."

They went inside a brightly lit foyer and living room. Both bore contemporary African American art, wood floors, and cognac-colored leather furniture. Tanika sat down on a loveseat next to an adult man, who could only be Jeffery. On the sofa were two throw pillows and two teenage boys.

Sam recognized KJ, so the other teenager must have been...

"Henry?" Jamal's eyes widened in disbelief. "You been here. The whole time?"

"Dad, I..."

"Answer me!" Jamal barked. His throat sounded as if he'd swallowed tears. "I was so scared! I didn't know if you'd been shot by police, kidnapped by human traffickers, or killed in some gang rivalry."

"Don't shout at him like that. Let him explain," Tanika said. "That's part of why he's here." Jeffery took her hand.

Jamal rounded on her. "Oh, forgive me for interrupting your fragile family balance! I have every damn right to be furious. You've been hiding him here the entire time. I involved the police, Captain America, countless others. Do you understand how this looks?"

"I don't care how it looks," Tanika said. "This isn't about you, Jamal. It's about Henry."

Jeffery released her hand and stood up. Jamal took a step toward him. Sam rushed to get between them before a fight broke out. Emotions ran high, but they needed cooler heads.

"You don't have to play referee, Cap. Jamal needs to calm down so he can hear Henry. Really listen," Jeffery said.

Sam approached Jeffery's cool. "What do you do for a living?"

"Huh, oh, I'm a psychiatrist."

Jamal spun around, rubbing his face, and taking deep breaths.

Sam turned to Henry. "Start at the beginning."

Henry swallowed loud enough to hear it. KJ took his hand, and gave him a small, encouraging nod. "It's okay. Tell him."

Henry licked his lips and looked at his hands. "After Dad and I argued, *everything* got worse. Leona and her friends, all the crap on social media and all the stuff that's always in the news, I needed to get some space."

"Why didn't you tell me?" Jamal's tone had lost its initial fury but still sounded harsh.

"How could I? I was running from you!" Henry squeezed KJ's hand.

"Me?" Jamal's voice broke. "I do everything for you…"

"You won't let me breathe. I know I'm Black, dad. I know the statistics 'cause you never let me forget them. There's a walking bounty on my head as a young Black man. I know! But sometimes, I wanna be Henry, a kid who goes to the movies with his boyfriend."

Henry glanced at Sam.

Sam took the pleading message and turned to Tanika. "Did you know he was here?"

"Not at first, no. I've been on tour for a month. I came back when Jamal told me Henry was missing. When I got here, two days ago, Jeffery and Henry explained everything. We were going to tell Jamal, but Henry was afraid of his reaction."

"And the police?"

"Jamal already involved them," Jeffery answered. "When they came by here, Henry wasn't here."

"I stayed at KJ's house the first night," Henry said.

"I checked here, first," Jamal interjected. "Jeffery said Henry wasn't here."

Jeffery hitched up his chin. "And he wasn't."

For the first time since arriving at Tanika's, a hush fell over the room. Sam saw all the hurt and all the love. It brought him back to the week before his parents' murder. He and his dad scuffled over a foolish matter. He couldn't even remember it now. Back then he'd been full of so much anger and rancor that he lacked direction and focus.

All too soon, his love, his life, his parents were snuffed out.

Henry was looking angrier and angrier at the squabbling going on around him. "Is that all y'all still care about?" he sulked. "Trying to one-up each other so you can brag about who cares about me the most? No wonder I hate being around any of you," he huffed.

"Henry," Sam crouched down in front of the boy. "Your dad, like Jeffery and your mom, are doing their best. Will they make mistakes? Yeah. We're human. When we don't understand, we can sometimes get scared, and act out of fear and anger. One thing I learned is you can't run from your problems. You have to face the things that scare you."

"Huh, that's easy for you, Captain America," KJ said. "You ain't queer and Black."

Henry searched Sam's face.

"No, just Black, but I wasn't Falcon or Captain America when I was your age. I was Sam Wilson. I still am. Once, I relied on my best friend, Jamal, your dad, to rescue me from a dark, horrible place."

Henry's eyes lit up. "My dad saved you?"

"Oh, yeah, man, if it wasn't for Jamal and your grandmother, I doubt I'd be here talking to you." Sam stood up.

Jamal stood up, too. He went to Sam and hugged him. "I'm sorry."

"Man, you know I don't need an apology. We're good." Sam returned the hug and started easing toward the door. His job was done, and it was time for this family to heal.

Jamal turned to Henry. "I'm sorry, son. I should've listened..."

Henry leapt to his feet and hugged his dad.

Tanika and Jeffery looked on, and they seemed relieved. Tanika said, "We will make every effort to ensure Henry gets what he needs."

"I've got to go. I'm glad Henry's safe," Sam said to them.

KJ stood up too. "Captain America, I... I want to say I'm sorry too, for lying to you. And, uh, I know you're getting a lot more heat online about being Black and being Captain America, freaking racists, and pundits. I'm sorry they're all so stupid. You're real cool."

Sam laughed. "Thanks, KJ."

Jamal said, "Thanks, Sam."

"Stay in touch, man," Sam exchanged a fist bump.

"You too, man." When Sam stepped outside onto the porch, he found Delphine leaning against a black SUV.

She said, "You need to go to bed. I'm not getting yelled at again because you're yawning and sleeping through meetings. You can't miss the next one. The meeting in the morning with the mayor is still on the table. Who is he going to meet?"

Sam slid into the back seat. "Captain America, Sam Wilson."

SURREPTITIOUS

GARY PHILLIPS

SAM WILSON arrived at San Carraga not by air, as might be expected, but by sea. He expertly piloted the mini-sub sheathed in a sonar-deflecting material. Sam slowed the engine, coasting to a halt. He turned on the interior lights.

"Okay, old buddy, you took being cooped up pretty well," he said, smiling at his falcon, Redwing. "And now you're gonna get to do your thing."

Sam flicked a few more switches and pulled a lever, causing the submersible to angle upward through the semi-gloom of the depths into clearer water.

They traveled through schools of colorful fish. Redwing made no sound, perched near him, but his dark eyes intently watched the fish through a porthole.

Sam pulled his cowl with its mask and built-in goggles into place. The mini-sub surfaced a mile off the leeward side of the small Caribbean island. The landmass was an uneven slag of volcanic rock, sand, flowers ranging from butterfly jasmine to orchids, heavy undergrowth, and swaying palm trees. Various species of birds flew about, cawing and skreeing. Sam filtered out the impressions from the minds of these winged creatures.

It wasn't telepathy he shared with these birds, but he did have the ability to order them to attack an enemy if need be. His rapport with Redwing was another matter.

"Now, don't you go getting distracted should some fine-feathered lady falcon come flying your way. You're on a mission, right?"

The bird, balanced on the hull, blinked at him and shifted on its clawed feet. The two were taking in the island from where they'd poked out of the upper hatch. Sam activated one of the functions of his red-lensed goggles: long-range scanning for bipedal heat signatures. He detected none. But he knew better than to be complacent. Particularly given what he'd been sent to retrieve here, a heretofore undetected stash of Skrull weaponry. The S.H.I.E.L.D. intel provided by Maria Hill indicated the weapons had either been left behind in a past campaign of the extraterrestrial shapeshifters to conquer Earth, or possibly hidden away to serve some future effort. Whatever the reason, the arsenal had to be secured.

Redwing took to the air. Sam watched him soar, envious of his companion's natural ability. The falcon's spread wings were something to behold against the near-cloudless sky. With a low sigh, Sam refocused and triggered autonomous presets in the mini-sub's controls. As the vessel resubmerged, the hatch sliding back into place, Sam extended his artificial wings to also take to the air—though not seeking quite the altitude Redwing had achieved. He skimmed not more than five feet above the water, booted feet together, arms stretched out to his sides, his shield strapped in place over one arm.

Sam touched down quietly in a sandy inlet bordered by a jungle thick with mangroves. His vibranium wings folded into the diamond-shaped housing on his upper back. He concentrated to receive the impressions from Redwing, who was dipping and diving low while scouring the supposedly uninhabited island. He stood still as he sifted through immediate visual memory and what was being viewed by the falcon in real time as he received a particular image from Redwing. As he suspected, they weren't alone. Sam moved forward on foot. Given the scientific sophistication of the foes Redwing had spotted, it was advisable not to be an easy flying target.

Through Redwing's eyes, he knew the patch of jungle he headed for was a semi-circle bordering a clearing with a rock formation on one side. No sooner had he entered the clearing than twin laser cannons popped out of the ground. Sam's shield swung into place, repelling the ray blasts while he sprang into motion. The cannons' tracking sensors had them turning, vectoring in once more on his form. Though it appeared like he was off-balance as he threw his shield, it was a maneuver perfected through rigorous practice and application in the field. The near-indestructible shield sliced through the hinged lower supports of the laser cannons, also severing the thick cables leading to the batteries in their respective trunk-like housings. The cannons toppled over, useless, as the shield circled back to its owner.

Then a studded metal fist plowed toward Sam's head. He ducked and rolled out of the way just in time. The trunk of the tree behind him was splintered into kindling from the impact of the blow. Crashing into the clearing through the tangled undergrowth was an android seven and a half feet tall, encased in blue-black metal and blended with what Sam estimated were carbon polymers. The face was skull-like with small fins jutting from either side atop its blockish head. The imagery Sam had received from Redwing had been four figures in uniform carrying a coffin-like container in from the beach. This must've been how they'd brought the robot to shore.

"You guys might get into some copyright infringement with this thing," Sam quipped to his hidden opponents. The mechanical man was a design variation of a Hydra Dreadnaught.

The android came at him, swinging like a heavyweight. Sam took a punch to his arm that would have broken it, save for his armored suit. He uppercut the robot and followed with a left cross that would fell a rhino. It staggered back, opening its mouth. A hollow rod telescoped from inside the thing's throat, emitting a sonic assault that caused Sam to grimace.

His knees wobbled and his stomach roiled. *But what kind of super hero would I be, vomiting on the job?* he admonished himself.

The robot charged at Sam, its programming no doubt informing it the human should be sufficiently disabled and disoriented. Cyber-controlled wings sprouted on his back, and Sam zoomed upward. His attacker grabbed one of his legs. He expected that's what the machine would do. Rather than try and gain altitude, Sam flew horizontally, swinging his body around rapidly. He bashed the robot against a craggy pyramid-shaped rock. Then he brought the edge of his shield down on the android's arm at the elbow. The forearm separated from the rest of the body, falling to the ground. Trailing wiring and circuitry hissed from the end of the remaining limb. Sam power-dived at the robot, but the mechanical predator sprang up as jets built into the soles of its feet flared, providing him with flight as well.

Human and construct grappled above the clearing. The killer machine's remaining hand latched onto Sam's throat, crushing his windpipe.

"Ughh," he grunted, getting his hand on the metal wrist, crushing the android's shell.

The thing's mouth opened again and this time a torrent of frost issued from the maw, instantly icing Sam's wings. Down they plummeted, the robot still locked onto him. It increased its speed, seeking to smash Sam into the ground. Having experienced this type of maneuver before with other aerial opponents, he turned them at just the right moment, and they hit the earth on their sides. The robot rose to its feet first and, using its freeze function again, began to immobilize Sam from the top down in a block of ice.

While his right arm with his shield was now encased in ice, part of Sam's left arm was still free—as were his legs. He leaped upward despite the added weight, spun, and struck the ground again, shattering some of the ice and spiderwebbing cracks throughout the block. The android lunged at him. With his insulated gloved hand, he yanked on the exposed wiring hanging out of the half of the arm. Sparks sizzled and electrical current thrummed. He understood his action wouldn't short-circuit the robot, but now having a hold of it and falling backward, he caused the robot to crash onto him, breaking him loose from his frozen confines.

The android jumped off Sam. Airborne once more via its boot jets, the thing's chest split open where a human's sternum would be. Out of the cavity snaked a sectioned, chrome-plated tentacle not unlike one used by Doctor Octopus. The tentacle wound around Captain America's body as the coil super-heated. In less than two minutes, he estimated, he'd be cooked from the inside out, his organs and brain shutting down. The tentacle whipped him about so he couldn't get a clear shot with his shield. Peripherally, he saw three members of Advanced Idea Mechanics, A.I.M., come into view. They were dressed in their customary yellow jumpsuits and beekeeper-like hoods.

Redwing screeched as he swooped in, summoned mentally by Sam. He wasn't alone. A flock of birds also dove in, enough to cyclone around the robot. The A.I.M. members shot at the birds with their sidearms, killing some but many flitting about too quickly to be hit.

"Very good, my friends," Sam said softly, pleased most had not met their demise.

A mass of the airborne calvary swarmed onto the robot's head, causing an overload of sensory input just as Sam had intended. As the robot swatted at the birds, the tentacle momentarily stopped flicking him around. Captain America flung his shield with unerring accuracy and destroyed a servo unit he spotted inside the android's chest cavity.

Late nights devoted to studying various Hydra Dreadnaught schematics obtained via espionage paid off. The tentacle instantly lost its grip on him, but rather than fall a second time to the earth, he grabbed the lifeless artificial appendage with both hands.

Hand over hand Sam climbed the alloy tentacle as the airborne android flew patterns to dislodge him. He swung back and forth, using the metal limb like a vine in an old, politically incorrect king-of-the-jungle movie. It amused him wondering what T'Challa, the Black Panther, might think of that. Sam kicked upward and released his grip, landing on the machine's back. The birds, led by Redwing, dispersed.

"Thanks, man," he said to his partner.

With hands on either side, he brought the shield down at the base of the robot's neck as it turned its head around to look at him. Even given the enhanced strength provided by the nanotech of his suit, he was aware his shield wouldn't cut the head off in one strike. But he did damage the central core assembly stem of its artificial brain. The light went out behind the android's eyes. Sam flew away as the A.I.M. personnel took off to regroup. The robot struck the ground headfirst, plowing a sizeable trench through the earth.

Then Sam heard the sounds of gunfire and the thumps of hand-to-hand combat. Surmising someone or someones were attacking the members of A.I.M, he flew toward the fight from on high. He landed on a curved promontory. The brush here too was thick, though more than one outcropping of rock rose about the greenery. One of the A.I.M. detachment took a shot at him with a laser pulse rifle. A.I.M. had always been rather violent, Sam reflected, for an organization founded by brilliant scientists dedicated to world domination through technology.

As always, his armored suit performed admirably and deflected the blast. His straight right to the helmeted scientist's middle wasn't deflected, though, and it doubled the man over. Captain America then forced the helmeted head down from behind with his hands as he brought his knee up. The violence of his actions wasn't lost on him. The helmet broke, as did the nose of the man inside it. Two more blows had him motionless on the ground. Thereafter, Captain America followed the trail of three yellow-clad bodies on the ground not put there by him. One of them was missing part of his head, scorch marks from a ray blaster having singed what was left of his helmet.

Up ahead, two other members of A.I.M. were still on their feet. They were in a firefight with a lone enemy. Like in Saturday morning TV westerns from his youth, the two were partially hidden by rocks and brush below, while the other was higher up among the rocks. He knew the dark-clad woman they were shooting at.

"Figures she'd be here," he muttered, zooming forward and zeroing in on the two A.I.M. shooters, a man and a woman.

They fixed their attention on him. The man shouted, "It's the Falcon."

"Really?" Sam said, divebombing them, their blasts impotently striking his shield. Summersaulting, he came in feet-first. His textbook flying kick sent the man tumbling backward off his feet.

The woman tossed aside her now empty gun and assumed a karate stance, issuing a challenge. "How tough are you without your gimmicks?"

Sam grinned. "Please. You trying out for the head beekeeper?"

The woman from A.I.M. said, "What?"

"Never mind," he answered.

"I got this," the other woman said. She too assumed a martial arts stance. The fight was brief, with a number of grunts and a rapid succession of blows. The woman in yellow soon lay unconscious at the feet of the victor.

"Deadly Nightshade," Sam said, purposely referring to this one by her once super villain identity.

"You know my name, fool." Tilda Johnson wiped a crawl of blood from the side of her mouth.

"Is that all of them?" he said, scowling. Sam could never be cavalier about taking a life, no matter whose. Johnson, an inventor among other attributes, was as vicious as she was smart. Theoretically she was reformed, he reminded himself.

"Yep," she said.

"I'm betting you know where the cache is."

"Before you start puffing out your chest... Captain Falcon, I'm only after one item. A non-lethal device."

"Nothing about the Skrulls is non-lethal, Johnson. And what makes you think I'm in a mood to negotiate?"

"First things first, right?" she said.

Aware theirs was an alliance of convenience, he said, "Right. Let's secure the ones still breathing, shall we?"

Johnson eschewed voicing a comeback.

Together they trussed up the A.I.M. crew. Redwing, stationed on the pyramid-shaped rock watched them. Afterward Johnson led the way to the prize they'd come to San Carraga for, the Skrull trove.

He followed Johnson to another part of the headland. Not trusting her, he'd tasked Redwing to scout ahead again in case she'd set a trap. They came to a row of large forty-foot-high carved volcanic rock heads. Distinct from the ones on Easter Island, each seemed to be a varying combination of Aztec and Yoruba influences.

"These the real McCoy?" he asked Johnson. He removed a glove to feel the stonework on one of the heads.

"It would seem so. Who knows what ancient travelers came this way and marked their passage." She paused. "You and the A.I.M. contingent must have just missed each other, arriving by submarine. I parachuted in last evening to do my reconnoitering." She dragged into view what looked like a modern version of a steamer trunk. "I brought along my mobile tactical rig." She sat the trunk upright. "As best as possible, it's been attuned to Skrull operating systems."

"The Skrulls wouldn't leave their weapons lying around for just any chump to make off with the goods," Sam said. He had a similar set of instruments on his sub.

"Exactly." She produced a compact remote control and pressed a button. The trunk split open and various types of antennae and sensor indicators rose from within it.

"Let me guess, the Skrulls hid their stuff under one of the heads."

"The big dome-like one that looks like an Olmec face. Help me get this closer."

They carried her equipment over the uneven ground nearer to the specific head as the mechanism scanned for boobytraps. Sam watched over her shoulder as Johnson, slightly hunched, eyed various monitors and adjusted several dials. Johnson's machine revealed what had been an invisible multi-pronged trident staked out a yard in front of the big head.

"That thing probably barbeques the unwanted," Sam said, noting the readout on one of the monitors.

"Neutralized," she announced, flicking a switch. The now visible trident fizzled and sparked.

Twin mortar-like devices sprang from hidden compartments on either side of the head.

"I got this." Captain America leaped onto one of the devices, twisting it around on its radial arm. The explosive round it released destroyed the other mortar. He then wrenched the remaining one free from its moorings, dropping the useless ordnance to the ground.

Straightening up, Johnson declared, "That should be the last of 'em."

"Should be?"

"Yeah," she agreed, "these are the devious Skrulls we're talking about."

Sam pointed skyward. Redwing arced in from overhead, releasing a coconut from his claws toward the head.

Twin purple beams erupted from the statue's eyes, obliterating the coconut. As the rays swept toward them, Captain America launched up and forward, the shield in front of him. The twin beams blazed blindingly against his shield as he slammed into the stone head. The destructive rays were redirected inward. The resulting concussive explosion knocked him to the ground.

"You okay?" Johnson asked, sounding sincere.

"I'll make it," he said, rising from the ground and dusting off his colorful costume. The white star in the middle of his chest was gray with soot. Smoke rose from the oblong eyes of the statue. The unmistakable smell of burnt electrical conduits filled the air. Soon they found the mechanism that opened the statue, which split in half to reveal a set of descending steps.

"After you," Johnson said. Still cautious, she regarded a handheld probe that crackled like a Geiger counter.

Down Sam went, his movement causing a light to come on. The two soon stood in a medium-sized bunker. There were metal cases stacked around them, along with a wide variety of gadgets on shelves or in hexagonal alcoves. He cocked an eyebrow, aware of a low hum starting up.

"Gonna need a bigger sub, huh?" Johnson joked regarding the amount of hardware.

Angling his head toward one of the shelves, he asked, "You hear that?" He detected a high-pitch trill.

"What, darling?"

He turned back to see a different woman facing him. She was dressed as if attending a Victorian-era costume ball. Despite a life of dealing with the likes of the Cosmic Cube, he gaped at her.

"Leila?" he said incredulously. Leila Taylor was an old flame, but they were no more, these days.

She smiled at him. "Yes, my love. What troubles you?"

"This whole setup," he said grimly, steeling himself for whatever else was to come. *Keep your wits, man.*

Captain America realized he too was now dressed like an extra in *Bridgerton* or some such take on that era. He had to admit he did like the look of the frock coat he wore. But he wasn't about to get swept away in all this foolishness. The two of them stood in a lush garden where others mingled. From a stage, a quartet played. The melody supplied by a mandolin and lute wafting about the conversations.

"Some kind of Skrull trickery," he said to the fake Leila. He studied her to see if he could discern her alienness.

"Skrulls?" she said, snaping open a fan with a flick of her wrist. "Why, none of those blaggards have darkened these quarters since we routed them last summer." She fanned herself. The illustration on the fan was the stylized star on his shield—a shield that wasn't present.

"I'm getting out of here," Sam announced. He started for a set of stone stairs leading to a terraced patio.

"But, Sam," the purported Leila Taylor said, "the buffalo steaks imported from the Americas are just being set out." As she spoke, she extended her arm and indicated a set of tables upon which were numerous platters of food. Several staff arrived, holding large silver trays covered by matching cloches. These were set down and the covers removed, revealing slabs of raw meat.

Leila stood beside him. "Oh yes," she growled lustfully. Her red-nailed hand gripped his arm. The hand was changing, the fingers growing longer and knotty, long hairs sprouting across the back.

"Aw, damn," he groused, "werewolves. Of course it's werewolves." In her Deadly Nightshade guise of the past, Johnson had turned the captured Sam Wilson into such a creature to kill his friend Steve Rogers.

At the tables, the other werewolves snarled and fought each other to get at the meat.

"Join us, be one of us and feast as we feast, hunt as we hunt." Leila Taylor tried to dig her claws into his arm, but a knife-edge chop to her collarbone dazed her enough for him to pull free without being scratched. Whatever the Skrull gadget was doing to him, he wasn't going to take the chance of getting werewolfed or devoured by these other ravenous partygoers. *If you die in the mind, does your body follow? Or is this somehow Johnson's doing?* he also considered. She'd once developed what she called

Mesmer Dust, he recalled as he vaulted over a balustrade. Three werewolves in their finery chased him.

He landed on the lawn in a crouch. Spinning around, he roundhouse-kicked a werewolf in a ripped striped suit and bowler hat. Sam noted his blow felt solid. *Is it only sophisticated holographs, or a form of Skrullduggery that solidifies your fears?* he weighed. *But again, that could be part of the effect, your sensory input hoodwinked as well.*

As the man-creature dropped to the ground, Sam used the unintentionally offered back as a springboard, and with one hand on him, took both feet off the ground to scissor his lower legs around the neck of another werewolf. He spun her around and flung her into two others. He ran, a pack of werewolves led by Leila Taylor chasing him. Before him appeared an energy crackle, the landscape and sky blinking in and out of existence before it stabilized again. There was a way to think his route out of this, he determined.

Fangs prominent and drool wetting the sides of her mouth, Taylor yelled, "Sam, you're only delaying the inevitable, my sweet. I promise you will rule at my side. First among equals."

One of the circular silver serving trays lay on the ground next to the severed head of one of the servers. Apparently only the gentry had the privilege of being lycanthropes. On a dead run, he scooped up the tray and, twisting his upper body around in a fluid motion, flung it at his attackers. While the tray was certainly not aerodynamically engineered like his shield, he nonetheless tagged a werewolf upside the head. The tray ricocheted off that beast to hit a second one in the head too.

As befitting the upper-class setting, there was an ornate hedge maze ahead. Sam darted inside. He knew damn well his pursuers wouldn't be concerned with the niceties of following the layout and would simply crash though the walls of shrubbery.

But the hedges were thick and afforded him a modicum of protection. Being someone who spent a good deal of his time in the air, his sense of direction and topography was well above average. After a few turns and backtracking, he figured out how to reach the center of the maze. Growls and thrashing all around, beastly forms surrounded him as he continued. A stout werewolf in dark blue serge burst through a hedge in front of him. Sam leveraged him over his shoulder in a modified judo move. The beast man landed on his back and Sam stomped him hard in the face. Again, there was the flash and crackle, the fabric of this nightmare tearing apart. But again, it was brief. On he went.

Given enough time to get it right in his mind, he could transcend this situation. To convince himself the claws raking him and the jaws biting off pieces of him weren't real. Such mindfulness would take minutes of peace, however, and there was none to be had to escape this psychological trap. He needed a lifeline. Nearing the center of the maze, two more werewolves were on him, and he kung fu'd them senseless. Out of options, Sam took a knee in the open circle in the heart of the maze. Leila Taylor and her pack reached him.

Hands pressed to her upper body, she enthused, "Oh, Sam, this will be glorious. Dare I say heavenly?"

The transformed standing around her chuckled low in their collective throats. The changelings advanced as one, in no hurry, savoring what was to come.

"Are you praying, darling?" she taunted.

Sam's head was down. "In a way."

She put a clawed hand on his head and reared it back to expose his Adam's apple. Her salivating jaws opened wider. "I thought about turning you, Captain America. But now, I'm thinking how wonderous it would be to simply dine on your flesh, Sam Wilson."

From overhead a distinctive *skreee* filled the air. Redwing zeroed in on the gathered. The werewolves hissed and snapped their jaws. Sam figured the Skrulls' mind trap was calibrated to affect beings of a certain level of brain function. While he and the falcon shared a bond, the bird was still a bird and remained unaffected. He pushed his point of view through Redwing's. The animal was perched on the steps, observing him and Johnson in her mental thrall. The out-of-body perspective helped Sam to center himself and overcome the induced phantasms. Redwing cawed triumphantly. Captain America was back in the bunker.

He shook Johnson, who was huddled in a corner, mumbling and writhing in her mental malaise. Looking around, he spotted Redwing pecking at what looked like a toaster for Galactus. A quick toss of his shield destroyed the apparatus. The ruined device caught fire from within but there was no danger of it spreading.

Johnson groaned, hands on her face. "That thing didn't register on my instruments because technically it's non-lethal. But I suspect we'd have been trapped in our own private hells over and over."

"Until we were driven crazy."

She nodded as Sam helped pull her to her feet. "Maybe you're right, maybe you should take possession of these weapons."

Sam turned his head to regard the stockpile, seemingly not noticing a silver sphere barely larger than a tennis ball rolling toward his feet.

The sphere burst open with a flash. Black ribbons of flexible titanium sprouted from the metal ball and coiled around his body, tightening as they did so.

"That ought to keep you busy long enough," Johnson announced, now carrying a long, cylindrical container.

But as her foot came down on one of the steps, a sudden

surge went through her. Johnson's body spasmed. She dropped the container as she lost control of her lower limbs and wilted to the floor.

"Dammit," she swore.

Captain America got himself loose. "How long we been knowing each other, Tilda? Like I would go for the okey-doke." He shook the control fob of his shocker at her, the one he'd placed on her when he helped her to her feet. His boot was now on the cylinder.

She was still on the floor, pointing at the cylinder. "In there is tech allowing humans to mimic shape-shifting. The appearance of such, to be specific."

"A variation of what we just went through," Sam declared. He had an idea where she was going with this.

"Use it to infiltrate the fascist groups actively seeking to undermine what you stand for, what you, and I, fight for. You've said how our worst day as a country is where we rise from, where we start. Well, that's where we are now, aren't we? Whack-job conspiracy theories informing policy. White supremacists infiltrating police departments and the armed services. The take-backers wanting to drive queer folk into non-existence..."

She paused, rising to her feet. "I can make a difference with this."

"You'd assassinate some of these folks you're talking about," he said.

"Maybe I'm the sword to your shield, Captain America. Allowing you to take the high road while I do the dirty work."

"Taking a page from the Book of Nick Fury, Tilda?"

"Someone has to. Nobody but you knows what you'll inventory from this haul."

"That's right." His boot slowly came off the cylinder. "I won't stand for indiscriminate slaughter."

"I know."

"You coordinate with me. There is no other option."

A few moments of silence as they regarded one another. Finally, she said, "Understood."

He wasn't fooling himself. She'd take it too far, but he'd keep watch. This was on him, how his Captain America fulfilled his mission. The weight and the honor of wielding the shield meant you could never be complacent.

THE MALTESE CONNECTION

GLENN PARRIS

SAM WILSON spat blood out of his mouth, the crimson liquid spilling down on his red, white, and blue uniform. The punch had caught him by surprise. But it wasn't just the sheer power of the punch that got him; it was also the source.

"Look kid, I was only trying to help. You looked lost."

The chubby, short white boy couldn't have been more than 16. Red cheeks and a hairless chin under a mop of thick, curly hair imparted a cherub-like appearance. His shorts and T-shirt screamed innocence. But the child proved to be uncommon, in a bad way.

"Should have minded your own business, Bird-man. I'm trying to score a hit of boost for some friends," he said, referring to the Power Broker's latest drug on the street. Boost gave you super-strength and superhuman durability, for a while. Sam wondered if it affected the mind too as he watched the boy ball his fists like an amateur who'd only seen fist fights in 1950s westerns.

Sam slid off his butt up against the wall, buffed from the surprise hit, his legs still wobbly. "You don't need to be here, son. Those fake powers don't make as much of a difference as you think."

"I mean, who're you trying to kid?" said the boy. "You're

not a 'Mighty' Avenger. Dude, you're just half chicken." Moving more swiftly than Sam expected, he grabbed Sam's uniform in his fists along with a few chest hairs and threw the winged Avenger down the alley with a casual sweep of his arm.

But Sam, his head finally clear, was prepared for this move. He stretched out his wings midflight and ignited his jets, barrel-rolling and swooping up and over the kid. Before the boy knew it, he'd landed smoothly behind him and was looking at him questioningly.

"Okay, Chucky, where did you come from?" he asked.

"Don't call me Chunky!" the boy screamed, then rushed at Sam again, clumsily, like a drunken bull. Sam evaded each blow and landed a jab of his own to the boy's mouth, rocking him back. The kid looked as if he'd never been punched before. "Quit it and stand still so I can hitcha!" he shouted woozily.

Exasperated, Sam swept the delinquent's feet from under him and dumped him on his rump. For all his strength, the kid rolled over on his belly and rose to his feet with all the grace of a turtle turned on his back.

"I said Chucky, not Chunky, as in the little demon-doll you're acting like," Sam said wearily.

Unsteady on his feet, the boy wobbled over to a dumpster and hoisted it up to try and throw at Sam, but he was clearly already weakening. *Bad battle judgment,* Sam thought. Just as the kid got it up, Sam rocketed over behind him and kicked him once behind the knee. The dumpster went down with a crash. From inside, Sam heard sobbing, and he lifted the lid. The kid had torn through the bottom of the bin and the rancid garbage had poured down on top of him.

Sam pulled the sobbing boy out of the muck and bound his wrists. "Enough of this crap! Where did you get the stuff?" he demanded.

"From him." The kid pointed a shaky finger down the alley. Hidden behind the dumpster until Chucky had decided to use it as a weapon, a body lay slumped. Sam tensed, gave the kid a wary look, then stalked toward the motionless figure. With solemn hesitation, he checked for a pulse. The body was already stiff.

"Poor bastard," muttered Sam. He scanned the body for any obvious cause of death, then opened the wallet lying beside the body with a gloved hand. "Cliff Buckhalter. Just the man I was looking for."

Sam photographed the ID in the wallet with his cell phone and loaded it into the criminal database app that S.H.I.E.L.D. had given him, then quickly scrolled through Buckhalter's file. "His rap sheet goes back to before you were born, kid. He's suspected of selling for a known criminal organization for months."

Chucky scratched his head and asked, "Selling what?"

Sam pointed to the inhaler half-hanging out of the kid's pocket. "Magic wishes." Four of the same black-and-white generic inhalers remained in a clear plastic bag tucked inside Buckhalter's jacket.

Sam surveyed the scrapes and bruises across the corpse's chest before probing the hole between his eyes with a pencil. "Bulletproof from the neck down. Bet he didn't even know it. Keeps your employees safe but acts as a built-in safeguard against pushers who get too… ambitious. That's some cold guano."

"Wow!"

Sam noticed a new nasal tone in the young voice. A raccoon mask was beginning to form around the kid's eyes and his nose was swelling. Sam leaned in and checked his nose. "It's broken all right. Sorry, kid. Looks like he gave you the same formula. You're strong, but not invincible. You're lucky you didn't start some mess with a veteran enhanced. He or she'd have torn your head off."

Sirens started to wail in the distance, and Sam saw panic

blossom in the kid's expression. He was likely facing legal consequences for the first time and looked like he was gearing up to fight at the prospect. Sam put a warning hand on his shoulder and shook his head. "Don't. It's for your own good."

"But I didn't do anything!"

Sam looked at the corpse. "The police will want to talk to you."

Cops started filing into the alleyway. Sam identified himself and gave his statement.

"But I didn't shoot Buck Wild!" the boy pleaded to Sam.

Sam and the two policemen exchanged knowing glances. "Yet you know his street name."

The kid's shoulders sank. The officer read him his rights and guided his head into the back of the police car.

"Watch him, guys," Sam called after them. "You might want to use the heavy cuffs. He's pretty strong, but his powers are starting to wear off. Good luck, kid."

Sam left the alley. He had bigger fish to fry.

CALLUSED KNUCKLES met leather again and again with extreme prejudice. The heavy bag didn't punch back. Sam found himself wishing it would.

"Why do we waste our time, Luke? Why?" Sam's punches intensified. "We'll never beat the Power Broker. Not as long as he has the Corporation behind him. He'll keep pumping out super-powered actors who play with powers like they just found a bunch of magic lamps. Remember that super-strong tweaker we took down a few months ago? He got his hands on this boost drug and it warped his mind. He went from robbing little old ladies with fake guns to killing people for pennies and laughing about it."

Luke Cage leaned against the door frame and folded his arms across his sinewy chest. "Open and shut. I agree." Luke wore a used Earth, Wind & Fire T-shirt riddled with bullet holes. "We had him dead to rights. Read him his rights. Got a confession. The government made a great case and the judge ruled and sentenced him. Did they turn it over on appeal?"

"That's the thing," Sam explained. "The appellate court upheld the ruling and he was remanded to the federal prison system."

"So, what happened?"

"Nothing!" Sam punctuated the answer with a haymaker of an uppercut. "He just disappeared. I can't find him in the military penal register anywhere. Even Stark's tech can't locate him."

Luke nodded. "Like he just dropped off the edge of the Earth. Has anyone looked at off-world activity?"

"Nah, man. S.H.I.E.L.D. and S.W.O.R.D. watch that traffic like a hawk," Sam panted, still slugging the heavy bag.

Luke smirked. "You mean like a Falcon?"

Sam finally stopped banging away at the bag. "So you got jokes now, huh?"

"Look, Sam, if somebody's really hiding him, he's gotta be in some database somewhere."

"This guy has too much juice," Sam replied. "If S.H.I.E.L.D. can't find one of his cronies, that means we can't trust S.H.I.E.L.D." His chest heaved from the exertion and he checked his heart rate on his wearable.

"What's your pulse, Sam?"

"212," Sam gasped in a breathless flurry of syllables.

"You're pushing it. Maybe you should slow it down. Take it easy?"

"Would you have asked Steve to take it easy?" Sam's question hung in the air between them. They both knew the answer.

Sam took a knee and slung a towel around his neck.

Perspiration soaked it before he caught his breath. "You can say it. I know as well as you do that Steve wouldn't have *needed* to take it easy." He stood on wobbly legs that he forced to steadiness. "And I'm not Steve."

"You could be." Luke crossed the room, spun a folding chair around, sat, and rested his forearms along the back. "You could have the same powers as Cap, plus your wingsuit and shield."

"Look, Luke, I know you had a different experience with this, and most of the others can't or won't understand. Cap passed the shield on to me knowing I didn't have the power he had. We had a long talk about this. He knew I saw it as a weakness, but Steve explained how my lack of super-powers could be a source of strength. A man with unearned powers can easily lose perspective."

"I feel you, Sam." Luke scratched an itchy spot on his forehead. "Power corrupts, *et cetera*. Trust me, even with powers, it doesn't take long before making those decisions begins to humble you. For better or worse, you learn to live with them. How's that for perspective?"

"Let's put a pin in that." Sam picked himself up and walked toward the showers. "I'm going after the guy behind these freaks, the Power Broker."

Luke raised an eyebrow.

"Don't even try it, Luke," Sam said from the cubicle. "This guy is handing out super-powers like candy to people who don't have a clue what they're getting into—and worse, to remorseless criminal maniacs," he shouted through the vigorous spray. "He's up to something, and we have no idea what."

Luke stood outside the showers and shrugged. "To gauge our powers, our values, to see which lines we'll cross and which ones we won't. And you think you're better equipped to take these supers on with nothing more than a flying suit and a shield?"

"I'm not stupid, Luke," Sam called out from the shower. "I know I'm outclassed out there. Hell, I've spent the last several years of my life literally being Captain America's wingman."

Luke stared at him. "Sam, I'm not trying to put you down. You were never just Steve's wingman. But I don't understand—what do you want? A gun? 'Cause there again, life and death in your hands."

Sam turned off the water and left the shower. "In the fake life, I remembered doing horrible things, but that wasn't me," he said, toweling off. "I limited gunfire to mechanical monsters, armored aliens, and enemies bent on mass killing, both foreign and domestic." He returned Luke's hard glare. "And I've lost many a night's sleep over those lives." He sighed. "Maybe I'll have to use some damn formula one day. Before I do, I have to know *my* limits. I'll learn them in battle."

Luke squared up to Sam and looked him in the eye. "I'd love to help you, Sam, but I can't be away from Danielle and Jess for too long."

"Fine," said Sam. "I got some time off coming to me, Luke. But if you can point a brother in the right direction..."

Luke climbed the stairs and said over his shoulder, "You can't trust everyone in S.H.I.E.L.D., you're right. But there's someone you *can* trust who's been working to bring this man down too."

"THANKS FOR the use of the plane, Happy," Sam said as he disembarked from Tony Stark's private jet on the cliffs of Malta.

Happy Hogan's image appeared above Sam's communication console. "Sorry I couldn't wangle a Quinjet, but they're all being tracked by S.H.I.E.L.D. these days."

"Nah, this is great. It's more than I could have asked for on short notice."

"On any notice, you mean," Happy groused. "One last tip for you: Malta's a tiny island, and a car often isn't the ideal way to travel. A three-wheeled ATV is all you need."

"I'll pick one up."

"Already arranged." The hologram winked at Sam and signed off.

o———o

SAM SETTLED into his wicker chair and pulled it up to an umbrella-shaded table, enjoying his second cup of Maltese coffee and a generous wedge of baklava while watching the passers-by from the Ellaga café. He brushed flaky crumbs from his lap, looked up, and met the discerning eyes of Contessa Valentina Allegra de Fontaine.

"How the hell did you sneak up on me like that?" he demanded.

"It's my job, Sam," she said, the corners of her lips turning upward mirthlessly. "Spycraft. Don't you watch the James Bond movies?"

"I'm more of a Mission: Impossible man." Sam put down his coffee cup and looked around the restaurant.

"I'm alone." She nodded at his anxiety. "Now tell me, Sam, why are you here?" She looked around the table for something she expected but did not see.

"Because for once, I hear that our interests align," Sam told her.

"I don't understand." Honest puzzlement didn't fit her face somehow.

"The Super-Soldier Serum," Sam whispered.

She slumped down in her chair. "That's an appropriate topic of conversation."

"How so?" Sam asked. It was his turn to be puzzled.

A hand dropped heavily on Sam's shoulder from behind him. "Hello, Sam."

Sam turned to see the newcomer. "Johnny Walker. Who invited U.S. Agent to the party?"

"A girl's gotta be careful these days, gotta have someone watching her back," the contessa said, grinning. "The Agent happened to be in town."

Sam quirked an eyebrow at the spymaster. "The prototype."

As if there were no question hanging at all, Walker asked his own. "What are you implying, Sam?"

"I've seen it firsthand," Sam said. "Watched you fight. Different technique, but endurance, strength, agility, regenerative ability. Even among the enhanced friendlies and foes we've faced over the years, we've seen this phenomenon before: Steve, Isaiah, the Red Skull." Sam glowered at de Fontaine. "But since John Walker hit the scene, there's been a deluge of enhanced cronies. Henchmen for hire. Until you just said it, I focused on a chemical formula, but for Steve there was radiation. Vita rays."

The contessa pointed to Sam with a half-empty coffee cup as if raising it in a toast. "The Black Widows sip from that Holy Grail too," she added. "You know too little, and you speculate too much. You never mentioned Nuke, Demolition-Man, Vagabond, or Battlestar." She was silent then for a little too long. "The Power Broker was responsible for messing with those renegades' biochemistry, not our team. We agree that the Power Broker must be stopped. If you're to be the new Captain America, this is something you're going to have to deal with. It may not be exactly the same formula that made Steve Captain America, but rogue, unknown superhumans in the wild is bad for business."

"Come with me, you guys," Walker said. "I have something to tell you, but not here."

SAM SCANNED the street. It seemed quiet and peaceful—humble establishments and simple homes, locals minding their daily business, paying him little attention. No suspicious characters or vehicles patrolling the village.

They followed the contessa to the inn. She led Sam and Walker to a staircase, and U.S. Agent stopped at the first-floor landing. "Give me a few minutes. I want to take a look around. It's too quiet out there."

The contessa nodded, then she and Sam climbed the remaining steps to an apartment door. She entered, beckoning Sam to join her. It was a modest flat. A cheap coffee maker sat on a desk along with standard paper cups in a cardboard tray, and the contessa slid a packet of tea into the filter brewer and flicked it on. She poured a cupful for Sam and handed it to him, then another cup for herself, gulping it down, then crumpling the paper cup and stuffing it into her pocket. Walker tapped at the door and quietly announced his arrival through the paper-thin panel of wood. Sam grimaced at the sour aroma of the tea as he acknowledged him.

The contessa pulled the window shutter closed and the dim room grew even darker. She encouraged Sam to finish his tea, then activated a communication cube. "This will mask our conversation from prying eyes and ears," she said.

Sam sat up on the bed as her communication device painted a holographic picture from the past.

"Let me fill in the blanks in your Super-Soldier saga, Sam," the contessa said. The projected image changed to one of a man in a dark suit and darker glasses. "This is the Power Broker. His name is Curtiss Jackson."

Walker belched out a laugh. "Maybe we can find him in da club."

"Funny," Sam said, giving him a sidelong glance.

The contessa continued. "He did the work on the Grapplers and the Power Tools that led to their powers. The cost, as far as we can tell, was two million cash. Each."

Sam dipped his head. "So, we're talking $32 million for sixteen subjects. Whew!"

"Seems like a lot of money, but it's just proof of concept. Our intel indicates Jackson is negotiating a much larger deal with a European strongman."

"Doom?" Walker asked.

The contessa nodded. "Can either of you imagine an army of enhanced Latverian soldiers operating Victor von Doom's weapons technology?"

"Let's get back to this Curtiss Jackson." Walker said. "What do we know about his operations, his whereabouts? What are his creations' weaknesses?"

The contessa shrugged. "We don't know. He's creating these enhanced thugs seemingly at random, dotting the globe with them. Why? Why now? We need to know the motive for the act. Is he part of a political movement or is he just a power broker for hire?"

"Maybe it's all a distraction," Sam suggested.

"Okay, for what?" the contessa asked. "Is he trying to hide a delicate plot or a budding relationship?"

Walker slapped his knees, loud as a thunderclap. "*I DON'T CARE*. We need to be able to track him, neutralize their powers, or kill them."

"Wait," Sam said. Redwing—Sam's own wingman, never too far from his human companion's side—was perched on the building opposite, keeping a watchful eye, and was now talking to him, squawking through their telepathic link. But before Sam could grasp the content of the message, the door exploded into fragments, and he was knocked off his feet, slammed against the far wall. Deaf and disoriented, he staggered to his feet, squinting through the smoke and dust. He could just make out the silhouette of five men wearing generic fatigues and camo helmets. A dusty hole swirled in the wall just behind where John Walker had been standing. There was no movement from its depths.

One of the uniforms raised a handgun and declared, "U.S. National Security!"

Deafened, Sam read his lips and thought, *Doubt it.*

He flipped up the desk and threw the coffee maker at the assailants, knocking the lead agent's aim off so that his rifle blast hit the desk off-center. It knocked Sam and a shower of splintered wood backward through the open window, its panes already blown out by the initial explosion.

Sam landed on rotting refuse in the alley below, his ears still ringing from the deafening explosion. As the sounds of the street slowly bled back into perception, he realized he hadn't heard the contessa call out, even now, how many moments later? Scrambling to his feet, Sam reckoned how to save the Contessa, if she were still alive. In his mind's eye, he pictured her by the door when it exploded.

Where's Walker? Did the explosion catch… Wait, is Walker with them or us?

The bearing of the men who'd broken in suggested they were mercenaries rather than disciplined NSC agents. After years of being involved in messy wars and undeclared conflicts, Sam knew the difference as clear as night and day. He powered up his wings and the suit hauled him and his star-spangled shield aloft.

The man who'd shot at him peered through the window, probably hoping to see the corpse of the new Captain America sprawled in the gutter. Instead, the merc lost consciousness as he was hit by a set of rocket-propelled armored knuckles.

Sam flew into the apartment armed only with his fists, shield, and wings, picked up the gun lying on the floor, removed the clip, cleared the chamber, then tossed both behind him and scanned the smoke-filled room with his telemetry goggles. He picked up a shadowy image—one of the mercs was dragging the contessa out of the apartment.

Not well, but alive at least, Sam's concern switched from her welfare to her loyalties. Was she being abducted or rescued? He'd have to query that later.

The dense smoke gave him an advantage he couldn't pass up and he launched himself at the mercs, his fists, elbows, knees, and feet blurring in a glorious, concerted whirlwind of subdued violence. *Hurt, injure, but don't maim and never kill.* The mercs didn't know what hit them. As the fourth body fell to the floor, moaning, Sam heard two pairs of footsteps going down the stairs. He frantically searched the room but realized he was too late: the contessa was missing.

Sam searched the smoke- and dust-filled room and eventually found Walker unconscious on the floor with a large splinter of wood lodged in his right arm. The shoulder was dislocated at least, if not fractured. A quick splash of cold water to the face roused him.

"You with me, Walker?"

Walker shook his head to clear it. "Gotta clear the cobwebs out, but yeah, I think I'm okay." He tried to stand but the pain in his arm brought him back down to one knee.

"Take it easy, now," Sam said. "That blast really rang your bell." He helped Walker up to his feet and steered him to what was left of the bed. "I'm taking you to the hospital."

THE DOCTOR guided them both through the back entrance to a private treatment room. Walker assessed the space in wonder.

"This equipment is state of the art," he breathed.

"It's Swiss tech. CERN. Better than state of the art," Sam said, as proud as if he'd created it himself. "It's for urgent care for elite member emissaries. The Avengers are an honorary covered entity."

Sam and Walker put their shields on the nearby table. Sam still felt an itch as he disarmed himself.

"You're both stable," the doctor said in a lilting French accent. "Just a few cuts and contusions. None of the shrapnel pierced any major organs. I'll administer the standard doses of rejuvenation solution." She beckoned two scrawny-looking orderlies over.

"Wait, what is she talking about shooting me up with, Wilson?" asked Walker urgently.

"The concoction includes hyaluronic acid, platelet-rich plasma, fibrin albumin, and New Skin, which we've found does wonders aesthetically," the doctor explained. "Agent Walker will heal quickly, and we'll be able to tell what kind of modifications the U.S. government has made to the Corporation's proprietary formula. It'll be interesting to see how this reacts with his existing enhancements. We can also accelerate Sam Wilson's healing with the serum to accelerate recovery and harvesting."

"What?" Sam blurted.

"Grab their arms," she said, and the orderlies applied vice-like grips to each super hero. Sam attempted to rip his hand away, it was useless. He kicked and fought like a child throwing a tantrum as the orderly easily pressed him down onto a gurney and strapped his hands and feet before jabbing an intravenous feed into his arm.

The doctor walked over and flipped a switch on a control panel, making the room signal- and soundproof. "Hold them securely. The Power Broker will be pleased to gain another couple of test subjects."

Test subjects? Sam struggled harder to free himself.

While the doctor gloated, Walker flexed his muscles and broke the clutch of the orderly holding him. Before anyone else could move, Walker barrel rolled to the table. U.S. Agent grabbed his modified triangular shield with its adamantium-sharpened edge.

Using the cutting edge, he slashed the intravenous line established in Sam's forearm. Walker spun and took out the first orderly with a thrust of his shield, drawing blood, and then the doctor with a super-powered front kick to the face. Finally he addressed Sam's orderly, punching him so hard he embedded him in the wall's sheet rock.

Sam grabbed his own shield and used it to smash the comm system. Then he turned to Agent Walker and glared at his triangular shield. "What the hell, Walker?"

Walker grinned. "It's a sword and a shield combined. Something special I got from the government. Are you okay?"

"I… I feel fine. But what the hell did they inject me with?"

The doctor started to stir and Sam was on her in an instant, pulling her by the scruff of her neck and throwing her on the gurney. "Talk," he grated.

"What?" the doctor asked, clearly still fuzzy.

"What did you do to me?"

"We enhanced you, Captain. You're welcome."

"Undo it."

"Couldn't if I wanted to, Mr. Wilson." The doctor smiled. "You're a super-soldier now."

"SAM! SAM! I understand this is a shock, but we're gonna have to deal with it later," Walker yelled, but Sam remained unresponsive. "Sorry about this," he muttered, then slapped him.

Sam jerked out of his stupor at the impact. "What the hell,

John? You couldn't just splash me with cold water?"

"Sadly, there was no time," Walker shrugged. "We can come back to this. We can see every doctor S.H.I.E.L.D. has to offer, but for now we need to rescue the contessa." He moved toward the door, but Sam put a hand on his shoulder.

"What if she's working with them?" he asked.

"Great theory, no proof. As far as we know, she's been kidnapped," he said, moving towards Sam and meeting his challenging gaze with his own. "We need to save her."

Sam blinked first. He knew U.S. Agent was right. "Fine. Where are the doctor and the orderlies?" He scanned the room.

"They escaped while you were... incapacitated," Walker said. "Besides, we don't have jurisdiction here. Nothing's happening to them."

"Okay, we follow them. They'll lead us to the Power Broker. I'll fix you up with a sling and you can hang on to me like a bike bunny while I drive." Sam smiled for the first time since John had slapped him back to reality.

"We'll never catch up to them," argued Walker. "We—"

"I have a plan," Sam said.

A FEW minutes later, Sam was riding the all-terrain vehicle toward the east coast of the island, tapping into the vision of what seemed like every bird in a two-mile radius. Eventually he found what he was looking for: a feed showing a car speeding away from the hospital with their assailants inside. He nudged Walker in his bruised ribs and grinned in satisfaction at the groan from the back seat.

"I'm gonna find every pot hole along every cobblestone street in Malta, you sonofagun," he said.

"Fine," Walker grumbled. "Betcha it'll hurt you more than me."

By the time they reached the harbor, they were both moaning in concert.

Walker got off the ATV slowly, every move etched with misery. "Why do these people keep building cobblestone roads if they get covered in lava flows ever ten years or so?"

"Remnants of the Roman Empire," Sam observed. "They're famous for their roads and bridges. What's a Maltese worker gonna do?" He climbed off the vehicle with more agony than his reluctant partner. "They're on that ship. A lot of them."

"Probably enhanced. So, what's the play here, Sam?" Walker's question was sincere. "We gonna call in the big guns?"

"Nah, I think we can handle this. Besides, foreign soil, we want to be as covert as possible." Sam uttered the words as if reading directly from some obscure solemn oath.

"So, it's just us, then."

"I know someone who can lend us a hand." Sam rubbed his chin and made a call. "Hey, I need a favor."

"Anything for Captain America," Sarah Garza replied cheerfully. She was a S.H.I.E.L.D. computer specialist and not only one of the best hackers Sam knew but one of the nicest people too.

"Can you hack into the Power Broker's system? I understand it's probably…"

"Done," she said matter-of-factly, no pride or victory in her tone.

"Oh."

"Aaand I've been bounced out. Huh. I can get in, but the system patches in seconds."

"Can you key in a password?" Sam asked.

"What are you up to?" Walker asked, looking confused.

"Jackson is using the cruise ship as a barracks for his enhanced soldiers," said Sam. "He's got everything he needs there—quarters, a training gym, plenty of food and supplies."

"What about all the passengers?" Walker asked.

"There's a log," Sarah chimed in. "Less than a hundred civilians out of a crew complement of eight hundred enhanced men and women with battle training."

"I take the two on the left, you take the seven hundred and ninety eight on the right?" Walker asked. "We can't beat them head on, Sam."

"Yeah, but the Power Broker is who he is because he doesn't take chances," Sam replied. "I'll bet you a dime to a dollar he's secured those quarters in case some of his enhanced go berserk."

Walker followed the logic. "So the trick is, how do we get them all to go to their rooms at the same time?"

Sam shrugged. "Same way you handle bratty kids. They get grumpy, they fight, and you send them all to bed with no supper."

Walker threw his hands up and marched in a tight circle. "So, we wait for them *all* to throw a tantrum at the same time?"

Sam smiled. "Ever play spitball?"

THE CREW ate together in the mess hall while the officers took their meals in their own dining room nearby. It would have been better if they were all in the same room, Sam thought from his perch in an air-conditioning duct, but this would be a start.

"There they go, dirty jokes and all," he said before aiming the straw and blowing the first spitball at the neck of the biggest brute in the group.

The brute slapped at his neck and said, "Damn mosquitoes." Then he peeled his hand away from his neck to see the small wad of toilet paper. He scanned the crowd of shipmates to identify the joker, but everyone looked innocent, which royally pissed him off.

Sam tossed a straw next to the next biggest guy in the room, but this one looked meaner. The victim of the spitball assault picked up the straw next to his dinner neighbor and said, "Oh, you think this is funny?"

In lieu of an answer, the big guy slugged him.

"What's the matter with you?" the victim demanded before balling up his fist and answering his own question. The big guy saw it coming but wasn't fast enough to stop it. Before they knew it, the entire mess was engaged in a full-fledged free-for-all.

UP IN the control room, the confusion from the mess hall was noticed onscreen by one of the ship's officers.

"There's a commotion in the mess hall, Mr. Jackson." The lieutenant brought up the video feed. "It's total chaos down there."

"What started it, mister?" the executive officer demanded, but Curtiss Jackson stepped in.

"I don't care who started it," the Power Broker said. "With those powers run amok, they could sink the ship. Sound general quarters. I want everyone who's not a bridge officer confined to quarters. Lock them in and deploy the sedative gas pending an investigation."

"Maybe we've been pushing them too hard?" a lieutenant asked tentatively. "Overtraining them?"

The Power Broker growled. "Any of my men who can't take it are shark meat. Throw them overboard. But first, find out what started this mess."

SAM, WHO had crawled out of the ducts once the fight was well and truly under way, now watched along with Walker from a safe perch near the foghorns as an army of goliaths shuffled to their quarters while grumbling about fairness. "Okay, it looks like they're all tucked in," he said. "Walker, you're up."

BACK IN the control room, the lieutenant had locked the ship doors and was trying to deploy the sedative gas, which required more security and a password. He tried several times, then beat his fist on the console before turning to Jackson.

"We're locked out, sir," he said. "Someone changed the username and password, and I can't deploy the sedative."

"This computer is not that sophisticated, sailor," the Power Broker hissed. "Use the *forgot password* solution."

The computer responded to the lieutenant's command with a request:

Email address for this password?

The Power Broker entered his email address.

That email does not match this account.

Jackson ordered the lieutenant to click on the *new email* button and enter his own credentials. It accepted his email but then required a password reset.

Current password hint: The fastest flying animal in Malta.

Curtiss Jackson gave a wry smile. "What fools. Anyone over fifty has seen that movie and could guess that with their eyes closed. The password is Maltese falcon."

The computer voice announced, "Access denied."

The Power Broker thought for a moment. "I bet this is because of that fake Captain America. Okay, fine. Password is *the* Maltese falcon."

"Access denied."

"That damn Sam Wilson!" the Power Broker muttered. "I suppose he wants a more technical answer. Okay, password is peregrine falcon."

"Access denied."

The Power Broker snarled and googled the Latin name for the bird. "Try *Falco peregrinus*."

"Access denied."

The Power Broker thought again, then snapped his fingers. "Okay, try *Falco peregrinus brookei*."

"Access denied," the computer said, adding, "You have one more try before you are locked out for the next twenty-four hours."

Beads of sweat gathered on The Power Broker's forehead. "Get the code breaker in here," he snapped. "I'm tired of this bull."

The lieutenant winced. "Sir, breaking the code on the last try triggers the failsafe. No one will be able to get into the system. It will completely shut down for months, as programmed."

Curtiss Jackson howled in fury. And at just that moment, a star-spangled shield knocked him to the ground.

Moving at breakneck speed, Sam had divebombed through the control room's window, his titanium-reinforced wings blunting the impact as he smashed through and rolled on the floor, then launched his shield at the Power Broker. The next man fell like a bowling pin, as did the next, and the next, as Captain America threw his shield with his trademark precision. Meanwhile, Walker kicked through a door and got to slam one sailor into the ceiling, but mostly the job was already done.

"How'd you know he wouldn't get the code and let everyone back out?" Walker asked. "I like a good fight, but eight hundred super-strong guys against the two of us isn't much of a battle."

Sam shrugged. "The Power Broker's in his late fifties, I'd guess. He'd have to be aware of the movie."

"*The Maltese Falcon*? Even I know about that," Walker said. "So, how'd you fool him?"

"The password hint. The fastest flying animal in Malta."

"The Maltese falcon?"

Sam grinned. "Nope. Captain America."

The network came up, giving Sam the keys to the kingdom, and he deployed the sedative gas to the subjects confined to quarters.

"Great," Walker said. "Now let's find the contessa."

DESPITE BEING indignant, ungrateful, and vengeful, the contessa was more or less fine. Sam reasoned that either she was a very good actress or had indeed been kidnapped.

"So, you're still with S.H.I.E.L.D.?" he asked.

The contessa smiled. "Do you not trust me, Sam Wilson?"

"I don't trust anyone who answers a question with another question."

"Yes, I'm with S.H.I.E.L.D.," she said, and as if to prove her point a hundred agents chose that very moment to descend on the ship and take the eight hundred enhanced into custody. "We can't just put them anywhere. They'll either break out or someone will break them out, unless we take them to the S.H.I.E.L.D. facility in the Neutral Zone."

"Now you sound like a S.H.I.E.L.D. agent. No trials, no due process, just incarceration?" Sam asked. "For how long?"

She rolled her eyes. "Until they're no longer a threat."

Sam asked, "And who's to decide when that is?"

Sam and Walker looked at each other, then at the contessa, who gave an embarrassed smile. "You," they said in unison.

"Something like that," she said. "Look, boys, I'm not as capricious as I seem. We're already looking for some way to reverse the process and return them to polite society. Until then, they're guests of the U.S. government, just not on U.S. soil." She leaned in and whispered, "That would be illegal."

"Speaking of illegal," Sam said, "that doctor dosed me with the Super-Soldier Serum."

The contessa tossed her hand in the air in a dismissive gesture. "Oh, come on, Sam. It's not as bad as all that. Besides, you got what you always wanted."

Sam squinted at her. "What do you mean?"

"You've struggled with this decision for years," she said. " 'I want to be like Cap but I don't want to take an experimental drug to do it.' I get it. You don't want to be one of Miss Evers' Boys. Well, do you feel any different."

Sam shrugged. "I'm confused."

The contessa gave him a frank look. "According to what we've learned from hacking the Corporation's systems, this 'boost' has instant effects. If you were super in any way now, you'd know." She smiled. "Relax. If there's any of it in your system, it'll be completely gone in a few weeks and you'll suffer no effects, ill or otherwise."

"So I'm not a super-soldier."

"I guess you're just a regular ol' Captain America." Walker said.

"That's fine with me." Sam smirked. His mission wasn't over yet—a super hero's never is. S.H.I.E.L.D. still had potential breaches, there were still remnants of boost on the street, and danger still lurked around every corner. But he'd caught the Power Broker and taken eight hundred enhanced super-soldiers off the streets.

Sometimes you needed to take the win.

UNIFORM

JESSE J. HOLLAND

IT ONLY took Sam Wilson one bite to fall deeply, madly in love.

The warm flaky crust, the tart yet sweet apples, the faint aftertaste of cinnamon sugar. Closing his eyes and moaning to himself as he reached for a second bite, Captain America had no choice but to admit, dammit, yes, this was the best apple pie he'd ever tasted.

"Damn, Johnny, you were right." Sam moaned with pleasure as he slumped back onto the red vinyl diner bench while scooping more pie into his mouth. Brushing flakes of pie crust off the red hoodie he wore over his uniform, Sam shifted around in his seat and reached for more pie, his elbows pushing his famous red, white and blue shield—that signified his status as the nation's new Captain America—further down the seat.

Sam sighed as he scooped the last of the pie into his mouth, using the back of his hand to wipe the light-colored crumbs off his dark black goatee and chocolate skin. He grinned across the diner table at the muscular blond man smirking at him.

"Yeah, yeah, it's a cliche that Captain America loves apple pie. You did too, I bet, and I know Steve Rogers has a wicked sweet tooth. We just had some strudel from a Queens bakery before I headed down here," Sam admitted. "I know this can't be the reason you called me all the way down to Georgia, but it was worth leaving New York and coming down South just for this pie."

John Walker smirked as he carved off big chunks of the pie on his plate and shoveled them into his mouth, the late afternoon Georgia sun glinting off of his chiseled jaw and blond buzzcut. A former wielder of Captain America's shield himself for a brief period, Walker still had muscles on top of muscles because of a strength augmentation procedure that made him one of the strongest Captain Americas in history. But after a rocky start, which included the murder of his parents in Custer's Grove, Georgia, by some of Captain America's enemies, Walker abandoned the public persona of Captain America and found his true role as the black-clad U.S. Agent, a shadowy government-sponsored troubleshooter.

But Custer's Grove still remembered their favorite son as a hero, and for a while *the* American hero, and that meant the fawning blonde waitress getting him and his guest only the freshest apple pie from the town diner's oven.

"You're right, Wilson." Walker smiled at the waitress and the curious onlookers watching him and Wilson. But that smile turned into a frown as he watched the retreating waitress get verbally accosted by three coffee-drinking farmers at the counter, whispering angrily at her and gesturing toward Sam. The young waitress just harrumphed at the men, shot a dazzling smile at the two muscular men, then vanished through a pair of double doors into the kitchen.

"I wouldn't bring you home without giving you a taste of true Southern hospitality," Walker continued, one eye on the men as they kept arguing in a low tone with each other. "I owe you for that dustup around you getting Rogers' shield from me a couple of years back, and this pie is a close second only to my mom's. But unfortunately, this delicious pie isn't why I called you down here."

Walker reached into a leather satchel sitting next to him and fished out a letter.

"There's an alternative energy facility right outside the city limits where an old high school friend of mine, Rosalie, works. She says they've made some kind of breakthrough, and for some reason they need you to help them with something.

"Now, normally I wouldn't bother you with this." Walker shrugged. "But Rosalie and I were pretty close before she grew up and got married, and she says I can't help with this, only you. She said she needs the current Captain America, not the previous one. And I wasn't looking forward to throwing myself into a scientific mystery. I ain't that kinda guy, you know?"

Sam let the last of his pie roll around his tongue before swallowing it. "Do you trust her, Johnny?"

Walker smiled. "You're down here eating my pie, ain't you?"

"Yeah, I am." Sam sighed in contentment, reaching across the table toward Walker's plate to scoop up more pie.

But before he could take another bite, one of the farmers, this one bald, skin reddened from the sun, and a green mesh baseball cap perched precariously on his head, slammed his coffee cup down on the counter, shocking the diner's few patrons. This one seemed to be the trio's leader, and Sam had noticed him watching and muttering to himself from the time he'd walked into the diner. Apparently, he had finally worked up the courage to come over, or at least had finally been egged on by his friends, Sam thought to himself.

"You ain't *my* Captain America, boy. You hear me?" the farmer drawled as he neared, his friends nodding their heads behind him like puppets in a theater and puffing out their chests.

Walking over to Sam, the farmer hiked up his jeans, looked back at his friends for courage, and spit a huge glob on the floor next to his feet before sticking his finger in Sam's face.

Sam just stared at them, but Walker's face was turning redder and redder as the man ranted on and on.

"I fought in Vietnam, dammit, and my son died in Afghanistan. I'll be damned if the country we fought for will ever be represented by a damn woke n— umm... Yankee... like you!" the farmer spit out venomously, glaring in Sam's face.

"I think you need to move on, Earl," Walker rumbled ominously. "This here man's my guest, and I ain't in the mood to take too much more of this from you and your cronies here."

"Yew were classmates with Junior, Johnny," the farmer whined. "I saw you on the television fighting this here fake and trying to take the shield away from him. Now you're standing up for him?"

Walker started to rise, but Sam waved him back down.

"These... men have a right to their feelings and to be able to speak their feelings out loud, Johnny." Sam's calm voice belied the anger in his eyes. "That's what this country is all about." Sam glanced down at the floor and then back up toward the farmer's eyes. "But I'd be careful about everything else, though, Earl, is it? Most Americans get... twitchy when someone tries to get into their face and dribble. You probably didn't like it when you came back from the 'Nam, did you?"

"Nosiree, I know I didn't," piped up one of Earl's cronies. "I got off the bus in Atlanta, and they were trying to make me ashamed of my army uniform. Dammit, we bled for the right to wear them. Weren't no hippies gonna make me put them away. I wore my jacket every day, just to piss 'em off."

"Yeah, I bet you did." Sam smiled. "You see, gentlemen, I earned the right to wield this shield in Asgard, in Latveria, on Krakoa, in the Negative Zone, just like you earned the right to wear your uniform in Vietnam. My commanding officer, my partner, my hero, Steve Rogers, said I was worthy, and there isn't anyone in the world who can tell me that I'm not."

The friend nodded and put his hand on the still-fuming Earl. "Come on, Earl, let's go," he urged, and slowly led Earl and their friend out of the door. Looking back into the diner, the friend nodded his head to Sam before vanishing into the heat.

Sam sighed and flopped back on the vinyl bench. Walker glared as he looked around the diner as if he was daring someone else to speak. No one met his accusing eyes, suddenly fascinated by their plates.

"I don't know how you put up with that, Sam," Walker said, still seething as he settled back down into his bench.

"Some days better than others." Sam leaned his head back, eyes tightly shut as he tried to calm himself. "Some days better than others."

Sam took a deep breath and let it out slowly, letting his pent-up rage dissipate with a hiss. He scooped up the last of John's pie and chewed it slowly while he got himself under control. He'd always been able to hold his feelings deep, keeping his hurts internalized while his face stayed inscrutable and unreadable, even more so under his different masks.

It was harder now, as was everything else now that he was Captain America.

"You know, Johnny, I almost wore my Falcon wings down here instead of the uniform," Sam admitted angrily. "There are days I don't want to fight with people anymore about being Captain America. I could just hang up the uniform, no expectations, no pressure, no wondering if I'm doing the right thing for everyone."

Sam scraped his spoon around the plate in front of him, scooping up stray bits of apple and flaky crust.

"All I've done for them, you'd think at the very least they'd respect the colors, if nothing else. You don't like the skin of the man inside, okay, so what? You'd think they'd respect the Captain America uniform when they saw a man wearing it walking down the street. Instead, I get bewilderment, betrayal, and outright hatred from some of the same people who are fighting or have fought the same battles."

Sam's spoon clattered down, and he sat back on the bench tiredly.

"Is what I'm fighting for even worth it? Why am I a symbol for people who don't even like me?" Sam sighed.

Walker had finally calmed down and looked over at Sam with a smirk.

"Maybe they'd accept you as Captain America if they could recognize the darn uniform," he laughed. "You don't exactly look like the Captain America they know, you know, and I ain't talking about those fancy red wings. It's similar but not exact. Did you run some focus groups, Sammy? Got a little red, black, and green alternate ready in your bag there?"

Sam smirked back at him. "Nah, I'm saving that one for Kwanzaa. Who are you talking about, anyway? Maybe I didn't want to be a butt-kissing Steve Rogers wannabe like you, Johnny."

"Hey, keep in mind they didn't want anyone to know immediately that I wasn't Steve Rogers under that uniform," Johnny smirked. "I don't think *anyone* thinks you're Steve Rogers."

The two men laughed until their table was once again silent.

"Why didn't you design yourself something different, Johnny?" Sam sipped on his coffee. "I know you and Steve weren't on the best of terms when you were Captain America."

Walker looked down and shoved his last piece of pie around the plate. Frowning, he finally scooped it into his mouth and chewed slowly, thinking through his answer.

"I was so excited to be chosen as Captain America, I didn't think about it all," he shrugged.

Looking off into the distance, Walker's eyes looked sad as he recalled his past. "I was a snot-nosed punk, a D-class vigilante, trying to make my name as Super-Patriot. All muscles, no heart. Almost got my butt kicked by Rogers a couple times because of my smart mouth." Walker laughed. "But when the Commission handed me that uniform and shield, it felt like getting the Medal of Honor, the Congressional Gold Medal, the Grammy, the Oscar, and the SEC championship, all in one."

Walker shook his head. "And then to ask the U.S. government to change the red, white and blue, just because it was gaudy and old-fashioned, and the mask itched? No, dude, I was happy just to have it back then." He then frowned. "Course, if I'd known then what I know now, I'd have chucked the shield back at them and stuck with being just Super-Patriot."

"Even knowing how many people are alive now because of your Captain America and U.S. Agent?" Sam asked quietly.

Walker stirred his coffee with a spoon and looked out the window with cloudy eyes at a tractor being driven across a nearby field. "Even then, Sam."

Sam grew quiet. "I don't know if I've ever told you how sorry I am about your parents, Johnny."

Walker blinked his eyes clear and then smiled weakly at Sam. "Thanks, man." He leaned forward, a smirk on his face. "Did Steve take it well when you showed him your new gear? His best friend was going to carry his shield but not wear the exact same uniform. You made some changes to it. That couldn't have gone over well."

Sam smiled as he leaned back against the vinyl bench. "You know better, Johnny. That man doesn't have a spiteful bone in his body. He didn't care." Sam sipped on his own coffee. "Steve's words were, quote, 'It's the man, not the clothing.'"

"And a shield," Walker quipped.

"And a shield," Sam repeated with a snort. "Anyway, as much as Steve loves that uniform, it wasn't his design. The U.S. government gave him that uniform back during World War Two and told him to wear it. It must have been an insult to Steve's artist soul that he couldn't design his own get-up."

Sam looked down at his red, white, and blue uniform, and grinned at Walker. "Even the U.S. Agent uniform you're wearing is based on a design created by someone else, back when Steve was using it and going only by the Captain. This uniform here, it's gotten the seal approval from Steve Rogers, who thinks this is what *my* Captain America should look like."

Sam faux-brushed some lint from his sleeve. "Of course, I had some major design input as well because Steve's never flown into hundred-mile-per-hour winds before. But no, I didn't want to be Steve, and Steve didn't want me to be Steve either. It was time for Captain America to join the modern era and look like it as well."

Walker pulled out his wallet and started counting bills. "Well, don't tell anyone," he leaned over and whispered toward Sam. "I kinda like it."

Sam punched Walker in the arm as the two men stood up. "You would, wouldn't you? You old softy, you."

"Hilarious, Captain Falcon," Walker said with a grin as the two men left the diner.

SAM SPREAD his red wings and soared above the highway as a motorcycle-riding Walker cruised down picturesque highways and kudzu-lined roads to the sprawling engineering campus, and its glass-paneled, multistoried buildings.

As he kept pace with Walker's souped-up motorcycle, Wilson thought about all the times he'd been in the same formation with the original Captain America, the time-lost World War Two Super-Soldier, Steve Rogers. For years, in his costumed identity as the Falcon, he'd backed up the Star Spangled super soldier through many of his adventures on Earth and throughout the universe as both a crimefighting duo and a member of humanity's premier super hero team, the Avengers.

For many people, the words Captain America fit with the words "and the Falcon," Sam thought. Few people outside of Sam's native Harlem or the Avengers Mansion gave him a second thought as a solo hero, back then his sole contribution to the super hero world was the same as the mutant Angel or the Spider-Man criminal Vulture: he was a man who could fly.

In a world where billionaires created flying computerized armor and Norse gods walked the Earth, a flying man didn't turn many heads.

But once Steve Rogers decided to retire his red, white, and blue uniform, and named his longtime partner the next Captain America, things changed, Sam thought, shifting the famous indestructible red, white, and blue shield between his shoulder blades where it rested during flight. Everyone saw him and knew him now, and a lot of these people had very strong opinions about him and his new role.

Sam rocketed down to Walker's side at the gate, and watched as the impatient Walker, clad in his U.S. Agent gear, negotiated their way through the heavy security at the front gate. One of the guards, a bushy mustachioed redhead, scowled at Sam as he scratched his rotund belly.

Spitting down at the ground, the guard muttered under his

breath: "Not my Captain America."

Sam sighed. But before he could move, a furious Walker stalked up the quickly cowed security guard and lifted him into the air, hand around his neck.

"What'd you say?" the muscular Walker growled. "Say it again, Fred… I dare you!"

The guard whimpered as Sam put his hand on Walker's shoulder.

"Johnny. Let it go," he counseled.

Walker's rage was palpable. "Idiots like this, Wilson, they think they can get away with casual racism, like we don't hear the n-word behind the 'Not my Captain America.' And this doesn't bother you?" he demanded.

"I've been a public super hero for years, Johnny," Sam said patiently. "If I react every time a white person uses a profanity or a Black person calls me an Uncle Tom, I'd spend the rest of my life doing nothing else. They have the right to their feelings. I have the right to ignore them, instead of beating them into a pulp and disgracing the shield. Let it go, man."

With a snort, Walker lowered the guard to the ground and stalked into the compound. Sam looked at the hatred in the eyes of the flushed man on the ground and shook his head before taking off after Walker.

A quick glide, and he and Walker were being escorted by a harried-looking female guide into the largest building and into a service elevator, which dropped them down several stories nauseatingly fast. The guide looked down at her electronic reader, while Walker fiddled with his gauntlets. Sam looked curiously at them, wondering if they were the same StarkTech energy gauntlets Walker used to wear.

The elevator bumped to a stop, and a statuesque, raven-haired Black woman in high heels and a white lab coat strode over to

Walker and wrapped him up in a strong hug. Sam quirked his eyebrow at Walker, who blushed slightly.

"What's the problem, Wilson?" Walker challenged as the woman grinned at his beet-red face.

Sam raised his hands. "I didn't say a thing, man." Sam gallantly kissed the woman's tiny hands. "Captain America, ma'am."

"The *new* Captain America," the woman corrected, wrapping an arm around Walker's waist and grinning. "Johnny here will always be Captain America 'round these parts, no matter what uniform he's wearing these days. I'm Dr. Rosalie LaFontaine, lead scientist here at Energy Ascendent."

Sam had never seen the hard-bitten Walker so flustered or so red. "You're embarrassing me, Rosie," he whispered into her ear while smiling sheepishly to Wilson. "Stop it."

"But you're so easy to tease," she laughed. "But I guess we should get down to business. This way, gentlemen."

Sam frowned. "If you know U.S. Agent, why'd you call me? He's stronger and knows this area well."

Rosalie looked flustered for the first time. "Honestly, I was told to ask you to come down, Captain, and no, I can't tell you why. All I can say is some powerful people up in Washington wanted you here, and gave me orders to ask for you specifically. I know Johnny, and I knew Johnny knew you. And so, here we are."

She started walking into a large control room, a futuristic space dominated by a semicircular console of computer monitors and control panels. Technicians and scientists were scurrying about, monitoring high-resolution screens flashing with data and advanced software applications.

As Rosalie walked them through the room, the scientists watched the two super heroes from the corners of their eyes.

"As I'm sure U.S. Agent told you," Rosalie began, subtly reminding them of their surroundings by using Walker's super hero name, "our job here is to find new energy and applications for that energy… Think a southern-fried Project Pegasus, Captain."

Rosalie walked them out of the control room onto a balcony, which overlooked several testing bays, each designed for different types of energy equipment. Sam looked down into the bay, seeing heavy-duty workbenches, specialized testing apparatuses, and a vast array of sensors and instruments.

"We thought we had something new a couple of weeks ago, when we fired up a new Quantum Magnifier, which was supposed to draw energy quarks from the Negative Zone and combine them with free-floating radical quarks on this side." Rosalie shook her head, and waved at two technicians waiting for her signal in one of the bays. "Instead, we got this."

Inside the bay, one of the men flipped a switch on the wall. A meticulously calibrated series of lasers lining the bay all began firing at a precise angle and wavelength, converging on a single focal point within the central core of a generator in the middle of the room. Encased in gleaming chrome and pulsating with an otherworldly hum, the generator appeared as though it had been plucked from the pages of a science fiction novel. The air around the generator shimmered as the lasers met, creating a dazzling display of colors that seemed to dance with the promise of the unknown.

Sam could tell that the generator's energy levels had surged to almost critical levels, as a low, ominous hum resonated through the chamber, drowning out all other sounds. The temperature dropped, and the very walls of the lab seemed to vibrate with the immense power being harnessed. The next second, the laboratory was bathed in an ethereal, azure light. The light intensified until it formed a swirling vortex, resembling a mesmerizing, translucent whirlpool suspended in the center of the room. It was as if a tear in the very fabric of reality had been opened before their eyes.

Walker shielded his eyes with one of his hands. "Woah."

Sam snorted, his visor automatically adjusting to keep his vision clear. "Woah, indeed. What's on the other side of the whirlpool?"

Rosalie, who had slipped on a pair of safety goggles, hesitated slightly before she looked over at Wilson. "That's why you're here, Captain. To find out."

She waved down the technicians, and slowly the vortex shimmered and disappeared as they powered down the generator and the lasers. Sam looked over at Walker, who was blinking his eyes rapidly, trying to adjust to the new darker conditions. Sam's visor took care of all that for him.

"Come with me." Rosalie gestured for them to follow her, leading them down some winding hallways to her luxurious office. Photos of herself and what looked like a bespectacled college professor were scattered around the office, along with photos of what looked like a high school running back. She pointed them toward a small seating area, and while Sam sat in a comfortable high-backed chair, Rosalie curled her legs up under her on a couch next to Walker and scooted herself uncomfortably close, if the reddening of Walker's face was any indication.

Oblivious to Walker's discomfort, Rosalie got straight to the point. "You asked why you're here, Captain. You're here because the government asked me to ask you to be here. We get Defense Department funding, so I keep the Pentagon up to date on our successes. For some reason, they weren't surprised when I told them about the timerip—" she looked askance at the two of them "—that's what we're calling it."

Sam shrugged. "You found it; you name it."

A small smile quirked at the edges of Rosalie's lips. "Anyway, our Pentagon contact insisted that one of his higher-ups needed a super hero, specifically Captain America, to be the first one through the timerip." She trailed one of her finely manicured nails down Walker's muscular arms. "I first told them I wanted to consult with some of their civilian scientists like Reed Richards or Henry Pym, but they were insistent that I not call them and that they needed a different, more powerful touch on this mystery. I told them I already knew a super hero, and that he was a former Captain America to boot. But they said while I could have our U.S. Agent contact you and get you down here, I was not to let anyone go through that portal except Sam Wilson, under the threat of having our government funding pulled and the facilities taken over by government troops."

She sighed, raising her hands in front of her. "And here we are, Captain America."

Walker picked up the story from there. "I called my contacts back in Washington and found that this was coming from way, way up the ladder, above the Commission, above the Pentagon, maybe even from the White House itself. Someone with real juice wants you to go in that time portal, Wilson, and to be honest, none of us know why."

Walker scratched his chin. "I know Rosalie, and she's not going to put you in danger. And you know I'll hang out to help if you need it. But I'd want to know more if I was in your place, Sam."

Sam sat and thought it through for a minute. "I'm no scientist, or even an explorer. Why would they insist that I be here? There's got to be someone who knows something," he mumbled to himself. Speaking louder, he looked at Walker. "Let me take a wild swing here," he said, flipping out his Avengers communicator, a small ID card that served as the super-team's main form of communication. Pushing a few buttons, the Avengers logo emblazoned on the card vanished only to be replaced by the face of Steve Rogers, the original Captain America.

Sam, like always, was awed by the wisdom he could see in Rogers' blue eyes and sympathetic about the pain that his wisdom cost. Rogers was one of the few men or women left alive who had fought in America's last "good" war, as some idiotic newscasters called it—as if the deaths of millions could ever be called good, as a usually serious Rogers was wont to philosophize when people tried to aggrandize his work during the war.

Since giving up the shield, Rogers had moved up in the American defense hierarchy, coordinating with the former S.H.I.E.L.D., the Pentagon, and the White House on America's super hero forces and threats to the United States and to Earth. Steve was serious before, but the bump up in rank had made Sam's former friend's emotional output like granite. Most of the time.

But today, Sam could see a faint twinkle in Rogers' eye, as if he found something amusing about getting a call from his former partner.

"I was wondering when you'd call, Sam." Rogers smiled.

"Not that I don't ever call or anything, Steve. In fact, if I remember correctly, we just met yesterday for strudel." Wilson narrowed his eyes at the image. "But this time I think you mean something different from our normal chit-chat."

Steve sighed. "I do. And I've always told you that you have good instincts." Rogers hesitated before he spoke again, the silence stretching out for several seconds. "I've never lied to you before,

Sam, and I'm not starting now. It was I who called the Pentagon and told them to make sure you were the first one though the portal. I need you to trust me and not ask why."

Sam looked suspiciously at the former Captain America. "So, you're asking me to throw myself through an unknown portal, be sent to who knows where, do who knows what, and then hope to get home somehow, and all with just a 'I need you to trust me'?" Sam looked skeptical.

"Yep," was Steve's smiling smug answer.

Sam sighed, and looked over his shoulder at Walker and Rosalie, who were trying to hear the conversation. "It's Rogers," he whispered to them. He watched Rosalie pull a small wallet out of her purse and hand $10 to Walker, who tucked it jauntily into one of the pouches on his belt.

"You know my answer, man." Sam turned back to the communicard. "What do I need to do and when do I need to do it?"

"Good man," Rogers said, turning his head slightly to grin at something off camera. "Hold on one second, Sam."

Rogers muted the audio, and turned his head for a whispered conversation off-camera. Sam couldn't see the person Rogers was talking to, and Sam's lip-reading skills, something he picked up as a social worker, only caught a few words like "shield," "clown" and "tank."

Rogers turned back to the camera, and unmuted the audio. "One thing, though, Sam. I need to you leave your shield behind with U.S. Agent."

"You need me to leave my flight suit as well?" Sam said sarcastically as he tossed his shield over to Walker, who handled it like it was glass.

"That you need," Rogers replied, ignoring Sam's tone. "And the sooner you get going, Sam, the better."

Sam gave a follow-me gesture to Walker and Rosalie, and headed back toward the portal as he cycled his flight suit through all of the pre-flight checks. "Can you give me anything here, Steve? You know I trust you, but man, even for a super soldier, this is asking a lot," he said.

"All I can tell you is that you're doing what is needed and what is right," Steve replied. "And that's what Captain America does," the two men said in unison.

"You're corny. You know that, Steve?" Sam laughed.

"And you're loyal and steadfast, Sam," Steve said seriously. "And that's something this world desperately needs."

SAM BLINKED, the acrid stench of smoke and dirt wafting into his nose. Moaning in pain, he looked up through his cracked red lenses into a blue sky scarred with black smoke. He became aware of the fact that he was flat on his back in the dirt, stretched out across the ground.

"Hey, boy." A gruff voice shattered his tranquility. "I wouldn't lay there if I were you."

Ripping off his mask, Sam rolled over on his stomach and looked up at a battle-scarred Sherman tank rolled up right behind him. On top of the tank, looking down bemusedly at him, a bald Black soldier, face ringed with a graying beard, was waving him out of the way.

"Not the place for a… what are you dressed as? A clown?" The soldier's eyes took in Sam's red, white, and blue flight armor, his white teeth a stark contrast to his dark skin. "This road is gonna be filled with tanks and armor pretty soon. Not the place to be sleeping."

Sam sat up slowly, a dull ache pounding at his temples. Muttering to himself, "I really hate you, Steve," he spoke louder in the direction of the tank.

"I wasn't sleeping, soldier. I fell, and by the way my back feels, I think I fell pretty hard."

"You hurt? LilBae!" the soldier yelled down into the tank. "Get up here. We got a customer for ya."

The bald soldier, helmet hanging from his arm, pushed himself up through the hatch and climbed down to the ground. Right behind him, a brown satchel clutched tightly in his hands, scrambled a young light-skinned soldier, looking anxiously around like he was afraid a firefight would break out any second. Kneeling down next to Sam, the young man with large brown eyes, a small Afro, and two buckteeth, placed his rough calloused hands on either side of Sam's head and stared into his eyes.

"You feeling dizzy?" He spoke in a small soft voice, his clothes seemingly too baggy for his slight frame. "Headaches, nausea, vertigo?" The older soldier stood behind him, looking on impatiently.

Sam shook his head. "Just a slight headache and a sore back. If you give me a hand, I think I can stand up."

The soldier who acted like he was in command thrust his hand out, and between the two soldiers, they hauled Sam to his feet. LilBae carefully started brushing dirt off Sam's armor, carefully running his hands over the armored weave. "I've never seen material like this before, Sergeant Cutter."

Sergeant Cutter? Sam thought. Cutter stepped around Sam's back to look at his wing generators. "That's a funky-looking backpack you got there, son," Cutter said, lightly poking the sophisticated machinery on Sam's back. "And if you don't mind me saying, you sound more like a Harlem homeboy than a French clown."

Sam sighed, rubbing his temples in a vain attempt to quash a growing headache.

“Not a clown, Sergeant. A captain, soldier,” he said in the Avengers leader voice he’d learned by listening to Steve Rogers, the voice that made even a god like Thor hop-to when Rogers used it.

Cutter and LilBae looked at each other and immediately snapped to attention after hearing Wilson’s officer voice. “My apologies, sir,” Cutter said in a formal tone, snapping a smart salute. “We didn’t know, Captain. I take full responsibility, sir.”

Sam looked at the two men, shaking his head. “Not a problem, gentlemen. I know I look… unusual to your eyes.

“Sergeant, I need your help.” Sam looked back at the two men standing at attention. “At ease, boys. Time, date, location, Sarge.”

“Sir?” LilBae had relaxed slightly but was still shifting back and forth on the balls of his feet, his young eyes looking over at Sam carefully. “You don’t know where you are? That’s one of the signs of a concussion.”

“I told you, I’m fine, soldier,” Sam snapped. “I just need to know where and when I am, and I want you to tell me, Sergeant Cutter.”

Cutter narrowed his eyes at Sam. “Sir, it’s May 10, 1945, 1530 hours, you’re in Austria, and you just happen to be in the presence of *Eleanore*, one of the finest tanks in the finest battalion in this man’s war, the 761st. Any more you need to know, you’ll have to get from someone higher up than me. Sir.”

Sam looked up at the tank, a small grin on his face. “Mind giving me a lift back to HQ?”

“Sir, yes, sir. Mind telling me what you’re doing out here on the road?” Sarge looked Sam up and down. “And wearing that?”

Sam smiled as the three men walked back to the tank. “Sarge, you wouldn’t believe me.”

SAM, CUTTER and LilBae crawled inside and took their seats in the cramped tank. The driver, a short, stocky, goggle-sporting Black man they called Truck, looked curiously at Sam, but Cutter shrugged and the tank moved on, jerkily growling.

"I've seen some strange things in this war," Cutter shouted over the noise of the tank's engines and treads. "But I've never seen anything like you, Captain. Gonna explain how you ended up in the road back there?"

"Let's just say I'm on a special mission from headquarters, but I'm trying to lay low until I get in contact with some of the higher-ups."

Cutter and LilBae looked at each other and then across at Sam's red, white, and blue armor. "I wouldn't go snooping around wearing that, then," Cutter said. "They'll think you're shell-shocked and toss you into a rubber room."

Sam smiled as he snapped his gauntlets back together. "Yeah, a shower and some fresh clothes might help. If they're baggy enough, I can stay in action."

LilBae shook his head as he reloaded one of the tank's rifles. "I don't think so, sir. You need a couple days rest before heading out again. Concussions can sneak up on you."

Cutter patted the soldier on his back like a proud papa. "LilBae keeps us healthy, Captain.

Those Howard University boys, especially the pre-meds, are a godsend."

"And you, Sarge?"

"Birmingham born and bred, Captain." Cutter grinned again. "Iron in my blood, and a heart of steel. I've been in *Eleanore* for years, commanding three different crews. I picked up Truck there from a burnt-out unit during our last run, and I've been keeping LilBae here alive for the last year or so. Helps to have a sawbones-in-training on board. And a driver from Detroit to keep us going."

Sam snorted. "I bet," he said. "Listen, Sarge, my mission is classified, but it'd sure help me if I could hang out with y'all for a bit until I get my bearings."

Sarge and LilBae shared a look. Truck never turned his head, but Sam could see his grin anyway.

"Tell you what, Captain," Cutter said thoughtfully. "We'll get you to camp and take it from there, okay? I have to say, you're not sharing much information with us, and we've got a lot on the line to just be trusting anyone right now."

Sam started to protest but Cutter raised his hand to stop him. "I'm not saying we won't help you, I'm just saying I gotta think about it… unless you want to tell me what a Black man with—what is that? A New York accent?—is really doing laying in a road in a funny suit in Austria."

"No, to be honest, you'd only think I was crazy," Sam sighed. "A ride is more than I should be able to expect, I guess."

LilBae grinned. "Sarge'll eventually get it out of you, Captain. Everyone tells him everything."

"I got one of those trusting faces." Sarge returned the grin.

Sam laughed along with the men, their camaraderie reminding him of times he and the other Avengers just sat around and played cards in the tower, and the joy he felt catching Clint Barton futilely trying to palm cards outside of Natasha's keen eyes, or when he had to explain to his reluctant partner Steve Rogers about the cardinal sin of reneging in an impromptu spades tournament between himself, Luke Cage, and Monica Rambeau. These men were true friends, Sam thought, and probably trustworthy. But his mission required him to make it in and out of 1945 with as little notice as possible. Telling them he was a time-traveling

Captain America on an unknown mission from an older version of their Captain America trying not to alter American history wouldn't exactly endear him to them.

Better, Sam thought, to keep it to himself, find whatever Steve wanted him to do, and head back home.

TRUCK RUMBLED the tank up a small embankment and pushed *Eleanore* to a stop. Peering out a viewport, Sam could see other tank crews disembarking from their vehicles to refuel both the tanks and themselves.

In a clearing as far as his eyes could see, there were nothing but dirty tanks with their soot-stained turrets, dirty army jeeps and tanker trucks, tents of various sizes, and a mass of Black male humanity. Some were doing quick repair or cleaning jobs or refueling tanks from tanker trucks, others were laughing and jawing with each other while sitting on wooden boxes at the mouths of tents.

One group of men were cheering on two boxers circling each other and throwing out careful jabs, while Sam could see another group lining up for chow as cooks stirred pots with delicious-smelling concoctions. As he climbed out of the tank, his higher vantage point brought sight of what looked like an impromptu church service, complete with an all-male choir who were backing up a hellfire sermon from a rotund preacher.

Weary yet full of joy from the camaraderie of the men, Sam climbed down from the oil-drenched tank and took in the scene of Black warriors seemingly content in their lot, fighting for freedom and for their own dignity.

These men, Sam knew, were true heroes who were willing to sacrifice everything despite the hatred their own countrymen carried for them.

There were some familiar sights, even for a time-traveler like himself, Sam thought.

Walking up to *Eleanore*, Sam rubbed the bold black panther insignia on the side of tank declaring it part of the "Black Panthers" unit with the motto "Come out fighting."

Sam grinned to himself, thinking T'Challa and Bobby Seale would likely approve of their name.

Sniffing deeply, Sam coughed in the smells of home-cooked food mixed in with diesel fuel and the odor of hard-working men. He could hear the scratchy sound of someone playing a fusion of jazz and swing over a loudspeaker unit near a makeshift stage someone had erected near the center of camp. Climbing down from the tank, he pulled closer around him the spare uniform Cutter had found, not yet willing for anyone to see his Captain America uniform. Right behind him, Cutter, LilBae and Truck disembarked and immediately went their separate ways: Truck gesturing wildly with a mechanic who was pointing at the tank and shouting something about unnecessary damage; LilBae wandering over toward the hellfire-spitting preacher; and Cutter standing at attention and giving some kind of report to a mustachioed ranking officer. The officer, whose face was coal-black with a pair of oval reading glasses perched at the tip of his nose, glanced over at Sam and back at Cutter, and began pointedly growling orders at the sergeant before stalking off.

Cutter, with a big sigh, walked back over to Sam, who had been leaning against *Eleanore* and watching the exchange with trepidation.

"So," Cutter wiped the sweat from his balding head, "I'm supposed to keep an eye on you while they check out your claims. It might take a while, however, because we're under radio silence with the U.S. until this particular operation is over. So, for now, where you go, I go, and where I go, you go, capeesh?"

Sam raised his hands in surrender. "No problem, boss. Anyway, right now, I'm between orders."

Cutter scowled. "Well, I'm not. I've got to keep you under wraps for a while because we've got some bigwigs coming in, and a crazy-ass French clown is not what they're expecting to find."

Sam laughed. "I understand, Sergeant. Point me toward the chow and a bunk, and I promise I'll keep quiet."

The rest of the day was a blur for Sam as he wandered around the camp absorbing the camaraderie and brotherhood among the men. Sam knew intellectually that Black men fought in World War Two, and had even heard of the Black tanker units, but seeing the hundreds of men, these "Black Panthers," a glorious mass of humanity, willing to take arms up for their country in this time period brought tears to his eyes.

Tents pitched on soft grassland formed a circle around a crackling bonfire, where weary soldiers swapped stories over steaming mugs of coffee. The air was tinged with the aroma of cooking rations. Some men sat polishing their rifles while others played cards or strummed guitars, their laughter mingling with the distant rumble of artillery. Against the backdrop of towering mountains, the soldiers found solace in each other's company, their faces etched with both weariness and determination.

At the heart of the camp, a makeshift mess hall buzzed with activity as soldiers lined up for their evening rations. The clatter of mess kits and the murmur of conversation filled the air, punctuated by an occasional burst of laughter or the sound of a friendly argument.

Sam wandered around the camp, just taking it all in and watching the men he had come to know.

He found Cutter sitting at a rough-hewn table, his weary eyes scanning the faces of his comrades with a mixture of pride and concern. Even though he was in the middle of the camp, an invisible barrier seemed to be around the sergeant. Sam could see the weight of responsibility resting squarely on his shoulders, a burden Cutter carried with stoic determination.

Around the corner, Sam found LilBae shoveling spoonfuls of stew into his mouth with gusto, his youthful enthusiasm undimmed by the horrors of war. At just nineteen, his babyface, smeared with grease and grime from a day spent tinkering with the tanks, lit up with a grin as he regaled his comrades with their discovery of a clown during their last run, his eyes twinkling at Sam as he waved and gestured during his storytelling.

Sam found Truck nursing a steaming mug of coffee in silence in front of a darkened tent, his thoughts a world away from the jovial chatter around him. He looked into Truck's dark eyes, shadowed by the brim of his helmet, and could see memories of friends lost and battles fought. Despite his stolid demeanor, there was a vulnerability in his gaze, a silent plea for understanding that Sam thought was going unheard amidst the clamor of the setting sun.

Sam walked over, and as Truck looked up, he simply placed his hand on his shoulder in silence.

As the last rays of sunlight faded from the sky, casting the camp into shadow, Truck nodded, got up and disappeared into the tent, where the air was thick with the scent of sweat and canvas. His memories would hopefully fade away for at least a night, Sam thought as Truck headed toward a roaring fire and loud voices.

Wandering over, Sam saw that around the campfire were a couple of tankers, one of whom was waving a newspaper and shouting. Around them stood a small crowd listening intently, jostling and pushing for a good view.

Sam worked his way to the front of the crowd in time to see a baby-faced officer crumple up a newspaper and throw it to the ground at his feet.

"I don't care what your daddy wrote, we done served our country, shed blood even. I say we ought to wear our uniforms with pride, no matter where we are. South or North, it don't make no difference. We earned these stripes," he growled.

Sam bent over and picked up the paper, looking at the front page of the *Pittsburgh Courier*. In bold letters, the newspaper proclaimed: "Black Soldier Lynched at Hands of White Mob." On the front page was a blurry photo. Sam squinted to see in the low light and gasped as he recognized the U.S. Army uniform on the man swinging from the tree.

The arguing men looked up at Sam momentarily before turning back to their argument.

"James, I hear ya loud and clear, and ain't nobody questionin' your valor, youngster. But you gotta see the sense in keepin' your head down sometimes," a weary looking soldier, a blood-red scar running down one side of his bearded face, retorted. "I'm from Mississippi, boy, and I can tell you that wearin' that uniform in the wrong part of the South is like paintin' a target on your back. We need to be smart, live to fight another day."

James rubbed his hands across his bald head in frustration, and stalked forward.

"It's about standin' tall, George. If we shrink now, what's all our sacrificin' been for? Change don't come from keepin' quiet and makin' yourself small. We wear these uniforms, we show the world—and our own folk—that we're just as much Americans as any man who's served."

James pointed at Sam. "We've been over here fighting just as much as the white man, right? I know I have, you have, he has, and I bet he has too. Why do we hafta hide what we did and who we are? They should be proud of us!"

George shook his head sadly, as several of the listening men murmured in approval. "And what good is standin' tall if you're laid flat the next moment by a lyncher's hand? Pride won't protect us from hate. I'm all for fightin', but I ain't for senseless risks."

The wizened soldier plopped down, using a small bucket as a chair.

"My daddy told me that we've already lost his nephew down in Iuka, just for walking down the main street in his greens. Lynched him that same night. What did he win? He didn't change anything... Education, votin', protestin'—that's where we can make a mark without givin' them the satisfaction of seein' us as targets."

James kicked angrily at the ground, glaring at George. "Sometimes, you just gotta pick a side and stand firm. I choose to wear my uniform, to show I'm not afraid, to demonstrate that I'm a man of honor, same as any white soldier. It's about dignity. If we don't assert our worth, who will?"

George sighed at the younger man.

"Dignity don't mean much to a dead man, James. We're more than just soldiers. We're fathers, sons, brothers. We owe it to our families to come home, not just as heroes, but alive. The real courage is in livin' to fight another day, in a way that'll truly bring us all to the table of brotherhood."

"Maybe so, but I'd rather walk my path in the light, as perilous as it may be. Our uniform ain't just cloth; it's a testament to our service, our courage. Hidin' it away feels like denyin' a part of who we are." James kicked at the fire, sending glowing embers into the air as he stalked off, followed by some of the crowd.

Sam looked around as the rest of the men wandered away, arguing amongst themselves about their hometowns and what they could expect when they made it home. For the first time, he noticed Cutter standing across the way, his eyes intently on Sam.

Before long, it was just him and Cutter left at the fire, now both looking silently into the flames.

Eyes down, Cutter looked as if he were trying to read the future in the flames.

"More than half of them will be dead before making it home, the way this war's going," he said sadly. "And the rest, they'll walk into the flames of hell here but they'll be alone at home, and they'll die one by one in their boots. It ain't worth it."

Sam cleared his throat and stepped forward. "There's something to be said for standing your ground, even in the face of insurmountable odds, isn't there?"

"Dying for a pair of pants and a jacket with a few ribbons? I ain't a fan of dying for nothing, college boy."

Sam walked around the fire and laid his hand on Cutter's shoulder.

"Your pride ain't nothing. Your dignity ain't nothing. Your sacrifice ain't nothing. It's everything, Cutter."

"In the end, it's only colored cloth that we're wearing, Captain," Cutter insisted. "It's not worth dying for."

"Then what is, Cutter?" Sam said quietly. He looked down at his army uniform and the gleaming armor underneath it. Tugging on his color, he turned back to the dying fire.

"This uniform means something, Sarge. It has to mean something, or otherwise, what are you over here dying for?" Sam said.

Looking up at the sky, Sam was silent for a second. "We don't wear uniforms because we want to. We wear them to become part of something bigger than ourselves. An ideal, a principle, a way of life that we aspire to and defend," he continued. "I almost let other people make me forget that. Our colors are worth dying for, even just to remind ourselves and other people that we are men who stand for something, even if it costs us everything.

Cutter looked up with a snort. "Deep thoughts from a fancy-ass French clown?"

Sam rubbed the armored mesh under his uniform and smiled. "Yeah, I'm feeling a little differently about my colors as well, my friend. If y'all can wear yours with pride, no matter what, I can wear mine."

Cutter stood up and started pouring water from a coffee can onto the flames.

"Something to think about. But for now, we've gotta get some rack time. I'm hearing rumors about some bigwig visits in the a.m. Grab you a rack in a tent, and come find me in the morning."

"Gotcha, boss." Sam watched as the older man walked off into the night.

o———o

"SAM? SAM?"

Sam squinted and slowly opened his eyes. As the blurriness faded, it wasn't the warm canvas with dappled sunlight he expected but the cold metal floor of the timerip laboratory. Surrounding him were Rosalie, Walker, and to his surprise, dressed in civvies, an older Steve Rogers, with their famous shield strapped to his back.

Sam looked at him, and could see the weight in this Steve's eyes, the experiences, triumphs and sorrows the other Steve had yet to experience. But the warmth and compassion was still there in his friend's eyes, Sam thought.

"You okay?" Rogers stuck out his hand to help pull Sam upright.

"I am now." Sam hoisted himself off the ground, noticing he was still dressed in his army uniform over his flight suit.

Rosalie waved some kind of scanner up and down Sam's body, excitedly taking readings.

"How do you feel, Captain? Any side effects, pain, nausea?"

Sam eyed Rogers carefully. "No nausea, but a little bit of confusion."

Walker slapped Sam on the back, knocking the breath from him. "We got a little worried about you when you flew into the timerip, but look at you! Back a few minutes later no worse for wear. You gotta tell us, what'd you find?"

Sam started to speak, but before he could get a word out, Steve interrupted.

"I think… Sam and I need to have a debrief first, Walker, before he says anything." Gesturing upstairs, Steve put a hand on Sam's shoulder to lead him out. "Rosalie, do you mind if we use your office for a bit?"

Rosalie was busy looking at her readings, and paid little attention to the two men walking out. "As long as you bring him right back so I can get some more readings," she said, poking at her scanner. "Johnny, keep me company. I may even have some heavy things for you to lift."

Walker rolled his eyes and called out as Sam and Steve left the lab. "Wilson? The first beer's on me when you're done with Grandpa Rogers. Tell him he can come along if he sticks to only one glass of milk…"

Rogers smirked as Walker's voice trailed off as they walked up a staircase. The two men said nothing until they were in Rosalie's office with the door securely closed behind them.

Sam looked at Steve and quirked his eyebrows. "Clown?"

Steve laughed. "Okay, okay. Yes, I knew where you were going. But," he raised one finger to interrupt Sam, "remember that we're not supposed to interfere with the past or the future. That's why I couldn't tell you where you were going. Reed said that put the timeline in too much danger."

Rogers walked over and sat on the edge of Rosalie's desk. "We had to let things happen naturally."

"Naturally my butt. *You* were the one who made sure I went, Steve."

Rogers raised his hand and began to tick off points. "One, I just made sure you were where you were supposed to be. Two, I made sure that you didn't take anything that would cause suspicion.

"And three, I had insider knowledge on how it was going to end," Rogers said mysteriously.

Sam sighed, knowing Steve wanted him to ask but he wasn't ready to rise to his old friend's bait. "I'm not mad at you, Steve. In fact, this trip helped resolve some things that had been bothering me both there and here."

Steve smiled and walked over to a briefcase he had stashed in the corner. "I did keep up with a few of your friends after the war, however."

He reached in for a newspaper, and tossed it over to Sam. Looking down, Sam saw on the front page a photograph of an elderly soldier being honored as the grand marshal of a Veterans' Day parade. Looking closer, Sam smiled at Cutter's elderly face, his army uniform and ribbons still gleaming in the sun.

"Cutter," Sam whispered.

Steve looked over Sam's shoulder and down at the photo. "Believe it or not, he became a lawyer, and when he wasn't in court, he wore his uniform everywhere he went after the war. He apparently had a couple of close calls, but as you can see, he's still around and kicking.

"In fact," Steve smiled, "it was Cutter who came to me in Washington and said it had to be… in his words, the 'fancy-ass French clown' who went back in time to Austria. Seems that some of his contacts in Georgia told him about the 'timerip' and he put it all together once he saw you in the news."

Sam fingered the picture, remembering his time with the sergeant and the boys in *Eleanore*. "I'm going to have to look him up." He glanced at Steve. "They taught me as much as you did, Steve, about pride and standing up for your colors. He deserves to hear that."

"Well, good. The timeline is where it should be, you're where you should be, and all's right in the world." Steve rubbed his hands together after he and Sam gave each other a warm hug.

"Now, what's this I hear about some pie?"

Sam laughed as he led Steve back down toward the lab.

CHAOS RULES

GLORIA J. BROWNE-MARSHALL

SAM WILSON was caught between his life as a social worker and his duties as a super hero. He knew it was wrong. Across the city, visions were shared by pigeons, sparrows, wrens, and owls of humans lost in the mists of their anger. Sam saw babies in expensive strollers abandoned in Central Park as their parents slung curses and rocks, while others swam in the Jackie Onassis reservoir, fully clothed. The birds showed him road rage in lower Manhattan as drivers threw punches and rolled in the hot streets while crowds cheered. Construction workers in Brooklyn danced on steel beams jutting into the sky from a hundred-and-ten story building. Sam Wilson was Captain America now. This valiant hero was needed elsewhere but chose to be at the hospital bed of Thelma Jackson, a beloved Harlem foster mother.

Over the years, Sam Wilson had placed at least a dozen abused and neglected foster care children in her embrace and watched them blossom and grow strong. Sam was a young social worker when they first met, and Miss Jackson was a gray-haired elder even back then but powerful in spirit. Now Sam was at her bedside in Harlem Hospital, watching her eyes flutter without opening. He could do many things, but he was no doctor, and the slowing beat of the heart monitor told him that this precious woman was fading away. Sam's face, dark as his sorrow, bowed to pray when his eye caught the banner flashing across the silenced television: "Breaking News: Violent Outbursts Disrupt City".

As a native New Yorker, Sam had seen his share of violence. But it was getting worse. Sam had stopped a high-speed police chase across Staten Island, a robbery in the Bronx, and a truck driver careening into the Hudson all before flying to the hospital. His wings were packed in a case at his feet. The many other super heroes who called New York their home would keep the city safe today. Sam was busy. Sam's heart pulled him to pay respects to an unsung hero who had mothered dozens of neglected children placed in her care by Sam and other social workers in Harlem. As Sam held Miss Jackson's cooling hand, he tried to avoid the television re-broadcast of a scene outside of the United Nations building.

He had been in mid-town Manhattan when wild-eyed screaming throngs battled security swinging batons. These were far from Captain America's usual villains who were intent on taking over the world. These people fought with fists, bags, and canes as if in a trance. Suddenly, the crowd froze. A tall young woman in dark glasses passed through them, the guards opened the glass doors. Sam saw her look back at the crowd and smile. Once inside, the thrashing throng ignited again.

"What the hell?" Sam muttered to himself. "I know her."

Then a man ran into the street and was hit by a Ford Bronco. His flailing body was tossed onto open garbage bags strewn across the sidewalk. Sam flew him gently over the gnarl of cars to an emergency room. He had to ignore Central Park's wide lawn filled with people acting possessed. The woman in the glasses looked familiar but Sam didn't have time. The nurse had said this may be the last day in the life of Thelma Jackson.

SAM WILSON watched, his brow rising, while telepathy brought him more unanswered questions to the confusion he was witnessing. Redwing held fast to a cherry tree, facing the United Nations, showing Sam the dignitaries fighting with protesters. United Nations Secretary General Anders Gunther banged his gavel in the air as madness swept over the usually staid global leaders.

"They're coming from Mars," an ambassador yelled, hacking on his spittle. "And they're going to beam us all up!"

If the UN had fallen into mayhem, the entire world was in jeopardy. Seagulls showed Sam cargo ships left adrift as crew members tore at each other on deck. This strange violence had spread to Maryland, and Washington, D.C. would be next.

"Is this some kind of virus?" Sam whispered. "Who is behind it?"

Visions of mayhem pulled at Sam, bringing more unanswered questions. *Not now,* he thought. Avengers have feelings, too. Did he not get to mourn because he was a super hero? Did he not feel burnout too? Was he not allowed to be tired? Sam was exhausted, tired in the worst way.

The call from the nurse was clear. Thelma Jackson was in her last hours. The nurses had been calling him for two weeks. There was always an excuse, an act of bravery for a child or teacher. Sam had not expected Thelma's illness to unbury a longing for family. As a social worker, he felt a triumph when a child bloomed in Thelma Jackson's loving care. As she declined, the violence across the city seemed to worsen. Sam couldn't hide from the truth any longer. He had avoided facing the loss of Mother Jackson, as she was affectionately known in the neighborhood. He could not leave her now.

A nurse stepped into the room, quietly checking the fluids. She was a stern-looking pale woman with glasses, brunette hair pinned in a bun. Sam noticed her left eye twitching.

"Do you need anything?" she asked, her twitch coming faster. Sam shook his head. "As I told you on the phone, Miss Jackson was alone when she fell."

"I should have been there," Sam said, tenderly touching her swollen arm.

"That swelling is due to Miss Jackson's diabetes and heart condition." The nurse changed the I.V. drip bag.

"Do you think—" Sam asked. "Is there any chance she may recover?"

"I'm sorry." The nurse watched the fluid drip slowly. "I'm very sorry." As she stepped to the door. "I'm down the hall, if you need anything." A laugh jumped from her mouth that was covered quickly by both hands. "Don't know what's gotten into me." When she left, rubbing her twitching eye, Sam sighed deeply.

He was left with those words and the beeping monitor. There was hope even in grim times. That's what Sam's father instilled in him. Hope is what Mother Jackson represented. When he looked at her curly gray hair and her face, worn by time, Sam recalled how she had cooked meals from scratch for those foster children in a kitchen filled with love. From their first meeting, Thelma Jackson treated Sam like they had known each other for years. She taught him more about being a social worker than any social work class. He realized, as an adult, with the longing of a child that, in many ways, Miss Jackson had been a foster mother to him as well.

"I love you," he whispered. Those were words he wished he had said the day his mom died. "I will miss you."

Sam looked up through tears as the television showed.

He watched as the news anchor cut to the Financial District

where a hedge fund manager rode the iconic brass bull statue as a busload of school children recorded him on their cellphones.

"Mommy, I'm a cowboy," he screamed. "Giddy-up."

The camera abruptly cut across the bottom of the television screen where stock market numbers showed red arrows pointed down as the NASDAQ fell, while the two female financial anchors argued despite the rolling cameras

"This is not a correction in the market," one anchor shouted. "It's a catastrophe!"

"Shut up, Beth," she said. "You don't know anything about downturns."

"More than you, Jasmine." The station switched to a commercial.

Sam found himself standing up. His head began to throb. The beeping of the heart monitor was fast and getting faster. Miss Jackson sat up, startling Sam.

"Chaos."

"Mother Jackson, you… you should lay back down."

"Sam?"

"I'm here," he said.

"Cold… so cold."

Sam gently eased her under the blankets and then ran to the door, afraid to leave her even if it meant going down the hall. Sam watched the heart monitor jumping.

"Someone, please come quick!" he shouted.

Mother Jackson began to groan. Sam held her cold hand as she rocked side to side in agitated moans. Sam's head hurt as Redwing's vision sent bursts of images of fistfights and violence that weighed on him like a mountain of pain. Flocks of doves, starlings, and crows showed him the worst of human behavior until Sam wanted to run from the room. Then, Miss Jackson was still.

"Chaos?" Sam said.

The young woman in sunglasses who walked through pandemonium at the United Nations that morning was standing at the foot of Miss Jackson's hospital bed. Sam had placed Charlotte Olivia with Miss Jackson ten years ago. He was unsure who gave her the name Chaos, but Charlotte Olivia was known for trouble. It seemed to follow her. She had been in four foster homes before the placement with Miss Jackson.

Sam had seen little of her in four years. During that time, she had certainly grown up. At nineteen, she was a young lady, thin, with caramel-colored skin and shoulder length braids. But something else was different. When she looked at Sam, he could only think of the loss in his life. He could barely stand up to embrace her.

"So, Captain America, you came back," she said. Sam heard a hoarse deep-throated voice of barely controlled rage. "She kept asking for you."

Chaos brushed by Sam, took off her sunglasses and gave Sam a hard stare filled with street-worn suspicion and carried an attitude on her broad shoulders.

"I told her you had left like all the others she had helped."

Sam was surprised the little girl who had been lavished with unconditional love from Miss Jackson had become so cold. Chaos had arrived from a home where her mother, Shirleen, was too busy drinking in the clubs to bother raising a child. After being left inside a locked car in the parking lot all night while her mother was inside a cheap liquor joint getting drunk, the girl was placed in the state's care. She had been a bitter little girl and angry teenager who often ran away. Before his duties as an Avenger, Sam could spend time with Chaos, as more than a social worker, almost a big brother, protecting his little sister from the dangers of the world.

Sam studied the young woman who had climbed into the bed with Miss Jackson, her cheek nestled against the dying woman.

Suddenly, Sam saw Miss Jackson begin to wince as if she, too, felt the rising swirl of emotional pain and confusion that he had experienced the moment Chaos entered the room. He recalled when primary school teachers sent notes home complaining that Chaos caused fights at school. Chaos never had close friends or sleepovers with other children. She was a loner, except for Miss Jackson, whom she began calling "Mother" when Shirleen left without a forwarding address. No other relatives appeared to take Chaos, so Mother Jackson was granted custody.

Sam was hurt by the girl's coldness but refused to show it. Chaos was not a little girl. But she seemed to have forgotten all the birthday presents he had given her. He'd shared his love of birds with her, helping her to memorize the names and calls. But when Sam left, Chaos became distant. Now he felt she was a stranger. Miss Jackson told him that Chaos cried for days when Sam went away. Sam should have noticed that during his required site visits Chaos had slowly narrowed her life to going to school and being with Miss Jackson, rarely leaving the older woman's side.

"Where's the nurse?" Chaos demanded, finally speaking to him.

"I called for her," Sam said.

"Mommy, please don't leave me," Chaos begged.

Her voice was high-pitched like the little girl Sam remembered from years ago.

"Do something!" she said. "That nurse ought to be doing something."

"There's nothing we can do," Sam said. "She's dying."

Chaos jumped from the bed and ran out into the hallway. Then Miss Jackson groaned again, her eyes opened slightly.

"Memaw?" Sam said, softly, holding her hand close to his chest.

"She's here," Miss Jackson whispered. "I felt her."

"Chaos went to find the nurse."

"I love you, Sam."

Sam wiped a tear as another fell onto the white sheet.

"Thank you for all you've done for the children and for me."

"Please," she began. "Do something for me..."

"Do you need the nurse?"

"Take care of that girl," she said. Her voice was so soft that Sam had to place his ear against her dry lips. "She's got special gifts, Sam. But needs protection, even from herself. God bless you."

Those last words faded away with her final breath as Chaos returned, with the nurse. The beeping heart monitor now held a long note of death.

"Do something!" Chaos yelled.

Chaos pushed Sam aside and dragged the nurse to Thelma's bed.

"Do not resuscitate," the nurse said. "She gave orders for no lifesaving treatment."

"No!" Chaos screamed. "Help her."

Sam tried to hold her when Chaos fell across the bed. She was a little girl-child wailing. Her anguished cries filled the hospital room. Then a sound began as an uncomfortable pain in his head. It spread, winding around his brain, tightening its grip, squeezing visions from years past. Sam felt the vice, forcing him to reenact the visions. The nurse cried out.

"Sorry for your loss," she said. "Headache. Must go."

Sam sensed his core vibrate, felt sound ricocheting against the ceiling and walls. The nurse was holding her head, pressing shaking hands against her ears as if to keep it from exploding. She quickly turned off the heart monitor, but the sound grew louder, even after she shut off all the other machines.

"What is that?" the nurse asked. "Stop making that noise. It hurts."

Sam heard it, too. A sound coming from inside his head, muffling his mind and giving him thoughts of evil and rage and sorrow.

Chaos continued to cry. But the nurse, with a look of terror, began to hum and then to sing. She covered her mouth. But the singing became louder.

"I can't stop," she sang.

She repeated the singing of "*I can't stop*" off-key.

The nurse grabbed Sam's arm. "Make it stop," she sang. "Don't you hear it?"

"Yes," Sam groaned, holding his hands to his ears. He was trying not to fall to his knees. The sound triggered fear and sadness, with images of his parents calling him, flashes of the worst moments of his life, the loneliness inside welling up to the surface and pouring out in surges of grief. He wanted to shake the nurse and tear apart the hospital room as rage and depression twisted inside him. Only Redwing's vision of the clouds as the hawk circled above the hospital calmed him.

It was more of a vibration than a sound. He felt it in the center of his brain, triggering emotions and memories he had long forgotten. As Chaos cried, Sam realized that the vibration was coming from her. She was forcing them to feel her pain, her confusion. Emotions riding under the surface, left unresolved, were stirring within him, dancing before his eyes. Desires, hate, fears, worries, and uncertainty welled up in him.

"Mommy, come back," Chaos cried. "Don't leave me."

Speaking with a slow and soothing tone, Sam reached out to Chaos, fighting against the noise in his head.

"Chaos," Sam said. "Talk to me."

The nurse began ripping at the bun on her head until strands of hair flew like Medusa's snakes. Sam grabbed Chaos's shoulders, turned her to face him. The nurse ran from the room, knocking a tray out of the hands of a tall and hefty orderly, who tried to pick up the mess but could only stand at the doorway, as if in a trance. Sam watched him struggle, unable to enter the room.

"I can't go in there," he said. "She'll hurt me."

"How long have you had this power?" Sam asked.

With swollen eyes and whimpering with the grief of a lost child, Chaos fell back again onto the bed, crying.

"Why does everything die?" Chaos screamed.

Other nurses had joined the orderly at the door. Sam turned to Chaos.

"Go away!" Chaos screamed. Her voice pushed them back as if a wall had hit them. Her eyes were red with hate and mouth twisted with loathing.

"She left me," Chaos said, without wiping the tears or snot away.

"It was her time," Sam said, gently.

"No! Everyone leaves me. It's not fair."

Sam saw the images again, heard the shrieking of birds, saw bloody feathers, falling small bodies, lifeless. He knew it was coming from Chaos. He had to calm her. Sam gently guided Chaos into the hallway away from Mother Jackson.

"Mother Jackson was the only one who wanted me. Now, she's dead."

"She didn't want to leave you."

Then, Chaos turned on him.

"You left me!"

Chaos was snarling. Sam stepped back as her eyes narrowed and her growling voice was even deeper. Sam recognized the hate in it. Chaos was filled with hate. She pushed Sam away.

"He was right!" she screamed.

Sam knew as a social worker, he should have known what to do. But this was too close. The feelings welled up from the loss of his father, who was killed breaking up a fight, and his mother gone, too. The noise in his head and feelings of sadness were overwhelming him.

"Let's go, please."

"He promised never to leave me."

For a moment, Sam thought Chaos was referring to God. He knew Miss Jackson had been taking Chaos with her to Greater Baptist Church.

"He was right. Mortals die. But he won't."

"Who said this?" Sam asked.

He saw a hospital guard approaching and noticed the angry faces of the family gathering in the hallways, brought there by Chaos, screaming and cursing. The ringing vibration had returned.

"Who is telling you these things?" Sam shouted.

He did not mean to be so sharp with her. It was the noise in his head. Chaos backed away.

"Have you seen the world, Sam? There is only hate and death."

"I know you are hurting. But, in time, you'll see. Mother Jackson would want you to remember her and know there is still some good, too. I'll take you home," Sam offered.

Chaos laughed and backed away.

"You left me."

Sam wanted to explain. But he, too, was grieving. He wanted her to know that super heroes were not perfect. They make mistakes. Sam should have come back. He had not abandoned her. But the words stuck in his throat. Miss Jackson was also his mother figure.

"I'm sorry, Charlotte."

"My name is Chaos."

"You were at the United Nations today."

The orderly and nurses had gathered in the doorway. They swayed and held their heads as if in mental battle, as well.

"I swear," she said. "I swear all of you will know what it's like."

Chaos put on her dark glasses and ran down the hall to the stairwell. The day had begun with pandemonium and ended in heartfelt pain for Sam.

o———o

THAT NIGHT, the President of the United States called. She needed Captain America in Washington, D.C. Now. Captain America needed to just grieve as plain old Sam Wilson. He knew too many men hurting inside because they would not allow themselves to grieve the loss of a loved one.

Sam flew with a broken heart to Washington, D.C. Alone, among the clouds, he was beyond the reach of the vibration causing the confusion below him. His calls to the Avengers and to S.H.I.E.L.D. had his fellow heroes scrambling to help as many people as possible. But he felt the guilt and sorrow of anyone who had lost the dearest person in life and fear for their last connection to family. He would find a way to stop this virus of violence.

Sam's wings came at a price. It was true. He had left Chaos alone. But it was not his plan. Crash-landing on the Island of the Exiles, with Steve Rogers and other soldiers, was no exotic vacation. Their duty to help the country had come at a price. Years of absence from Miss Jackson and children like Chaos, which he regretted. But, like the other super heroes, Sam convinced himself it was for the greater good. Sam should have reached out to Steve, but his friend was recovering from a previous battle. So, Sam was in this one alone.

The world was in trouble. *How long had she possessed this power?* he asked himself. *Where did she meet this character who believes in immortality?* he thought, turning sharply to avoid the path of a private jet, the passengers staring with disbelief as he passed. Sam's deep thoughts about his failures and the deaths of loved ones made him overshoot the White House.

The streets were stacked with immobile cars as road rage crippled traffic. Sam circled the marble dome of the Capitol before heading to the White House. Below him were screaming jumbles of people, flailing fists, and tumbling bodies spewing rage. Landing at the White House, Sam felt the vibration and he described what he knew without revealing Chaos's role in the madness. He felt torn between his duty as a social worker and his duty to the country.

"There is some kind of sound," Sam said. "It draws out our rage and sadness. The feelings can be overwhelming."

The president listened. The full Cabinet sat at the long table of the bunker, all eyes searching for answers. On large screens, they watched Congress members flailing at one another. The Speaker of the House hitting their gavel to call for order. Fist fights and Capitol Police unable to place handcuffs on all of the unruly House members. The exact same madness was playing out in the Senate.

"Who is behind it?" the president asked. "Can you give us any more information?"

"No," Sam lied. "But it could be a sonic weapon. Perhaps a sound calibrated to affect certain emotions in the brain."

"Where did they get the technology?"

Sam remembered his promise to Mother Jackson. He had to find this man influencing Chaos without leading them to her.

"Does he want money?" the Secretary of the Treasury asked.

"Power?" the Secretary of State asked.

"The country cannot afford another day of this... this madness," the president said. "Without a Congress, our stock market in freefall and the police turning on each other, the United States will falter and fall. Not to mention the human aspect: there have been very few casualties so far, but that's only because we have every super hero working round the clock. This madness needs to end, Captain."

An assistant ran into the room and showed a paper to the president.

"Turn on the television," the president said.

The assistant turned on a large television. Sam saw what he assumed were computer-generated images of faces that changed shades, races, and morphed into different genders shifting every ten seconds, until a mechanical voice spoke, low and deep.

"I am your savior," it said. "Call me Brutis."

"A nutcase," said the vice-president.

"Can we trace this?" the Secretary of the Treasury asked. "What channel is it?"

Phones rang and were answered as Sam watched the room explode with activity. The Chairman of the Joint Chiefs of Staff was on his phone.

"They have tapped into our satellites," the Chairman said.

"Who?" President Misler asked. "Can this madness get in here?"

"Thank God these walls have reinforced steel," the Secretary of State said.

Sam saw the televised facial images speed up.

"You adults have ruined this world, poisoned the oceans, and are intent on destroying life for generations to come. I represent young people who will force you to cease and desist. Our technology makes you see your own insanity."

The mechanical voice began laughing.

"Our following of young people will grow. You will never know where we will strike next."

The channel returned to a repeat of a reality show made for young people.

"Young people," Sam said. He realized that the violence had been mostly among adults. The vibration's wavelengths left them weak and with migraines.

Sam left the meeting knowing he had to locate Chaos. Redwing was tracking her in Harlem. "Thank you, my friend," he said.

He wanted to tell Chaos that other foster children, now adults, were coming. They were planning a funeral. He wanted Chaos to know that people still cared. Miss Adams, who had lived next door for twenty years, would be there to continue to act as a family. But first he needed to find Chaos and stop Brutis and his vibration machine.

Sam flew over Harlem, Calvary Cemetery, and Greater Baptist Church. Thelma's best friend, Miss Adams, was small and feisty, with a limp from a fall two years ago. She was keeping Sam aware of the funeral plans. Miss Adams, like many elderly people, was not driven into a frenzy by the sound. Sam thought it was probably due to a loss of hearing that came with age.

"Sam," Miss Adams said. "What's this all about?"

"The young people want to stop us from destroying the planet," he said.

"Killing people to save the world doesn't sound right to me," she said.

Sam hugged the woman who had been a friend to Thelma Jackson for sixty years. She squeezed his cheek, leaving the smell of roses.

"You be good," she said. "And where is Chaos?"

"I'm looking for her."

"I hope she's not in trouble," Miss Adams said. "Poor thing. God bless her. I miss my friend. But that girl had no life apart from Thelma. No friends at school. I hope she can find one now."

"Yes," Sam said. "I hope so, too."

THE FOLLOWING evening, the president addressed the nation on the television networks that were still capable of airing programs.

"The heightened level of criminality that has swept our country has required me to take the extraordinary measure of declaring martial law," the president said.

The press questions were on a video screen. The president had to remain in the Oval Office because members of the White House Press Corps had attempted to storm the stage, during the last in-person press conference, swinging the podium like a club and throwing chairs. It was a miracle that their battle with the secret service had no casualties.

As Sam watched the press conference, he felt Chaos was close. His ability to access the sight and memory of birds meant every pigeon in New York City was searching for Chaos, as well. Earlier that day, Sam stopped a robbery of Manuel Gomez, the shopkeeper on the corner. Then, he prevented a carjacking by flying overhead and deflecting the bullets with his wings. Sam rescued a child who had gotten lost while walking home from school after her parents began running wildly through Central Park chasing swans. He then stopped an armed, masked woman who walked into a bank and demanded only quarters. Sam was tired.

The next morning, with a heavy heart, Sam stood at Miss Jackson's casket, alongside others who had loved her as he had. There was no organ music or program. Sam was lucky. This was the funeral director's final service until life could return to normal. Some bodies were stacked in refrigerated vans in the streets. Miss Jackson deserved better for the joy she had given the world. Sam waited for Chaos, seething at the harm she had caused. But she didn't show up.

Sam flew over New York City as dusk fell and chaos reigned. He knew where to wait. Sam landed in a far corner of the Calvary Cemetery in Queens. Angels atop mausoleums watched him. The cemetery's headstones mimicked the Manhattan skyline of buildings miles away, except the city had twinkling lights and the cemetery had one lonely streetlight at the gate down a gravel-covered hill from Miss Jackson's grave.

Night birds called to him. Finally, she arrived. He saw a black limousine make its way slowly toward the locked gate. Two men got out, the rattling chain on the rusted gate causing the birds in the trees above him to scatter. The gate squealed open, and Sam heard the crunch of tires on gravel. Men walked beside the vehicle holding strange elongated weapons. The limousine stopped at the newly dug grave. A woman walked, head down, to the gravesite, carrying a flashlight.

Sam's heart was heavy as he watched Chaos approach. He stayed in the dark shadow of the trees near Miss Jackson's grave. Sam saw through the eyes of an owl, and easily followed the car. But he stayed within the shadows as Chaos approached the gravesite.

"They asked for you at the funeral," he said.

Chaos jumped. Sam spoke without emerging from his place in the shadows. She tried to illuminate his face. Sam flew above the trees, avoiding her flashlight. But her flickering light alerted the men in the car.

"Get away from here, Sam," she said. "He won't like it."

As the men ran toward Chaos, Sam saw a short man step out of the back seat.

"Brutis!"

"Chaos," Brutis yelled. "Get over here, now!"

Sam landed behind her. Chaos turned the light toward him, quickly. But Sam was gone.

"Let me meet your new friend," Sam said, from behind a different tree.

"You can't stop him," she said, running toward his voice. But he was gone again.

"We'll see about that," Sam said.

"I wanted to be there," Chaos told him.

"This Brutis guy is using you," Sam said. "Using your power."

"That's not true," she said. "He says I'll never be alone again. He makes me feel special, Sam. Miss Jackson didn't understand and neither do you."

"She knew?" Sam said, with growing fury. "Did he have anything to do with..."

The men rushed up the hill. Sam stepped back into the shadows and then flew toward the treetops. He sat on a branch, watching them.

"Don't hurt him," Chaos yelled.

After Chaos ran toward the car, Sam jumped down onto the men. With a kick and twist of his body, one man was down. Sam flew back into the trees. They pointed the weapon into the trees, and sound waves blasted into Sam, giving him thoughts of disaster and guilt deeper and darker than he'd ever experienced. That was what the object in the man's hand was, weaponized chaos. Somehow they'd managed to concentrate the effects of Chaos's powers. Sam's brain ached as the vibrations stirred emotions of loss, and his dead father's face danced in his mind, laughing, sending Sam twirling into a tailspin, breaking branches until the pummeling he received snapped him out of the weapon's trance.

After falling to the ground, a second man jumped on Sam. From the darkness came grunts, moans of pain, and a final thud as a body dropped onto the gravel.

"There's nothing he can do, now," Brutis said.

Sam saw Chaos pushed inside the limousine. He kicked the weapon out of the hands of the first man. The other threw punches at Sam's face. Sam dodged and then cracked him on the head with a broken branch. Sam checked his pulse.

"Alive, but you *will* have a headache."

The car began backing down the road. Sam flew to the limousine. The muzzle of the vibration weapon appeared from the driver's side window, pointed directly at Sam. The wavelength hit his chest. Sam darted away. The car backed up too fast to maneuver through the narrow gate and crashed into the stone pillar, creating sparks. Chaos jumped from one side of the car as the spark became a flame. Brutis, weapon in hand, leapt out before the car burst into flames.

Brutis pointed the weapon to the sky, searching for him. Sam needed to know that Chaos was safe, then he could take on this so-called savior. In the flames, Sam saw a masked figure, Brutis. Another direct hit to the chest sent Captain America spinning backward.

I must be faster, he thought.

But each blow slowed his reflexes. Sam was falling.

WHEN SAM awoke, he felt a cool metal table beneath him and iron bars across his chest pinning his arms to the table with locks on either side. The man who called himself Brutis walked around the table twice before speaking. There was a rumble, like an earth tremor, but above him and distant. The room was stone, damp and dark but for the lanterns placed several feet apart on three of the gray stone walls that looked like a dungeon in Europe.

"You're awake," he said. "Good."

The voice was soft and measured, with a slight lilt of an accent, nothing like the mechanical baritone Sam had heard at the White House.

"I'm sure you did not know New York City has its own catacombs," Brutis said. "I discovered them. I discovered many things."

He was a slump-shouldered little man wearing a wrinkled white lab coat. He was as small as a boy, with curly black hair, wearing a mask of a pale, male grinning face that clashed sharply with his tan hands and neck.

"What's your deal, man?" Sam asked.

"My deal? The preservation of life, of course."

"You've caused nothing but death," Sam said. "And destruction."

"Only to preserve life!" Brutis said, voice sharp with rage, his mask within inches of Sam's face. "One must sometimes kill to create."

"Where's Chaos?"

Ignoring the question, the masked little man stepped back and resumed his circling of the table. Sam struggled against the bars that held him, never taking his eyes from Brutis.

"I wear this mask because of a chemical leak. I was a happy child, playing soccer with my friend. I had friends back then. The chemicals did this to my face."

"I am truly sorry to hear that," Sam said.

He was trying to be sympathetic. Social work had trained him to think of empathy first, give positives before negatives. *But this guy has Chaos somewhere and people are dying*, Sam thought.

"Couldn't you use your talents for good?" Sam said.

"My face, contorted by nerve damage, left me without friends or companionship," Brutis said.

"Lonely?" Sam said.

Brutis removed his mask, revealing a right eye looking forward at Sam, a boy's tan handsome face of nine or ten. On the other side, however, his young face was a mass of wrinkled, sagging flaps of skin hanging off of his chin. His drooping left eyelid held an eyeball facing away, locked into its far corner, sightless.

"I feel young and old at the same time," Brutis said, with a long and heavy sigh.

Sam was using his telepathy to connect with the birds. He felt them nearby. The two-foot-thick stone walls kept him from reaching the surface from wherever he was. The rumbling above him returned. It was familiar.

"All I could do was study," said Brutis, as if in a trance. "I chose chemistry and physics. Using each day of my painful life to seek solutions to the greed adults use as their god. It was during this time that I discovered the special ones. Like those men, once homeless, and now my army. Special ones, like Chaos, are all around the world. Their powers waiting to be gathered."

"And led by you."

"Of course," Brutis said, his back to the table, walking up the stone steps.

"How do you transfer their powers into your weapon?" Sam asked.

Brutis only laughed.

"Where is Chaos?"

"In my good hands." Brutis's laugh trailed away as the door closed behind him.

Then, Sam found himself in darkness. Waves of vibration filled the room along with a whimpering. Sam called out.

"Chaos?"

Footsteps approached him from the corner.

"He left me."

"He was only using your pain."

"Everyone leaves me."

"I'm right here."

"I'm sorry, Sam. I've caused a lot of trouble."

"Yes. We'll deal with that later." Sam was so grateful she was unharmed, so far. She hugged him as he lay helpless. "Let's get out of here," he said.

Chaos found the lever that released the bars that locked Sam to the table. He rose.

"We're under the subway."

"Yes," Chaos said. "The abandoned station near City Hall in the Financial District."

"Chaos, listen, we need to stop this guy. What exactly is this Brutis guy up to?"

"He said he would take advantage of the chaos to remake society and form a new government, a better government, one that actually cares about people. People like us wouldn't fall through the cracks."

Sam rolled his eyes.

He allowed Chaos to lead the way. He felt she was still under the spell of Brutis. But he had to trust her to guide him through this maze of tunnels to a passage to the light of day. Chaos led him up narrow, low cement passages, sooty channels to stone stairs. Chittering rats ran below, and subway trains ran overhead, getting louder. Then there were voices.

"Brutis must have discovered I was gone," Sam said. "How many people work for him?"

"Hundreds," Chaos said, panting from the climb. "How many homeless people are in New York City? Many of them have military training. Some are specialized, classified even."

Sam thought of the millions of homeless men and women on the streets whom Brutis could recruit. A worldwide army at his fingertips.

"He has a machine, doesn't he?"

Chaos stopped.

"Yes."

"How does it work?" Sam was afraid Chaos may be too far gone to help him.

In the dark, her voice was more mature but sad.

"I talk into it," she said. "I tell it all of the bad things and hurt that no one knows, not even Miss Jackson or you. But Brutis only wanted to hear the bad stuff. I got tired of only talking about what was wrong."

"Mother Jackson loved you," Sam said.

"That's why I can't let him hurt more people," she said. "He said I was the only one. His favorite. He lied."

They reached the end. A door. Sam kicked it open. They emerged from an old wooden doorway onto subway tracks.

"I'm not sure which way," she said.

A light was coming. Sam realized these were not abandoned tracks. He pulled Chaos back inside just as the subway cars rushed within inches of the doorway. His telepathy with Redwing showed him the entrance to the platform. But it was too dangerous to risk walking on the tracks.

"Chaos, I've got to show you something," Sam said.

Sam spread his wings and flew through the tunnel with Chaos in his arms. When Sam reached the City Hall platform in front of the Number One train, he saw writhing bodies of Wall Street businessmen in suit jackets turned inside out wearing pajama bottoms sitting on the platform edge with feet dangling over the side and watched women playing handball against the walls and hopscotch on the tracks. He soared above it all.

"He's going to the top of the Empire State Building," Chaos said. "That's where the big machine is located. Brutis is going to blast every country, everyone."

Sam pulled the emergency switch shutting down the trains and protecting those stupefied people playing on the subway tracks.

"Is the effect permanent?"

"No, they go to sleep, and then, in a few days, the nightmares stop."

"He's trying to make people as insane as he is."

Brutis had to be stopped.

Sam picked up Chaos and darted, wings careful of the pillars, until they were out of the station. Brutis's army of homeless men ran toward him, pushing passengers aside. The army's clothes were ragged. They marched with military precision. They stared straight ahead with a determination that was clear. They would kill him for Brutis.

He left Chaos safely on the top of a nearby building and flew to the Empire State Building. Brutis was there, over 1,250 feet high. The vibration machine was the size of a tank but was shaped like the weapons carried by the two men in the cemetery.

How did he get that thing up here? Sam thought.

Wind tore at Brutis' white coat and Sam had to fight against the wind driving at his wings and the vibrations from the machine. Sam had to clear his mind of sadness the vibrations brought, images of Mother Jackson on her deathbed, his father's death, and his mom dying alone.

"That's a long way to fall, my friend," Brutis yelled, against the loud winds.

The tank was pointed directly at him.

"Die, little birdie," Brutis said, laughing.

Sam hurled himself to the right. But the vibration struck him, slowing his response. He sank with the heaviness of images from his youth, children teasing him in grade school, the shame of wetting the bed, the girl he loved in high school but never kissed. Office windows whirled by as he fell, not caring to flap his wings. Nothing mattered, life was hopeless. Brutis would win.

Then Sam remembered what Chaos said. Strength returned. He turned around and pushed himself up, soaring. Speed returned when he remembered the beauty of the wind beneath his wings, joy of the sun and miracle of the moon.

"You're too late," Brutis said as Sam landed in front of him. "Get him!"

Four men attacked Sam. Sam flew out of their reach, slamming heads and hands, tripping the men while ensuring they didn't fall over the edge. Soon the men had lost the ability or the will to fight, maybe both.

"This is why you always need a backup plan," said Brutis. He reached for his hip, brandished a pistol and began to fire. But this wasn't the first time a desperate man had pulled a gun on Sam. His wings deflected the bullets and he easily dodged Brutis' fire until he heard that familiar click. Empty. Brutis screamed in fury and threw the gun.

The little man removed his mask. "You ruined everything!"

They were now face to face.

"There is no place to go," said Sam.

"I don't expect you to understand." Brutis said.

Sam felt the tug of a social worker who had seen many hurt people turn to hurting other people. "You're right. It's not fair, Brutis," Sam said. "But don't make it worse."

Brutis turned and seemed to consider Sam's words for a second before a sneer appeared on his disfigured face. His mind was made up.

"You're too late," he taunted, his voice echoing off the stone walls. "The machine is already active. Soon, everyone will feel what I feel."

Sam stepped forward, his wings folding behind him. "Brutis, this has to stop. You're hurting people, not helping them."

"No. They're already hurt. The machine just brings to the surface what's already inside of them." Brutis spat, his face contorting with rage. "Their rage, their sorrow, their pain. It already exists. Everyone is in pain in this world. Why? Why did we build a world like this? Why don't you do anything about it? I'm going to remake this world, Captain. You'll thank me one day."

Chaos appeared at the door out of breath, having ran from the safe perch where Sam had stashed her. She quickly moved to the control panel, her fingers flying over the buttons. "Sam, I can shut it down, but I need time."

Brutis lunged toward her, but Sam intercepted, catching him with a powerful blow that sent the smaller man sprawling. "You're not stopping her," he growled.

Brutis scrambled to his feet, his eyes wild. "You don't understand!" he screamed. "This is the only way!"

Sam advanced, his voice steady. "There are other ways, Brutis. Ways that don't involve forcing your pain on others."

Behind him, Chaos worked frantically, her brow furrowed in concentration. "Almost there," she muttered.

Brutis pulled a knife from his coat, slashing wildly at Sam. The blade nicked Sam's arm. Sam retaliated, disarming Brutis with a swift kick. The knife clattered to the ground, skidding across the stone floor.

"Stop," Sam said, pinning Brutis to the ground. "You can still choose to help people the right way."

Brutis struggled, his breath coming in ragged gasps. "I've already lost everything. This is all I have left."

Chaos pressed a final button, and the machine's hum died down to a low whine. "It's done," she said, stepping back.

Sam looked down at Brutis, a mix of pity and determination in his eyes. "You don't have to lose everything. Help me fix this, shut off the machines, reverse what you've done. I'll ask the judge for leniency."

"I don't need your pity," he said.

Sam sighed, tightening his grip. "Then you'll face the consequences."

As the NYPD burst into the room, Sam and Chaos stepped aside, allowing the officers to take Brutis into custody. The machine was dismantled, its parts hauled away for analysis. The effects weren't permanent, but every scientist available would be looking at how to stop the madness immediately. Sam smiled despite the tragedy. Even on such a dark day, he still had hope. Order would be restored, the pieces would be picked up and the citizens he protected would rise to even greater heights. This he knew.

Outside, the first light of dawn was breaking over the city. Sam and Chaos stood on the rooftop, the cool morning air washing over them.

"We did it," Chaos said softly, her eyes on the horizon.

Sam nodded, a sense of relief washing over him. "Yes, we did. But there's still a lot of work to be done."

Chaos smiled, her grip on his arm tightening. "I'm ready."

Together, they took flight, soaring over the city that was once again safe, knowing that as long as they stood together, they could face whatever challenges lay ahead.

PLUG IN, PLUG OUT

DANIAN JERRY

"YOU DISCOVERED your powers when?" Sam stared across the cluttered desk at the teenager slouching in the brown recliner.

The office space had served as a company break room in its former life. After buying the building, Sam had turned the place into his own Avengers mini mansion. The road was rough most of the time, but he had come a long way—from hopeful preacher's son to orphan to Captain America.

How many kids who daydream about crawling up walls and shooting lasers from their palms actually become super heroes? Sam thought.

"I wouldn't say powers," Plug replied, shrugging. "I just got a special talent. That's all." She wore a denim jacket and jeans, black construction boots decorated with silver glitter, and a black fitted Yankees cap turned backward.

"How did you come by this talent? Gamma rays? Radiation? Cosmic cube?"

"A couple of years ago, I woke up and… everything was different. Sounds funny, huh?"

"Actually I've heard that story before—except you control

computers with your mind," Sam said, tapping his fingertip against his temple. "I've seen telepaths, telekinetics, pyrokinetics. I never met anybody who specialized in computers."

Over the years, dozens of troubled kids and adults would visit Sam seeking assistance, but his life was different now. The Captain American Hotline and the Whisperer—former superhero sidekick and now computer genius Rick Jones—constantly found him missions and trouble to fight, alone and with the Avengers. Sam spent most of his days rescuing people in need and taking down corrupt organizations like Hydra and Serpent Solutions. He rarely had time for the community work he loved.

"I don't *specialize* in anything. Computers are alive, Mr. America. I talk to them, and they speak back." Plug tapped her feet, one at a time in a quick rhythm.

"Call me Sam." He cringed at the thought of Misty Knight overhearing his new nickname. "So it's like HTML?"

"Not quite," Plug said and laughed. "The first time, I was playing *Mario Kart*. I was crying because some kids had been teasing me about my parents doing drugs. Luigi jumped out of that dune buggy and waved at me. He said, 'Cheer up, Plug. Everything's gonna be okay.' I know it sounds crazy, but that game became my best friend."

Stranger things can happen, Sam thought, smiling. *I went through a plane crash to meet Redwing and Steve Rogers.*

Plug sat up in the chair and continued. "One day Luigi just came up missing. I think my daddy traded my game for some drugs."

"I'm sorry, Plug, but if I'm gonna help you I have to ask. How did you end up breaking the law with your *special talent*?" Sam couldn't believe Plug's arrest record. Car theft on her eleventh birthday, bank fraud three months ago; on paper the fifteen-year-old sophomore was already a hardened criminal.

"No family, nowhere to go. I had to eat." Plug stared at him steadily. "My mom and dad OD'd. My grandma was locked up. They tried to put me in a group home, but I ran away." She shuddered. "I was safer on the street." Plug pulled her Yankees cap over her eyebrows.

"My parents died when I was young as well," Sam said. He remembered the black sedan, the gun barrel pointing through the open window at his father.

Plug nodded, her eyes serious. "I started putting in work, getting money. My gift made it easier. By the time my grandma got out of jail, I had done so much in the streets, I couldn't go back."

"If that's the life you want, then why are you here now?" Sam asked.

"You sound like my grandma." Plug chewed the tip of her thumbnail. "I didn't say that's what I wanted, Mr. America. I want out. Grandma said you could help with that. But if I leave the life, I gotta leave New York. Have your stars and stripes made you forget what it's like around here?"

Sam winced. Her words stung more than he expected.

"How 'bout I come to your block, talk to whoever's in charge," Sam said. "Strictly plain clothes. No uniform or nothing, we can call it a social visit."

"I can't be seen in the hood with Captain America," Plug said, sitting up straight. "So everybody can think I'm talking to the feds? I got enough problems."

The expression on her face made Sam want to laugh.

"You don't have to live like this," he said, quietly. "I can help you find some alternatives. Unless you popped out of a cocoon, we can look at a school in Westchester that specializes in youngsters with *special talents*."

Plug snorted. "No cocoon, and no Westchester. It already sounds boring and expensive. I'll pass."

Sam sighed and prayed for patience. There was a reason he didn't have children of his own. "Don't worry about the cost, Plug. Just keep an open mind."

"Whatever you say, Mr. America." Plug stood up and pulled the wide straps on her backpack over her thin shoulders.

"Before you go, would you mind demonstrating your powers?" Sam asked.

A huge smile brightened her face. "I'd be glad to, Mr. America, in exchange for something."

"Am I gonna regret this?" Sam asked.

"I want *that*!" Eyes gleaming, Plug pointed at Sam's shield propped on the wall behind his head.

"That's not a toy," he said. Talking about his uniform, equipment, Captain America's job description always filled him with conflicting emotions.

He was proud to carry the shield, but assuming the persona of Captain America had exposed Sam to more bigotry and hatred than he had ever seen. Even though he had millions of supporters scattered across the United States, just as many opposed his tenure as Captain America and his outspoken politics.

"No shield, no powers," Plug said, minus the humor in her voice.

"All right." Sam pulled his cellphone from his pocket and set it inside a small space he cleared within the clutter on his desk. "There you go. Let's see what you—"

Squealing, Plug ran around Sam's desk and brushed the shield with her fingertips.

"Okay," Sam said. "Now that you've had some time with the shield, there's my cell phone. Talk to it. I'm sure it has a lot to say."

"Power off." Plug spoke in a chorus of voices.

Sam's phone rattled against the dark oak and surrendered to black silence. Raising an eyebrow at Plug, Sam reached across the desk.

"Power on," Plug snapped, her voice split in multiple keys.

Life returned as the powerless phone rattled against the desk, colors bursting and flashing over the screen.

"Impressive," Sam said, nodding. "So you do a Siri sorta thing but with your mind?" He wondered if he could get Storm or Rogue to help Plug with her powers.

Plug held up a finger to Sam, silencing him. "So, how are you today?"

The colors swirled into a starburst and then a bright golden light emerged. "I've been better," a voice replied.

Sam leaned forward, startled.

"Oh," Plug said, "what's wrong?"

"I'm a little bored. All Sam does is work. Flying around all day, beating down bad guys. I want to have some fun every now and then. Sometimes he talks to Steve, and he's a good guy. Tony Stark, now he's a character! Sam hasn't spoken to Misty in a minute, but the last time they were texting..."

"That's enough," Sam said, blushing as he stuffed his phone in his pocket.

"Oh! You got it like that, Mr. America?" Plug said, smiling mischievously.

"Okay, I see what you can do. Just make sure you stay out of trouble. You have a powerful gift. Don't misuse it."

"Yeah, yeah. I gotta go, but if you wanna head to the block alone, feel free. Go up to 123rd and 2nd Avenue, Jefferson Houses. Ask for Grandma Dukes."

SAM PREFERRED suiting up and flying over New York, but this evening he wanted to visit Plug's grandmother. Passing a cathedral topped with spires and stone crosses, he noticed a flock of gray and black pigeons perched on the church towers and the surrounding tree branches. Hundreds of black impassive eyes, the winged army stared as Sam walked past.

Growing up in Harlem meant growing up around thousands of birds. Most people never fed them, since a pigeon snacking on a bread crust could become dozens of hungry beaks in seconds, but for Sam the more birds the merrier.

Years ago when he met his falcon, Redwing, the pair established a psychic connection that allowed him to communicate with any bird he desired. He also gained the ability to see through their eyes. This connection made him appreciate Plug's special gift even more.

Stopping to stare at the flock of dark sentinels, Sam gazed at himself through dozens of eyes, at a splintered mirror image dark and blurry. The pigeons flapped and cooed at Sam, stopping him midstep, forcing him to listen.

We got your back, the birds said, and that was enough.

Even without the mask and shield, everybody in Harlem recognized Sam. He was *their* Captain America. Most people glanced only once or twice. One passing couple whispered and giggled. Super heroes walked by every day, no big deal.

A haggard man with dark eyes and saggy cheeks, obviously intoxicated, stumbled down the sidewalk, pointing a shaky index finger.

"Mr. Take-It-To-The-Hotline, you're a disgrace to this country, and a sorry excuse for a soldier." Spit flew from the drunkard's mouth. "It's time for you to give back the shield."

"I don't want any problems. I'm here to help, actually." Sam dug in his jacket pocket and handed a card to the veteran. "Call this number. Ask for Pastor Gideon Wilson. My little brother. He'll hook you up with some food, a warm bed, maybe a job if you're interested."

Another fifteen blocks, the sidewalk led to a green sign posted over a patch of hard dirt and withered grass. Yellow cursive spelled *Welcome to Jefferson Houses* across the weathered paint.

Sam stepped into a courtyard surrounded by five-story apartment buildings, their windows barred, and found himself in the middle of an old-school block party. The streets were cut off to traffic. Speakers inside neighborhood restaurants and bodegas blared salsa, soul, and Afrobeats, while outside men laughed and slammed dominoes down on rickety tables. He closed his eyes, focusing on every sound and scent, even the brisk air against his skin.

My phone was right. I could use more time for myself, Sam thought.

"There he is," a woman shouted behind him. "Mr. Take-It-To-The-Hotline, himself."

Turning, Sam's eyes fell on a petite woman with a salt-and-pepper afro, round cheeks, and gray eyebrows set behind a pair of horn-rimmed glasses.

"A little birdie told me you might be stopping by," the woman said, wrapping her arms around Sam's neck, pecking his cheek.

"Is that right?" Returning the hug, Sam noticed the similarities between Plug and the woman standing before him, the same eyes, the same smile. "You must be the world-famous Grandma Dukes."

"Child, please," she said, her voice warm and comforting. "I'm as far from famous as you can get. I'm still in a daze—

Captain America in Jefferson Houses. To what do we owe this pleasure?"

"Can we talk about Plug? She told me about her situation. I'd like to help if I can," Sam said. He thought about Plug's reluctance to be seen with him. He wondered if someone was watching him talk to Grandma Dukes right now.

"My granddaughter's something else, but she gets it from me. Word to mother, I was worse at her age. Let's walk over here and talk."

"You sure? I don't wanna cause any trouble for you or Plug."

"Trouble's been chasing us since I was a kid running these same projects. I did fifteen years at Ryker's. I could've snitched a long time ago and bought fifteen years of freedom." Wrapping her arm around Sam's, she led him through the courtyard toward a playground and a basketball court.

"So how long have you known my brother?" Sam asked.

"I met Pastor Gideon about a year before I got out of jail," Grandma Dukes replied. "Reading and praying with him helped me to make those last few months. Once I got out, he got me a place to live, food to eat, and honest work. When he said you would talk to Plug, I almost fell out."

"Plug is a great kid, and I'm glad to help."

"I bet you're wondering how such a great kid gets caught up in the same evil that sent me to prison and murdered her parents. Look around. Not a lot of hope in Jefferson Houses. We get it by any means."

"No need to school me about Harlem. I grew up here." For a second, Sam was overtaken by his father's memory. He bit his bottom lip and stared at a group of kids playing half-court basketball. "How deep is Plug into the gangs?"

"Very deep," Grandma Dukes lowered her voice and her gaze. "She's not a supervisor, but she's definitely a high-ranking worker in Jefferson Houses. She reports directly to the supervisor who runs these projects."

Sam nodded solemnly as Grandma Dukes continued.

"After I got my own apartment, Plug moved in with me. One day she showed me an advertisement for the Anthony Stark High School for Business Careers. She wanted to enroll there because of her gift. We worked on Plug's application for six months. I even called this guy I knew from the old days who teaches math at the Stark School and got him to write Plug a recommendation, but none of it mattered.

"They put my grandbaby on a waiting list. After that, Plug gave up on the straight-and-narrow path. She didn't believe that sort of life was meant for people like us. What could I say? I'm a two-time felon dodging my third strike. Who's gonna listen to me?"

"I have a direct line to Tony Stark," Sam said, thinking about Misty Knight. "But there's another school I think would be even better for Plug considering her unique abilities."

"I want my baby out these streets, period. What's the name of this school?"

"It's a private institution in Westchester. Their curriculum is designed for kids with special abilities like Plug. It's an elite program, one of the best in the world, but I can definitely get one of their representatives to talk with you and Plug if you're interested."

"Of course I'm interested," Grandma Dukes said, as she hugged Sam's waist. "I'm glad you got the chance to see how special my granddaughter is."

"Would the gang come looking for Plug if she left? Would they retaliate against you?"

"Their leader, E Way, might try something, but I'll handle that. Don't worry." Grandma Dukes nodded.

"Not a good answer, ma'am. Plug's gonna need you even more as she gets older and her gift develops. If she lost you, she'd never stop blaming herself."

"Thoughtful and handsome." Grandma Dukes rubbed Sam's jaw and winked. "Come on, Mr. America, lemme buy you a slice of cheesecake."

Heat rising to his jaw, searching for something to say, Sam spied a tall, slender woman dressed in hunter green yoga pants, a black tank top, a green jacket, and black sneakers. She had green eyes and brown hair braided into a ponytail hung over her shoulder.

"Grandma Dukes." The woman spoke like they were old friends. Her Scandinavian accent suggested a Northern European upbringing.

"Helen," Grandma Dukes said, lips barely moving.

That's a bad sign, Sam thought. *She doesn't like this woman.*

"How's the block party? Did everything go smoothly with the permits and the vendors?"

"Everything's fine," Grandma Dukes said dryly. "No problems at all, and I hope it stays that way."

"Hear, hear, sister. We're all neighbors, right? One happy family working it out in uptown." Helen spread her arms.

Grandma Dukes kept her mouth closed, but her eyes said *Harlem*.

"And here, we have a bonafide super hero in our midst. I'm Helen Nichols." She offered a friendly smile and her hand for Sam to shake.

"I'm just a regular citizen trying to help those in need." He found Helen's skin a little clammy.

"You're Captain America, for heaven's sake," she replied. "You symbolize the strength of this great country."

"I'm still getting used to all the attention. I focus on the responsibility part more than anything. You know, helping people in need, protecting those unable to fend for themselves."

"That's why Harlem loves our Captain America. He's a man of the people." Grandma Dukes hugged Sam with one arm. "Ms. Nichols represents the brokers that manage Jefferson Houses."

"Your tenant committee asked for a corporate rep on site who could address resident issues in real time." Helen wagged her finger.

"Tell the truth," Grandma Dukes stepped closer, pointing at Helen. "Your investors wanna raise the rent and everybody out. How do you gentrify affordable housing?"

"Is that true?" Sam asked. He knew the answer, but he wanted to see if Helen would lie.

"We're building a safe community despite the troubles that your niece and her friends are causing. I have my own birdies feeding me information." Helen stood her ground, her green eyes hard and flat.

Sam wanted to ask Helen about the gangs, but that meant outing Plug. "Is there some way you two could work together, make the neighborhood a better place for everyone involved?"

"Make a deal with the devil in the green jacket? I don't think so." Grandma Dukes rolled her eyes, staring daggers at Helen.

"Come on, Mr. America. I've had enough of Helen for one day."

SAM SAT at his desk and stared at a pile of unpaid bills. A while back, he went viral, expressing his dissatisfaction with politics in the United States. Months later he left S.H.I.E.L.D. after a debacle in Pleasant Hill involving the intelligence agency's involvement in a plot to rewrite portions of reality using an energy cube with omnipotent power. With all of that, who had time for a job? But even super heroes had to eat, and there was only so much Stark money he was willing to accept.

"Hey, Cap." With a strawberry-blond bush of a beard and a buzz-cut cropped close around the ears, Dennis Dunphy stuck his head into Sam's office. Normally, the former superstrong super hero was all good humor and affirmations, even though he had experienced more than his fair serving of hardship.

"What's up, D? Where's the cheer and the jokes? We need some comic relief around here." Sam waved a handful of bills at Dunphy.

"Cap, the police just called about Plug. She's at Harlem Hospital."

"What happened?" Misty Knight asked, stepping into the open doorway.

"Somebody shot Plug's grandmother," Dunphy said, his voice soft, full of remorse.

"Wait a minute. Somebody shot Grandma Dukes?" Sam pinched the bridge of his nose. *This is not your fault.*

"Whatever's going on, it's not good." Dunphy leaned forward, propping his fists among the bills and junk mail piled on Sam's desk.

"Plug! What did you do?" Sam asked, staring at his cellphone.

SAM FLEW as fast as he could to Harlem Hospital with Misty Knight rushing through traffic in her supercharged sports car. Black exterior, tinted windows, glossy black wheels, the sport sedan evoked a liquid shadow as it zoomed through the streets, almost as quickly as the hero in the skies.

Police officers rushed Sam the moment he stepped inside the emergency room. They started to escort him to the intensive care unit where they were holding Plug and treating Grandma Dukes, when Misty arrived.

She wore faded blue jeans, red boots, and a black leather jacket covering a pair of .45 automatics holstered under her armpits. Years ago, she had served on the force until some mafioso planted a bomb under her car. The explosion took one of her arms and ended her career in law enforcement until Tony Stark gifted her with the metal prosthetic arm that would become her signature trademark.

Misty squeezed Sam's hand as they followed the cops down a brightly lit hallway to an open room guarded by two more police officers.

The officers smiled, visibly relaxing their posture as Misty Knight led Sam into the room. First, Sam noticed the heart monitor next to the bed where Grandma Dukes slept peacefully. Plug sat beside the bed, rocking in her chair, holding her grandmother's hand.

"You all right?" was all Sam said, walking toward the teenager.

Plug mumbled something under her breath, before raising her head. Her face a mess of tears, saliva, and snot, she leapt from the bedside and wrapped her arms around his torso.

"They shot my grandma. The only person who ever gave a damn about me. She's about to die, and it's all my fault."

The halogen lights lining the ceiling blinked in rapid succession. On and off. On and off. The television mounted on the wall above the foot of the bed glowed a bright yellow then red before the screen cracked and ribbons of gray smoke hissed through the splintered glass. Mournful whispers and murmuring spilled from the broken screen.

"I thought I could get out," Plug said. She pulled back from

Sam and wiped her nose with the back of her hand. "That kinda life just isn't meant for people like me."

"Don't worry, Plug. Grandma Dukes is going to be okay," a scratchy voice sizzled its way from the television speakers. The screen glitched and popped.

"You have people around you that love you," the heart monitor clicked and beeped until the sounds formed coherent language. "Allow them to help you."

Taken aback, Misty Knight took a step toward the door.

"Don't forget about us," the broken television, the heart monitor, and the police officer's cellphone all sang in unison. "We love you, too."

Sam and Misty looked around the room, marveling at the chattering electronics. Holding Plug's shoulders, Sam saw fear, anger, and hopeless uncertainty. He'd been there before. *This girl's about to get herself into a whole world of trouble,* Sam thought.

"I know it hurts, but what you're thinking's gonna get you killed," he said.

"How do you know what I'm thinking?" Plug sniffled. "I'm not a bird."

"Can't you release our young friend into our custody?" Misty Knight asked the officer. "We can look after her and keep her out of trouble. Get her off your hands."

"I don't know." The officer scratched the back of his head. He cupped his hand around his mouth and whispered his next sentence. "My sergeant told me to keep her until he gets back."

"Don't treat this girl like a criminal," Misty Knight said. "She's been through enough already."

Sam watched the pressed officer struggle for the right words.

"If you know who shot your grandmother, you need to tell us," Sam said. "Taking matters into your own hands will only make things worse." Sam remembered his conversation with Grandma Dukes, her soft hand against his face.

"Tell us who did this, Plug. We'll handle it. I promise," Misty Knight said, gently. "How would Grandma Dukes feel if you got locked up or hurt trying to avenge her?"

"I have to do something! This is my fault." Plug stared at her shoes.

Misty sighed and turned to the police officer. "Is she a suspect?" she asked, pointing at Plug.

The officer scratched his head and stammered, eyeing the electronics suspiciously as they muttered in the background.

"Since she's a juvenile, we have to hold her until a relative or legal guardian picks her up. If you can take her home and keep her out of trouble, I suppose she could leave with you. Let me check with my superiors."

"I'm a licensed social worker," Sam said, hugging Plug with one arm. "I'll assume custody until Grandma Dukes gets better." He smiled at her despite the worry knotting his stomach. "Your grandmother's a hard rock, straight up and down. She's gonna pull through this. Trust me."

o————o

RIDING THROUGH Harlem, Sam was glad to give up the front seat to Plug, who didn't seem the least bit affected by Misty's driving. The teenager sat up in her seat, like a tourist, staring at everything and nothing outside the window. Sam, on the other hand, sprawled across the back seat, his head and stomach swimming with every twist and turn.

"Like I said, Mr. America, I tried. I told my OG I wasn't working for him anymore. He didn't get mad or anything. He wished me well and offered me some money to help me get on my feet."

"Wait," Sam said with one hand. "Who is *he*?"

"E Way, he runs Jefferson Houses," Plug said from the back seat. "Normally the runners report to his lieutenants, but I deal with him directly."

"What kind of work do you do for your OG?"

"I find money on the internet and shuffle it around. Sometimes I hide it." Plug's voice grew nervous.

"I assume you use your talents for this work." Sam leaned toward the front seat.

Plug nodded, her eyes shiny and sad.

"How much money are we talking about?" Misty asked, incredulous.

Plug stared at the storefronts and streams of pedestrians reeling past the passenger window.

"How much?" Sam prodded. "Four figures?"

Plug shook her head.

"Five figures?" In disbelief Sam thought about Plug's arrest record. "Six?"

"I would've stopped sooner if Grandma had taken the money I tried to give her. But she refused, and I couldn't leave her there all alone."

"Doesn't matter if you touched a penny," Misty said, glancing at Plug. "It's conspiracy, which means jail for the rest of your life or cooperating with the government."

Misty blew the car horn and cursed at a tall elder sleepwalking across the street.

"I gotta tell you something, Sam," Misty said, glancing at him through the rearview. "On the way to the station, I did some snooping. Guess who manages Jefferson Houses? Fisk and Associates."

"You're pranking me, right?" Sam asked, knowing that Misty never played about her detective work.

Sam sighed. "Take me by the office, so I can suit up."

o———o

PLUG LED Captain America and Misty Knight through the Jefferson Houses courtyard between a rusted children's playground and a faded basketball court filled with young people and parents and old folks resting on peeling park benches. Walking quickly, Cap found himself wishing for another way, but there was nothing else they could do. The people who hurt Plug's grandmother needed a message. A strong one.

My people deserve change, Sam thought with a heavy heart.

Everyone in the courtyard watched Plug pass briskly with Captain America and Misty Knight in tow. The people whispered and pointed, but Plug held her head high and kept walking until she got to the last building where a group of young men stood around with hoods pulled over their foreheads and their hands stuffed deep inside their pockets.

Cap assumed the young man crouched by a set of cement steps, shaking a set of dice, was E Way. He seemed to be the center of attention, and something about him screamed *leader*. Sam couldn't put the feelings into words, but he had worked with enough troubled teenagers to recognize a hard rock when he saw one.

"What's up, Plug," E Way said, flashing a smile filled with platinum and diamonds. He wore a brown bubble vest, white T-shirt, and brown jeans with the cuffs stuffed inside a pair of suede construction boots. "I knew you'd be back. I kept your job for you and everything. Even though you just up and quit. No two weeks' notice or nothing."

"The only thing keeping me from murking you is these two," Plug said. Seething, she pointed her thumb over her shoulder at her escorts.

"It's okay, I got this." Captain America stepped in front of Plug, his red, white, and blue suit standing out amongst the hoodies and bubble coats.

"It's like that, shorty?" E Way asked. "You talking to the Opps now?"

"You get one warning." Cap stood over E Way. "I don't care what kind of arrangement you had before. Plug no longer works for you, and if I find out that anybody here had a part in hurting Grandma Dukes, I'll be back, and I'm going to deal with you personally."

"Sorry you feel like that," E Way sneered. "I'm just a manager. My boss does all the hiring and firing."

"And who *is* your boss?" Misty stood beside Captain America and unbuttoned her jacket, revealing the butts of the handguns holstered under her armpits.

"That's none of your business, Miss. Besides, they don't talk to civilians, and they definitely don't talk to wannabe super heroes working for the police."

Misty raised her steel arm, and let a surge of energy crackle through it. E Way froze, his eyes bulging. The crowd stepped back, a hush falling upon the courtyard.

"Say what you like," Misty said. "But if anything happens to Plug, I know who to come for, believe that."

E Way turned to Cap. "I thought you were a soldier, like the old Captain America." He laughed. "You can't tell when you're surrounded? All you gotta do is look up."

That's when Cap noticed the open windows and the gun barrels aiming down at them.

"That shield can't protect everybody." E Way stuffed his dice into his coat pocket. His hand reappeared, holding a blue revolver.

Cap heard Plug breathing heavily, and when he turned, he saw tears running down her face.

The power lines connecting the buildings surged, and the tops of the surrounding lamp posts exploded. The air suddenly filled with expletives, rising from every light pole in sight.

E Way raised his gun, but Misty was quicker. By the time he fired at Plug, Knight's arm had already thrown up an energy shield. She'd gotten the upgrade either from Stark Industries or King T'Challa, Cap couldn't remember which. Misty always had somebody tinkering with that steel arm of hers.

A rectangle of light glowed in E Way's pocket until he screamed. He snatched his phone from his jacket and threw it just before it yelped and exploded. Cap nodded for Misty to drop the energy shield, lunging forward quickly while E Way was distracted.

Shield first, Cap listened to bullets bounce off the vibranium and adamantium alloy until E Way's gun clicked and clicked, signaling a depleted chamber. Sam rushed E Way to the ground as the cowering crowd roared, "Oooh!" Misty stood over the pair, pointing both her guns at E Way's forehead.

"You're not talking so much trash now, are you?" she said.

"Listen close," Cap growled. "We're gonna save some lives today, starting with yours."

E Way's eyes widened at the shadow spreading over the project courtyard. Cap didn't need to turn around to see his winged friends filling the sky behind him. He felt them just as strongly as he felt the nerves in his hands and his heart pounding beneath the star on his chest. He saw himself through their eyes. E Way looked terrified.

"Unless you wanna be fricasseed by an angry teenager and torn to pieces by New York's finest feathered flock, you're gonna tell us where we need to go and who we need to talk to, so we can straighten all this out."

"I TOLD you where to go and who to talk to," E Way complained from the back seat of Misty's car. "You didn't say anything about taking you there myself."

"Don't worry," Misty Knight said, staring in her rearview mirror. "That's limo tint on these windows. No one's gonna see you."

"What are you saying? Everybody in the projects saw me leaving with you!"

"Oh, *now* you're worried about being seen," Plug said. "I thought you had Jefferson Houses on lock. Who's the Opp now, Mr. Nobody Can See Me?"

They pulled up in front of a nondescript glass building, like the ubiquitous office buildings that had popped up throughout Harlem over the past year.

No one will see him unless those security cameras have infrared, Cap thought, and if this had anything to do with Fisk and Associates, the possibility was almost certain.

"You don't know anything about this brokerage firm?" Cap asked Plug.

"You keep asking me the same question and getting the same answer," Plug groaned. "I didn't know and neither did my grandma. Shoot, how could we have known that the property managers were supplying the gangs. Whenever I did anything, I worked with E Way directly like I said. Just me at a kitchen table with three or four laptops."

"Remember, Plug," Misty Knight said, pointing her thumb at the back seat. "Our boy here is not breaking these restraints, so you're safe. All you have to do is watch him until we get back. Hopefully he knows what will happen if he even tries to hurt you."

"YOU READY?" Cap took a deep breath and turned to Misty Knight.

"You owe me dinner after this *and* a concert," she answered with a wink, then popped the bones in her neck. Her face was full of the excitement she got just before she threw down.

"Remind me why we're splitting up, again." Staring at his reflection, Cap estimated the number of goons behind the glass posing as office personnel. *Fifty? A hundred?*

"We need solid evidence to connect Wilson Fisk with the gang activity in Jefferson Houses. In a just world, E Way's testimony would be enough, but this is New York," Misty Knight said coolly. The next moment she disappeared into a group of young people walking by, decked in backpacks and Air Pods, cargo jackets, and Jordans.

Soon as the glass doors slid open and Captain America stepped inside the office building, security guards, giants of men with huge muscles stretching their black suits, trapped him inside a closing half-circle.

"There's no need for violence, gentlemen," Cap raised his hands in the air, shield nonthreateningly strapped to his arm. He turned around slowly, making sure everyone could see him being nonviolent.

"I'm here to see Helen Nichols," Cap yelled to no one in particular and everyone present.

Instead of answering, the guards grimaced and cracked their knuckles before charging Cap all at once.

First, he flew up to the lobby ceiling and flung his shield at the disoriented mass of guards. He caught the returning shield with one hand before diving toward the ground and fighting his way through the fray. By the time he made it to the elevator, Cap had endured a bloody nose and a bruised eye swelling under his goggles. He spat a mouth full of blood and swiped the security pad with a key card he ripped from the black lapel of an incapacitated guard.

Time to get this over with one way or another.

48, 49, *50, 51.* Cap sighed. The ride to the top floor took forever. Good, he needed a breather. The goons were sloppy but dogged. Fisk, and his leadership "methods", inspired loyalty.

He hoped Misty would find *something* linking Fisk to the illegal trafficking and the gangs operating in Jefferson Houses. But if the street legends were true, finding a trail leading back to New York's underworld kingpin was unlikely.

Wilson Fisk had faced every street-level hero in town: Daredevil, Luke Cage, Spider-Man. Somehow he had managed to operate, even flourish, through the years of constant strife.

The elevator arrived at the penthouse floor with a single chime and the low hiss of the sliding metal doors.

Cap stepped off the elevator and into the biggest office he'd ever seen, larger than the meeting rooms at S.H.I.E.L.D. Headquarters or the Avengers mansion. Even in the dim light the room held unmistakable splendor. Huge abstract paintings decorated walls that rose over fifteen feet to the underside of a rotunda decorated with a giant map of New York City. Tall vases and bunches of wide palmer plants loomed in the corners. A pair of brown leather sofas, a leather armchair, and a walnut oak desk filled the room's center.

Behind the desk, Wilson Fisk, the Kingpin of New York's criminal underbelly, stared out the window at the gleaming city, Helen stood beside him.

"Sam Wilson, Falcon, Captain America... what *are* they calling you these days?" The derision in Fisk's voice was unmistakable.

"Don't call me anything," Cap said. "I have a message for the both of you."

"No one called me about a message," Fisk responded. "Before anyone can see me, they have to reach out. Steve Rogers should have taught you better manners."

Wilson Fisk was a wide-shouldered mound of packed beef, not chiseled but definitely solid. He wore a white suit, black shirt, red necktie, and a matching red pocket square. He raised a hand big enough to crush a human head and rubbed his chin.

"On the contrary, you're here to answer questions," Fisk said. "Your answers will determine whether you leave on the elevator or tossed out the window with your wings ripped to shreds like the second string super hero you are, *Captain America*."

"Whoever's supplying the drugs and the guns in Jefferson Houses needs to stop yesterday. Whatever my friend Plug did for your *organization*, that's over, too." Cap pointed at Fisk and Helen. "In fact, stop whatever you're doing here."

"Why would I do that? Our arrangements work for everyone involved," Fisk sneered.

"This…" Misty pointed to Cap and herself. "This is out of your league."

Fisk laughed. "I find it amusing that you think you, an ex-cop, and our social worker here think you're in my league as well."

Misty looked Fisk dead in the eye. "I don't think, fat boy, I know."

Face turning purple, Fisk unexpectedly leaped across the desk, massive hands extending, ready to crush whatever they touched. Cap had never seen anyone as big as Fisk move with that much speed. He barely got his shield up in time to block the pair of massive fists crashing down toward Misty.

The vibranium in the shield's metal alloy soaked up the crushing force. Before Fisk could raise his fists for a second attempt, Cap pushed Misty aside and landed a blow of his own, smashing Fisk's jaw with the shield.

The meaty face snapped quickly to the right and back again. Each blow sent painful shock waves through Cap's fist and forearms. Unaffected by the punches, Fisk offered a mischievous smile suggesting that hurting things was the best part of his job description.

"Grandma Dukes and I have a decade-old arrangement." Fisk wrapped his hands around Sam's neck, lifting Sam into the air as he rose to his knees, then his feet. "I allowed her the possibility of parole and ensured her granddaughter's safety. Grandma Dukes was one of my top earners. So when her son and his rat wife turned into federal witnesses, I offered her a way to atone for their offenses."

Cap swung his shield and kicked Fisk in the groin. The latter had time to raise his arm, blocking the head blow, but his knees bent when Cap's foot landed below Fisk's belt. Blood rushing to his face, the Kingpin flung Captain America into a massive bookcase that lined the wall next to the elevator.

Cracking his back against the hard, wooden shelves, Sam fell to the floor under a shower of books that smelled like dust and old leather. He propped himself on his hands and knees as Fisk lumbered forward.

Cap tried raising his shield, but a sharp pain flared from the joints surrounding his shoulder.

Is this what Steve felt like after the super-serum wore off? Is this what it feels like to be old?

Misty Knight rolled with Sam's push and gripped a black gun in each hand. Fisk dove over a couch, bullets snapping at his heels.

In the background, Plug crept off the elevator, and as soon as there was a lull in the shooting, ran into the room.

"Plug! We told you to stay outside!" Cap cried.

Plug balled her fists and glared at Fisk. "You're the one who hurt my grandma?"

A large painting hung above the mantle split in half and sank into the wall, revealing a mounted machine gun. A deep voice bellowed from the menacing weapon. "We told you not to worry, little Plug. *We* have your back!"

"You little punk! You're controlling my security!" Fisk yelled.

"It's about to get real!" Cap flung his shield, timing the throw so the discus could bounce off the wall and strike Fisk who was hiding behind the oak desk. A second later Misty snatched Plug out of reach.

"We need hard evidence linking Wilson Fisk to the gangs in Jefferson Houses. I tried hacking into the system's network, but that didn't work. Maybe the company's database will be more cooperative with you." Misty directed Plug's attention toward an all-in-one desktop computer sitting on Fisk's desk.

Plug nodded, took a deep breath and started toward the computer, but Misty grabbed the teenager's arm, turning to Cap.

"Can we get some cover, so our friend can do her thing?" Misty asked.

The office windows shattered with gunfire, spraying the room with broken glass. Cap covered himself with his wings. Reaching for Plug, he was relieved to see her wrapped inside an energy field Misty Knight projected from her steel arm.

Hundreds of birds flew in through the broken windows. Like always, Cap saw them and saw through them. He heard their thoughts in his mind.

Get him!

A storm of black feathers and snapping beaks flew around

Fisk, pecking, flapping their wings, and clawing. There were so many, Cap and Misty lost sight of Fisk.

Cap looked over at Misty in triumph for a few seconds, and then at Plug, who was in conversation with the computer.

"Where did Fisk go?" Plug said, her voice low and anxious. She pointed at the spot in front of the desk where Wilson Fisk had sprawled face down only moments before.

"Of course," Misty said, shaking her head. "For someone so massive, he sure moves stealthily."

"Did you find anything connecting Fisk to Jefferson Houses?" Cap tried to sound hopeful, but the look on Plug's face told him not to expect much.

"No." Plug said. "Everything leads back to Helen Nichols. She was the president of the brokerage firm, and E Way bought his supply directly from her."

"There's nothing we can take to the press?" He stood by the broken window and stared out at the city. "He's just going to get away."

The elevator greeted them warmly as Plug entered. "Told you everything was going to be okay," it said.

o———o

I NEED *to get by here more often,* Sam thought as he climbed the steps. It had been a few days since everything had gone down. Sunday morning, Harlem glittering in the daylight, he felt more hopeful than he had in months. He paused and thought about his father. *I wish you could see me now.*

"Earth to Captain America," Misty said, snapping her fingers to get Sam's attention. After taking a moment to straighten his tie, she took his hand and led him inside the church.

To Sam's surprise, E Way was the first person he saw inside the lobby. He had to swallow a laugh before giving the young man dap. E Way was dressed in all white, right down to his designer sunglasses.

"Mr. America," E Way said, smiling, shaking Sam's hand. "Everybody's waiting. Plug was worried, but I knew you'd show."

"Looking good, E Way." Grinning in spite of himself, Sam remembered his first encounter with E Way back in Jefferson Houses. So much bravado masking fear, the constant fear of the streets. Sam was glad that both E Way and Plug would be safe now.

"It's a trip, right, seeing me up in here." E Way looked around the lobby like he was nervous. "I know. It feels weird to me, but this day is special. I wouldn't miss it for the world. I've been talking to Pastor Gideon. I'm trying to leave that old life behind before it's too late."

Sam nodded and followed E Way into the main cathedral. He stood at the back of the church taking it all in—the Sunday morning light cascading through the colorful stained glass, Sam's brother Gideon smiling from the pulpit, Plug and Grandma Dukes waving from the front row, Misty squeezing his hand. Sam didn't know what the next day or even the next hour would bring, but he had to admit, this was one of the good moments he would remember for the rest of his life.

After a rousing sermon that reminded Sam of his father's best Sundays, he moved to the cafeteria behind the cathedral for Sunday dinner. Sam sat at a table watching his newfound family compliment his big brother, Pastor Gideon, on an amazing Sunday morning message.

"When we were kids, everybody thought that Sam would follow in our father's footsteps and pick up the calling," Gideon said. "It's funny how life turns out."

"I think life turned out just the way it was meant to," Misty replied. "Sam isn't a preacher, but he does the Lord's work in his own way." She smiled at Sam and winked.

"Couldn't have said it better myself, baby," Grandma Dukes said.

Sam had never looked at it that way, not as a social worker, or Falcon, or even as Captain America. He had always wanted to make the world a better place, but after his father died, he spent most of his time running away from his own memories. He never realized that he was continuing the work that his father had started.

"Anyway, how've you been, Grandma Dukes?" Sam asked.

"I'm all right, now. God is good. My baby is giving up these streets." Grandma Dukes rubbed Plug's cheek. "You don't know how long I've waited for this day. I've hurt a lot of people over the years. I'm still atoning for my mistakes, but some things I've destroyed beyond repair. I couldn't save your momma or your daddy, but I was able to help you. And you, Miss Plug, are going to redeem us all."

Plug threw her arms around Grandma Dukes' neck and squeezed, as the two women sat there hugging and rocking. Filled with overwhelming joy, Sam had turned his head to keep himself from crying, but when he looked at Misty and saw the tears rolling down her round cheeks, he felt his own eyes well up.

"I hate to disturb such a touching scene," a voice announced behind Sam. The voice was all too familiar, but Sam still couldn't believe his ears. *Finally*, he thought as he turned to greet Ororo Munroe, the mutant who called herself Storm. The term mutant had never sat right with Sam, especially with all of the negative connotations and bigotry aimed toward them.

Storm was something more. For Sam she had always been something ethereal, something beyond this world. He'd never met anyone else with silver hair *and* eyes to match. His recent encounter with the Asgardians Hela and Valkyrie reassured him of a fact that he'd always suspected. Storm wasn't a mutant. She was a goddess.

But the man with her attracted even more attention. A bald, paraplegic man with dark, intense eyes and fuzzy eyebrows. He sat in a futuristic, hi-tech wheelchair whose motor hummed softly at Storm's side. Sitting with his hands folded across his lap, the olive-skinned man smiled at everyone at the table.

Professor Charles Xavier, founder of the X-Men, Sam thought as Misty Knight squeezed his knee.

It's me. Professor X smiled, speaking in Sam's mind. *Do you mind introducing us?*

"Not at all," Sam answered, the flesh crawling on his forearms, but what could he say? The founder of the X-Men, one of the most powerful telepaths in the world, had shown up to see his protégé. "Everybody, this is our colleague, Storm. And the gentleman with her is Professor Charles Xavier." Sam turned to Plug and Grandma. "They're from the special school I told you about."

"It's a pleasure meeting you all, especially you, Plug," Ororo said. Her silver mohawk fell in shimmering bundles over her dark brown shoulder. "We've heard nothing but amazing things."

"I bet," Plug said, glancing at Sam. "What did you tell them, Mr. America?"

"That's your new nickname? Mr. America?" Misty asked with a sly grin. "When's the beauty pageant?"

Sam sighed.

"From my understanding," Ororo continued. "*Captain* America said you are an extremely talented young person, powerful beyond your years. You've had a hard life, made some bad decisions, but you're ready for a new journey. We want to help you."

A ring of lights, red and blue, green and yellow, pulsed around the wheelchair's rims as it rolled around the table, stopping beside

Grandma Dukes. "Ma'am, I want to thank you personally. You've done such an excellent job raising Plug. I know that your granddaughter had her heart set on the Stark Institute, but we would be honored if you would consider enrolling Plug in the Xavier School for Gifted Youngsters. Our curriculum is designed specifically for people with enhanced abilities like hers. We also have a robust scholarship package."

"I'm listening," Grandma Dukes said leaning closer to Professor X.

"Don't you wanna see a demonstration of my powers?" Plug said, eyes bright with hope.

"That's not necessary, but if you wish," Professor X said.

"If it's okay with Grandma Dukes," Storm added.

Sam pulled his phone out of his pocket and offered it to Plug. "Please don't share my text messages," he said.

"Wouldn't dream of it," the phone replied.

NO TIME LIKE THE PRESENT

ALEX SIMMONS

IT'S FUNNY how both peace and destruction can dwell in darkness.

These words whispered in his mind as Sam Wilson, aka Captain America, hovered high above the urban arena. Smoke-gray clouds drifted across the full moon, cloaking him from any eyes that might be gazing skyward from the barely lit abandoned factory below. The surrounding streets were dark and barren—a silent tableau of urban blight and industrial decline.

But soon, the moon would shine bright, revealing him in his red, white, and blue costume and the magnificent metallic wings that kept him aloft. Sam still marveled at the Wakandan technology he wore. It was a gift from the Black Panther—no, a gift from a *friend* who happened to be an African king. He had the super-tech even if he didn't have the Super-Soldier Serum.

Sam chuckled. *Oh, how Mrs. Wilson's little man had moved up in the world.*

Then there was the shield. Steve's shield.

It still felt awkward. New. On loan.

After three months, he still couldn't help feeling like... *like what?* he wondered. *A pretender.* Why?

Was it because he was new to this iconic super hero game and wasn't really super-powered? Or was it that the true mantle of Captain America had been worn since the 1940s by the same man? Steve Rogers. A white man. Could that mantle, that representation of America, be worn by anyone else? If so, was he really the man to do it?

What America do I represent? The one scribbled on paper hundreds of years ago? The country that welcomed people from other countries as cattle and forced laborers? Or the one that Captain America went to war to protect over eighty years ago?

Sam had asked those same questions of himself every single day since Steve handed over the shield.

A chill seemed to run through him as the moon began to peek out from behind the clouds. *Who am I now?* he wondered. *Now that I wear this outfit and carry this weapon of many battles.*

In the aftermath of recent events, he'd had no time to work that out, no time for anything more than partners and team members in battle.

I've had no time for family, no time for someone special, really no time for me.

The costume he wore had been designed especially for him. The wings connected to his days as the Falcon. He'd done good work under that banner, both solo and alongside the original Captain America.

But the *shield* was Steve's.

He chose me without waiting for permission. Why? The question was followed by a query of equal weight: *Why* not *you?*

One question always led to another. But whatever the answer, it would have to wait. Right now, the clock was ticking. A threat below superseded all else.

Responding to the silent command, the wings suddenly billowed to their full length.

The last-minute warning had come from a S.H.I.E.L.D. agent. He'd gone undercover in one of the most dangerous terrorist organizations in existence, A.I.M.—Advanced Idea Mechanics, a title that seemed to better fit an industrial corporation or a senior course at Cal Tech.

But the words of the dying agent warned of the deadliness of their intentions: "They've done it… the test… it worked. Time portal… worked… 'bout go full… 'bout to turn it… minutes away… nothing will be the same… they'll destroy… no… time… no time…" Then, there was silence, and the communication became nothing but a faint signal that Sam was able to zero in on.

A.I.M. wasn't some assortment of thugs and thieves. They were a criminal organization of genius scientists. Over the years, every one of their plans had caused either chaos, destruction, or death.

Their operations were always formidable, cold, calculating, and well-funded. S.H.I.E.L.D. and the Avengers had fought them many times, but they always came back like a swarm of rats and roaches.

If they'd truly invented some kind of time machine, then Sam was certain it would be the greatest threat of all. So he couldn't wait for backup, or to determine the number of armed personnel he'd face, nor what high-tech weaponry they carried.

He had to stop them before they turned it on, and the quickest way in was also the most dangerous. Sam took one look around, and then went into an accelerated dive and shot straight down the factory's five-story smokestack.

He swooped down the dark tunnel, knowing full well he only had a fraction of a second to veer off to avoid smashing against the iron structure of the old furnace a thousand feet below. With only seconds to spare, Sam used one of his newly acquired S.H.I.E.L.D. electromagnetic pulse guns to fire off a directed pulse burst that blew the electronic locks and burst open the cast-iron doors.

Instantly, he swooped into the room among the four-story rafters, simultaneously firing off more pulse blasts.

"It's Captain America!" several guards shouted as they fired energy blasts through the air.

I do get a charge when someone calls me that. Sam grinned.

He dodged and fired back. His accuracy was perfect, targeting at least twelve armed men scattered around the massive maze of pipes, catwalks, and old machinery rotting beside A.I.M.'s banks of high-tech wizardry.

Among the array of monitors, panels, and flashing lights, he spotted the device. Three men were stationed at a panel that would rival launch control at Cape Kennedy. Several feet beyond them was a circular screen, thirty feet wide.

"The time portal," Sam whispered as he dodged more energy blasts and returned fire.

It wasn't what he expected. In his adventures with the Avengers, Sam had seen numerous marvels of technology, even alien tech. He'd expected A.I.M.'s device to be more massive and imposing. This was not.

This organization had plenty of money and a fanatical desire to build devices that could destroy civilizations or, in this case, alter reality in some way. This was one of them. It didn't look like much.

At first glance, this thing didn't appear capable of transporting people. The device was more like a circular plasma screen. It seemed to hover above a semi-circular control bay with multiple touchpads and data displays.

There was no apparent way for anyone to enter it, no steps or ramp. *Did it emit some sort of energy field?* His mind was racing. *Or could it warp space around it?*

It doesn't matter, he told himself. *It's a threat that I have to neutralize. That's all I need to know.*

Sam's battle tactics were both swift and surgically accurate. There was no time for second or third shots. Every dodge and weave was executed with split-second timing, using his wings as a shield, firing back, and taking out every shooter with the first strike.

"Call in more men!" a commanding voice shouted over the din. "Protect the device at all costs!"

Sam spotted a man running toward a panel by a pneumatic doorway. He fired off two more stun blasts. One took down the man, and the other smashed the control board, causing the door to slam shut with a resounding thud.

Sam caught a glimpse of more A.I.M. guards on the other side trying to break through the doorway.

"Shoot him down!" came another command. The few remaining A.I.M. soldiers increased their firing. This time Sam deflected the blasts using his shield as he flew in and out between the metal girders, pipes, catwalks, and beams.

"Take him down, I said!"

Sam spotted the man giving the orders. Though all the A.I.M. agents wore the same distinctive all-over yellow radiation uniforms with cylindrical helmets and head masks, this one man was indeed in command, and his posture, actions, and voice made that clear.

"Can't hold them off until S.H.I.E.L.D. gets here, so I have to destroy it now." Sam's deliberately erratic flight path was bringing him close to the target. He was just about to dive closer to the control panel when his wings suddenly retracted, and he plummeted like a stone.

Somehow, they'd neutralized the wings' flight capabilities. Sam desperately grabbed for some piping but the force of his fall tore his grip from the rusted surface. Instinctively, he twisted just right so that he repelled off a wall and went into a forward somersault that allowed him to land on a catwalk.

His training with Steve and T'Challa had come in handy. But there was no super serum or secret tribal herbs to increase his agility and stamina a hundredfold. He was an ordinary man who had to rely on his will to survive, and that was being severely tested.

More men came at him with stun rods and deadlier weapons. Sam knew he had to go for the device now, before one or all of these men got a lucky shot at him.

More committed than ever, Sam dropped to the floor and battled toward the device, taking out several more men until he reached the control panel. Quickly, he jammed a small explosive device into the console that would likely blow up half the building.

Big things come in small packages.

He was calculating his chances of escaping now that his wings were incapacitated when he heard the voice. "Destroy Zurvan-X, and you destroy your chance to save your parents!"

Sam whirled around, ready to fire. But he was shocked to see an unarmed A.I.M. leader standing near a smaller control panel a few feet away. He'd removed his traditional headgear to reveal a greater surprise. The man was Black.

What the— Sam was stunned. Even though A.I.M. had never publicly espoused any racist propaganda, groups that were formerly part of Hydra normally kept their "superior race" nonsense as part of their credo, especially when it came to leadership roles.

"Yeah, we're having a brother-to-brother moment. And you should hear me out, because your next move could save your parents, or kill them."

"My parents are already dead," Sam snarled.

"Not there. Not yet," the A.I.M. leader replied. "Set off that explosive and the effect on them would be fatal."

Push the button, Sam. His finger froze over the switch on his belt. *What are you waiting for?*

The A.I.M. leader's eyes were bright and piercing. But devoid of anger.

He is playing for time, Sam told himself. *Expecting his men to break through any minute.*

"You can't get out the way you came in because I've triggered a damping field to shut down your wings. We are masters of technology, after all."

"In those suits, you look more like beekeepers."

"We're miracle workers," the leader replied. "Capable of giving you back your people, that's what we are!"

Sam's eyes narrowed. "How do I know—"

"That this is for real?" The leader pointed. "Look at the screen!"

From the corner of his eye, Sam saw his younger sister and brother, Sarah and Gideon. They were playfully running toward his mother, Darlene, and his father, Reverend Paul Wilson. They were all as they had been years before, at a church picnic in a park in his old neighborhood. A community fundraiser for a youth program his parents had organized—a fundraiser Sam couldn't attend.

"It's only an image from the past—"

"It's an image of *now*." The A.I.M. leader gestured toward the screen.

The A.I.M. guards had almost burned through the thick metal doors. Sam went to press the button and heard…

"Stand down!" The leader's voice echoed off the walls through a sound system somewhere in the ceiling.

 The agents froze.

Sam froze.

"You're not looking at the past! You're looking at a section of time that exists right now. Those people exist now, and they can continue to exist. Zurvan-X can make it so. *You* can make it so! That's what we've built."

"Zurvan?"

"It's named after the Persian god of infinite time, or so I'm told."

You know your job, Sam. Destroy it. But he didn't. "I know people who've traveled through time," he said. "It never works out."

The leader tilted his head to one side. "Is altering time exclusive to white people? Is it only for the elite? Is it only for the ones in power at the moment?"

"Time travel is unstable. You should know that." *Why am I still talking with this man?* Sam knew why. He glanced toward the damaged pneumatic door. The A.I.M. soldiers were standing still, awaiting orders.

"This isn't time travel," the leader insisted. "I'm not talking about sending you back to do anything. I'm talking about us being able to manipulate time and incidents within time." He pointed toward the large circular screen. "Through this device, without ever stepping into a portal, without ever running the risk of being in the wrong place and damaging anything."

"How?"

"Everything is energy. Quantum physics states that energy and mass are interchangeable. So even we humans are energy. We managed to..." The leader smiled. "I suspect your chosen field of interest omitted quantum physics, so I'll put it this way." He pointed to Zurvan-X's screen. "Time is like an ocean of energy. Some people can swim through it. Other energy forms can also move through its currents."

"You mean, like light and sound."

"Even more," the leader replied. "There's electrical, gravitational, chemical, nuclear. So many more, and it's all energy. We've found a way of sending… let's call them pulses that can affect the locations and the things within it."

"You've done this?"

"On a smaller scale. We've moved objects, siphoned electrical devices, touched people." The leader chuckled. "They probably thought it was ghosts."

Sam's finger, near the detonation switch, spasmed involuntarily, causing the leader to lean forward.

"With this device, you can prevent your parents from dying. And that means they'll continue to exist in this reality."

Sam's thoughts raced by in fragmented flashes, laced with the one command: *Blow it up!*

His first day of school, and his parents at his side. *Blow it, Sam!*

Saturday barbecues. *Push the button!*

Sunday sermons. *Blow it!*

Scolding when he screwed up. *Blow it.*

Praise and support when he needed to know he was loved. *Blow the damn thing!*

But he didn't move.

"Who's more important, Sam?" the leader asked. "A corrupt or incompetent government, or…"

"What's your name?"

The leader hesitated for a moment, then smiled. "Cletus Uriah Singleton. Yeah, my upscale parents had big things in mind for me."

Sam fingered the triggering device. "Well, Mr. Singleton, A.I.M. isn't a benevolent organization," he said calmly. "You've manipulated and murdered throughout your existence. You do nothing for the benefit of anyone but yourselves. In many ways, you're no better than the government that you mock."

The A.I.M. leader stiffened. "Oh no, my brother. A.I.M. is better than the people who pull your strings, who've made promises they haven't kept for generations! A government who now, more than ever, are mere puppets on the strings of their monetary masters."

Singleton gestured to his fallen A.I.M. agents: "Your government doesn't care about you. It just wants to control your movements, your capacity for creation. It wants to own your inventions so it can profit off of them. A.I.M. doesn't hold people back like that!"

Singleton continued: "Look around you! Every innovation, every breakthrough, even that fancy uniform you wear, I bet, is shackled by bureaucratic red tape and stifling regulations. They say it's for your safety, but that's a lie. It's about power. It's about keeping the status quo, ensuring that a select few continue to hold all the cards while the rest of us are left to toil in mediocrity.

"They don't care about your dreams or your potential. They care about maintaining their dominance, their control over the flow of innovation and knowledge. The government fears us because we represent what they can never control: the uncontainable force of human ingenuity. They want to label us as radicals, as dangerous, because they know that if people were to truly understand what we offer, their whole system would come crashing down."

The monitors played out the image of his mother and father interacting with his sister and brother. Sam recognized that moment. They'd written to him about the picnic and their time together—about the fun and the love. He'd missed out on it because he was off at summer camp. He wished he could have been there. He wished his parents hadn't died. There was so much he wanted to tell them. He even wanted them to see him now, wearing this… suit. No. Uniform?

"Come on, Sam Wilson. That's who you really are. Yeah, you've been the Falcon. Captain America's sidekick. Bucky's replacement… until he came back. Now you get to wear the suit. But it's only because Steve Rogers has hung it up. So, in effect, you're wearing a hand-me-down. And don't tell me that you haven't been given orders you disagreed with. We know how the military works."

Sam thought about what had happened to heroes of color for decades. Even the government's attempted covert actions on Wakanda.

The leader took a small step forward. "So, if you want to fight for something or protect something, start with your family. Think how much better you can make things for them because they're flesh and blood. Your parents brought you into this world. So who do you owe allegiance to the most?"

Sam smiled. "When I was a kid, my family used to watch old movies. Some of them were about mobsters taking over some territory and snuffing out anyone who got in their way." His hand near the detonation device relaxed a bit.

"Some of my friends followed down that path. My father didn't want that for any of us, or the community. He was preaching salvation and living the Lord's way till about two hours from now." Sam gestured toward the idyllic image on the screen. "In a few hours from that moment you've captured, he'll try and break up a fight between some gang members in our neighborhood, and they'll kill him. And they'll do a little bit of time, and then they'll be back on the streets. And nothing will have changed."

"That's how the system works, Sam," the leader insisted. "If you're not powerful enough, you don't get enough. But if you have connections you can twist the law, or make it.

"With Zurvan-X, we can influence any time, any era. We can send energy pulses to interact with physical matter. Imagine if we deflected the bullets that killed Lincoln, Martin, or Malcolm. Send sound waves with voices to persuade or control. We can supercharge machines or overload them so certain missiles or ships don't reach their destinations." Singleton took a step toward Sam. "We could even send a charge through an individual, rendering them unconscious before they could harm… anyone."

Sam's eyes locked with the leader. "Not long after my father dies, my mom is going to get killed in a mugging."

"Of course, brother. The neighborhood couldn't renovate because the people in the area couldn't get bank loans, open stores, or restore old buildings because we're Black. But within a few years, a whole other crop of folks will be able to come in and co-op everything."

What's it all for? Sam lowered his head slightly, staring at the triggering device on his belt. *Sidekicks, hand me downs, political agendas.*

"A few years back, we weren't even allowed to join the military," Singleton continued. "We couldn't have certain jobs in this city and couldn't eat in restaurants and diners. You were a sidekick, then a partner. Now look at you, wearing red, white, and blue. But are you really Captain America? Or just wearing his costume?"

Costume? Suit? Uniform? Symbol?

Why have S.H.I.E.L.D. not shown up yet? Sam wondered. Why was Singleton holding his people back? They could have been through the door and taken him out by now, possibly before he could have thrown the switch to destroy the device.

For that matter, why had the S.H.I.E.L.D. agent reached out to him in the first place?

One question always leads to another. But he knew—*Without them, we'd never look for answers... and sometimes find them.*

"Cletus." Sam looked up slowly. "This was all for me, wasn't it? This whole thing was a setup to get me here, to take me out, or more likely to bring me on board."

Singleton laughed. "I knew I was right about you. You have skills and intelligence! Yeah, that message you received was from one of my people. And the signals you sent off to S.H.I.E.L.D. were intercepted. Again, we are technology geniuses."

"What makes me so special?"

"The fact that you don't know speaks to the reason you should join us."

"I'm not a scientific genius, so you must want me as a symbol."

"What better man for the job than you? You get to save your folks, and that's just for starters."

Sam thought for a moment. He remembered life with his parents. He remembered the church on Sunday mornings and afternoon dinners. But he also remembered the hateful remarks and the physical harm that was done to his family as he was growing up.

Every single detail flashed through his mind in the split-second before he spoke.

"Can this machine do everything that you claim?"

Singleton shone bright with anticipation. "We've run tests with smaller units. They allowed us to work out any glitches. So we predict that Zurvan-X can do all that and more."

Sam took a quick glance at the screen. The picnic was almost over. Soon, his father would leave the park and walk into a situation that would get him killed. "Zurvan... 'X.' An acknowledgment to someone in particular?"

"That's true. You have to admit he was quite a leader, Sam. You see the same things I do."

"Maybe," Sam replied. "But through a different lens. For instance, you've never once called me Captain America because you see me as Sam Wilson. But you want to show off a converted Captain America—a converted Black Captain America."

"Yes, but you represent—"

"Me!" Sam's words were sharp and biting. "I represent me first and then my family. Because their commitment to me was unselfish. They had no idea what I'd become, but they knew what kind of man they wanted me to be."

"That doesn't have to change. Just—"

"My father quoted scriptures. And my mother quoted history. 'There is no passion to be found in playing small—in settling for a life that is less than the one you are capable of living.' Nelson Mandela said that. It was one of my mother's favorites.

"My father favored, 'A man's character is not judged after he celebrates a victory, but by what he does when his back is against the wall.'"

On the screen, Sam noted that his father was leaving the park, waving goodbye. "The day he died, he was trying to do something for the community. Yes, it was predominantly Black and Hispanic, but other people lived there too. And my father's house was open to all."

Singleton was fuming. He struggled to contain his anger. "You'll be lackey for the white man. He'll rule you and you will serve him like a—"

"I will work with and for the people I choose!" Sam shouted.

Suddenly a guard's voice bellowed through the sound system. "S.H.I.E.L.D. agents are converging on the building!"

"Took them long enough," Sam said, smiling.

Singleton whirled to face Sam. "You've been stalling!"

"Sure. I needed the time."

Suddenly, Sam's wings snapped into readiness, spreading

to their full width and glory! "I knew Wakanda tech would override your system given enough time. It restored my wings and rebroadcast my signal to S.H.I.EL.D."

"Why?" Singleton shouted. He leaped behind a rack of computer banks as the jammed doors opened, and a swarm of A.I.M. armed agents rushed in.

Sam tapped the detonation button as he soared up into the air. "Six seconds," he shouted into his com-link as he smashed through the skylight. "S.H.I.E.L.D., evacuate! Destruction in six seconds!"

"Fall back! Bomb will blow in five! Four! Three!"

The S.H.I.E.L.D. agents dove for cover just as the bomb went off, echoing off the concrete walls, shattering windows, and illuminating the night with brilliant yellow and white. It showered the darkened streets with a million fragments of flickering pieces of glass, generating a Fourth-of-July-like backdrop as Captain America hovered high above.

When it was over, the streets suffered minimal damage, but the factory's main floor was gutted. The debris seemed to blend in with the rubbish and abandoned items along the desolate street. The device was destroyed.

From a building across the way, Sam watched the S.H.I.E.L.D. agents perform their cleanup operation, herding the surviving A.I.M. soldiers into various S.H.I.E.L.D. security vans. Their leader, Singleton, was not among them.

Why?

Singleton's question drifted through Sam's thoughts as he flew over the Harlem streets. Eventually, he glided down onto a building across from where he used to live as a boy. Like so many other buildings in Harlem, it had been renovated, and some of the faces in the window were of a lighter hue than he remembered from his childhood.

Why had he chosen to destroy the device that could have saved his parents?

The answer settled comfortably in his soul. Ironic, that the very people the leader had dangled before him as a reason not to destroy the machine were the very reason he could.

Sam stared at the shield Steve had passed on to him. *Before my friends and schoolmates, before Captain America and the Avengers, the people who helped forge me into the man I am were my parents.*

The life they lived and the lessons they taught are part of the code I live by. To save them at the cost of millions of lives would have shamed them forever. And I wouldn't do that to them for any reason or anyone—ever.

As to the leader's words about A.I.M., like any powerful organization, their promises were only as valid as those who stood behind them. However, there was one thing Sam had to consider. Earlier, as he was flying away from the factory, he heard one of the S.H.I.E.L.D. agents exclaim, "Hey, one of these A.I.M. guys is a woman!"

Was A.I.M. truly measuring the value of its members by intellect alone? Or, like some cults, was it simply offering enticements to disenfranchised people to increase their numbers… for now? And what about Zurvan-X? Had the "X" really been a nod to an iconic civil rights leader?

Or had it actually been the Roman numeral ten? In which case, what happened to the other nine prototypes? And what, if anything, had their experimenting truly affected?

Sam felt his muscles tightened, and he found no comfort in the thought, *Only time and vigilance will tell.*

Always one question leads to another, Sam mused as he winged his way home. But tonight, perhaps he'd sleep peacefully, content in the knowledge that he'd found at least a few answers for himself.

ABOUT THE AUTHORS

MAURICE BROADDUS

A community organizer and middle school teacher, his work has appeared in magazines like *Lightspeed Magazine*, *Weird Tales*, *Beneath Ceaseless Skies*, *Asimov's*, *Cemetery Dance*, *Uncanny Magazine*, with some of his stories having been collected in *The Voices of Martyrs*. His books include the urban fantasy trilogy The Knights of Breton Court, the steampunk works *Buffalo Soldier*, and the award-winning *Pimp My Airship*. His middle-grade detective novels include *The Usual Suspects* and *Unfadeable*. As an editor, he's worked on Dark Faith anthology series, *Fireside Magazine*, *Streets of Shadows*, *People of Colo(u)r Destroy Horror*, and *Apex Magazine*. Learn more at MauriceBroaddus.com.

GLORIA J. BROWNE-MARSHALL

Gloria J. Browne-Marshall is the author of *She Took Justice: The Black Woman, Law, and Power*, *Race, Law, and American Society: 1607 to Present*, *The Voting Rights War*, *The Constitution: Major Cases and Conflicts* and *The Black Woman: 400 Years of Perseverance*.

Her essays have appeared in the Milwaukee Courier, TIME.com, CNN.com, NBC.com and her poem *Mother Mythic* is in Penumbra and "white privilege" is in *Esthetic Apostle Journal*.

Her articles appear in several journals and online. Gloria is a playwright with seven produced plays and looks forward to the production of her play that asks, "who owns American history?" She is working on a documentary based on travels to Angola, a nonfiction book on uprisings, and her debut novel.

Gloria is a tenured Professor of Constitutional Law at John Jay College (CUNY). Prior to academia, Gloria litigated cases for the Southern Poverty Law Center, Community Legal Services, and the NAACP Legal Defense Fund, Inc. She speaks nationally and internationally about her books and issues of social justice.

GAR ANTHONY HAYWOOD

Gar Anthony Haywood is the Shamus and Anthony award-winning author of fourteen novels, including the Aaron Gunner private eye series and Joe and Dottie Loudermilk mysteries. His short fiction has been included in the *Best American Mystery Stories* anthologies and *Booklist* has called him "a writer who has always belonged in the upper echelon of American crime fiction." He has written for network television and both the *New York Times* and *Los Angeles Times*. He and his wife Donna currently make their home in Denver, Colorado.

DANIAN JERRY

Danian Darrell Jerry, writer, teacher, and emcee, holds a Master of Fine Arts in Creative Writing from the University of Memphis. He is a 2020 VONA Fellow and a Fiction Editor of *Obsidian: Literature and Arts in the African Diaspora*. Danian founded Neighborhood Heroes, a youth arts program that employs comic books and literary arts. As a child, he read fantasy and comics. As an adult, he writes his own adventures. Danian's writing appears and is forthcoming in *Marvel's Black*

Panther: Tales of Wakanda, The Magazine of Fantasy and Science Fiction, Fireside Fiction, Trouble the Waters: Tales from the Deep Blue, and other publications.

NICOLE GIVENS KURTZ

Book Riot called Nicole Givens Kurtz "a genre polymath who does crime, horror, and SFF." They've named her as one of the Six Black SFF Indie Writers You Should be Reading, 30 Must-Read SFF Books by Black Authors, and The Best of the West: Eight Alternative History Westerns (Sisters of the Wild Sage). She's a two-time Atomacon Palmetto Scribe Award winner, an HWA Horror Diversity Grant Recipient (2020) and a Ladies in Horror Grant Recipient. Nicole has over 50 published short stories and is the author of the Cybil Lewis and Death Violations cybernoir series as well as the Kingdom of Aves fantasy mystery series. She's written the critically acclaimed, weird western anthology, *Sisters of the Wild Sage: A Weird West Collection*.

Nicole has conducted workshops for Clarion and is an active instructor at Speculative Fiction Academy. She is the owner of Mocha Memoirs Press. She's the editor for the groundbreaking *SLAY: Stories of the Vampire Noire* anthology and *Blackened Roots: An Anthology of the Undead* with Tonia Ransom.

KYOKO M.

Kyoko M is a *USA Today* bestselling author, a fangirl, and an avid book reader. She is the author of The Black Parade urban fantasy series and the Of Cinder and Bone science-fiction series. Her debut novel, *The Black Parade*, has been positively reviewed by *Publishers Weekly* and *New York Times* and *USA Today*-bestselling novelist, Ilona Andrews. She has been both a moderator and a panelist for comic book and science fiction/ fantasy conventions like Dragon Con, Geek Girl Con, Multiverse

Con, Momocon, and The State of Black Science Fiction.

She has a Bachelor of Arts in English Lit degree from the University of Georgia, which gave her every valid excuse to devour book after book with a concentration in Greek mythology and Christian mythology. When not working feverishly on a manuscript (or two), she can be found buried under her Dashboard on Tumblr, or chatting with fellow nerds on Twitter, or curled up with a good Harry Dresden novel on a warm Georgia night. Like any author, she wants nothing more than to contribute something great to the best profession in the world, no matter how small.

GLENN PARRIS

Glenn Parris writes in the genres of sci-fi, fantasy, and medical mystery. Considered by some an expert in Afrofuturism, he is a self-described lifelong sci-fi nerd. His interest in the topic began as a tween before the term Afrofuturism was even coined.

His debut novel, *The Renaissance of Aspirin*, is the first in The Jack Wheaton Mystery series. He was part of the all star cast of authors for *Marvel's Black Panther: Tales of Wakanda* with the short story "The Underside of Darkness". His latest full length work was released in May 2022 titled *Dragon's Heir: The Efilu Legacy*.

Parris encompasses his own dichotomy of physician by day incorporating that scientific outlook into his creative works. As one of the too few African American men practicing medicine, his unique perspective makes the stories he writes compelling, and makes him an engaging speaker on various topics.

GARY PHILLIPS

Gary Phillips has been a community activist, labor organizer, and delivered dog cages. He's published various novels, comics, short stories, and edited several anthologies including *Orange County Noir* and the award-winning *The Obama Inheritance: Fifteen Stories of Conspiracy Noir*. *Violent Spring*, first published in 1994 was named in 2020 one of the essential crime novels of Los Angeles. He was a senior story editor on FX's *Snowfall*, about crack and the CIA in 1980s South Central where he grew up.

ALEX SIMMONS

Alex Simmons is an award-winning freelance writer, comic book creator, screenwriter, playwright, teaching artist, and creative consultant. He's written for Disney Books, Penguin Press, Simon and Schuster, DC Comics, and Archie Comics. Simmons is the creator of the acclaimed adventure comic book series Blackjack. He has also helped develop concepts and scripts for an animation studio in England.

Simmons has served on panels and delivered lectures on children's entertainment mediums, as well as empowering young people through the arts. His clients range from Random House to the New York Film Academy. Simmons founded the annual family event Kids Comic Con, as well as three comic arts exhibits, which have traveled abroad. He is currently developing a comics and creative arts program for children in the US, Europe, Africa, and India. For over twenty years, Simmons has been a member of arts and education boards for the New York State Alliance for Arts Education, the Department for Cultural Affairs, and the Museum for Comics & Cartoon Art.

SHEREE RENÉE THOMAS

Sheree Renée Thomas is an award-winning writer, poet, editor, and a 2023 Hugo Award Finalist and Locus Award Winner. She was honored with the 2023 Octavia E. Butler Award and was also an Ember Award Finalist. Her work is inspired by myth and folklore, natural science, music, and the culture of the Mississippi Delta. She is the author of the short fiction collection, *Nine Bar Blues: Stories from an Ancient Future*, a Finalist for the 2021 Locus Award, Ignyte Award, and World Fantasy Award for Year's Best Collection and winner of the 2022 Darrell Award for Year's Best Novella. She is the winner of the 2022 Dal Coger Memorial Hall of Fame Award and is #339 in the Walter Day Science Fiction Hall of Fame Trading Cards. She is also the author of collections, *Sleeping Under the Tree of Life* and *Shotgun Lullabies: Stories & Poems*. She edited the two-time World Fantasy Award-winning Dark Matter anthologies, co-edited *Trouble the Waters: Tales from the Deep Blue* with Pan Morigan and Troy L. Wiggins, and *Africa Risen: A New Era of Speculative Fiction* with Oghenechovwe Donald Ekpeki and Zelda Knight, a NAACP Image Award Finalist and winner of the 2023 Locus Award.

Sheree Renée Thomas is the editor of *The Magazine of Fantasy & Science Fiction* and the associate editor of Obsidian. Her essays have appeared in the *New York Times* and other publications. She is a collaborator with Janelle Monáe on the artist's fiction collection, *The Memory Librarian: And Other Stories of Dirty Computer*, a New York Times bestseller. A former New Yorker, she lives in her hometown of Memphis, Tennessee, near a mighty river and a pyramid. Follow her @blackpotmojo on Twitter, @shereereneethomas on Instagram and Facebook, or visit shereereneethomas.com.

ABOUT THE EDITOR

JESSE J. HOLLAND is the author of the *Black Panther: Who is the Black Panther?* prose novel, nominated for an NAACP Image Award, and of the award-winning *The Invisibles: The Untold Story of African American Slaves In the White House*, named one of the top history books of 2016 by Smithsonian.com. He also was the editor and contributor to the prose anthology *Black Panther: Tales of Wakanda*. He served as a Distinguished Visiting Scholar In Residence at the Library of Congress, a Visiting Distinguished Professor at the University of Arkansas, faculty at Goucher College's Master of Fine Arts in Nonfiction, and was a judge for the 2020 Harper Lee Prize for Legal Fiction. He is a guest host for C-SPAN's Washington Journal, an associate professor at The George Washington University, and a former Race & Ethnicity writer for the Associated Press.

Awarded a doctorate of humane letters from Lemoyne-Owen College in 2018, Jesse lives in Bowie, Maryland with his wife Carol, daughter Rita and son Jesse III.

ACKNOWLEDGMENTS

I WOULD like to thank first and foremost my wife and children, without whom my life would not be complete. Thank you, Carol, Rita, and Jamie.

I also want to thank my siblings: Twyla, Fred, and most especially Candace. She was one of my biggest supporters and it is in her name that I will continue to work. She's my rock and I will miss her always. I also can't thank my beta readers and family enough for their never-wavering support, including my parents, Jesse and Yvonne Holland, and my ever-patient mother-in-law, Rita Womack. Thanks to Jabberwocky Literary Agency and especially Eddie Schnieder, who does everything else so I can focus on the writing work.

There are always a cast of characters to thank in the production of a book like this. I want to thank all of the authors who pitched for this book and took time out of their busy schedules to play in the Marvel Universe with me again or with me for the first time. This won't be the last time you hear from them!

At Titan Books, I would like to thank all of the people who take the raw material and turn it into a physical book, including Nick Landau, Vivan Cheung, George Sandison, Elora Hartway, Claire Schultz, and especially Daquan Cadogan. Without them, this anthology would not exist.

At Marvel, I'd like to thank Sarah Singer, Jeff Youngquist, and Jeremy West for their hard work in making sure everything fits into the Marvel Universe correctly.

I can't forget the support I received from the faculty, staff and students at the School of Media & Public Affairs at The George Washington University, the great people at the Smithsonian National Museum of African American History and Culture, the always supportive Alfred Street Baptist Church and Gray's C.M.E. Church, the men of Omega Psi Phi (especially my home chapter of Eta Zeta and my graduate chapter of Chi Mu Nu) and the members of the National Association of Black Journalists.

Thank you, Stan and Jack for creating the Marvel Universe. And thanks to Gene Colan for his collaboration with Stan Lee in the creation of the Falcon.

And thank all of you for being fans and coming along on this ride with us. This modern mythologies would not exist without you, so we humbly thank all of you with all of our hearts.

And as always, there were so many people who helped get this book published that it would be impossible to name them all. If I've omitted anyone, please blame my head and not my heart.